fading starlight

**Center Point
Large Print**

Also by Kathryn Cushman and available from
Center Point Large Print:

Chasing Hope
Finding Me

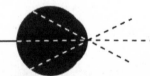

fading starlight

KATHRYN CUSHMAN

CENTER POINT LARGE PRINT
THORNDIKE, MAINE

This Center Point Large Print edition is published in the year 2016 by arrangement with Bethany House Publishers, a division of Baker Publishing Group.

The text of this Large Print edition is unabridged. In other aspects, this book may vary from the original edition. Printed in the United States of America on permanent paper. Set in 16-point Times New Roman type.

ISBN: 978-1-62899-998-3

Library of Congress Cataloging-in-Publication Data

Names: Cushman, Kathryn, author.
Title: Fading starlight / Kathryn Cushman.
Description: Center Point Large Print edition. | Thorndike, Maine : Center Point Large Print, 2016. | ©2015
Identifiers: LCCN 2016010907 | ISBN 9781628999983 (hardcover : alk. paper)
Subjects: LCSH: Hollywood (Los Angeles, Calif.)—Fiction | Large type books.
Classification: LCC PS3603.U825 F33 2016 | DDC 813/.6—dc23
LC record available at http://lccn.loc.gov/2016010907

Dedicated to those in the industry who
have supported me from the beginning:

Carrie Padgett, Julie Carobini,
Michael Berrier, and Shawn Grady—
writer friends since my very first
Mount Hermon conference

James Scott Bell—mentor, teacher, and friend

Dave Long
and the entire Bethany House team—
words cannot express what a blessing
you have been to me over the past decade

one

At this very moment, Lauren Summers's professional future was draped across the bony frame of a high-strung seventeen-year-old. The living room air seemed to crackle along with the television static as the swirl of pink and silver filled the ancient screen. Lauren grabbed the hands on each side of her—her best friend, Chloe, on the right and Chloe's mother, Rhonda, on the left—and they all waited.

The big moment had finally arrived.

"Oh man, she looks *amazing*." Chloe jumped up and made for the TV, planting herself only inches from the oversized box. "This is so incredible. Isn't this incredible?"

Lauren normally would laugh at her best friend's over-the-top enthusiasm—but not this time. Tonight, she waited for reactions along the red carpet.

Rhonda swatted the air. "Chloe, will you please sit down? The rest of us would like to see this, too."

Chloe rolled her eyes. "Mom, no talking. We need to hear this."

"And *see* it. Sit down so Lauren can watch her big moment."

Chloe let out an exaggerated sigh, but she did

come back to sit beside Lauren. She retook her hand and squeezed. Hard. "It's not every day your best friend's dress is on the red carpet at the VMAs."

"It's not *my* dress." Lauren was finding it hard to breathe. There it was, right there for the whole world to see, every camera focused directly on it.

Another dismissive gesture from Chloe. " 'Course it is your dress. We all know who did all the work."

Marisa Remington was posing for the cameras. She turned sideways and stuck out her left leg, barely managing to push her high-heeled sandal through the demure slit created by the wrap design of the dress.

"She did that on purpose, didn't she? Stuck her leg out to show some skin, trying to be sexy?" Chloe was quickly shushed again by her mother.

Lauren would have nodded an affirmative answer—because the speculation was indeed true—but she didn't want to encourage further conversation. She wanted to hear this. Every word.

Renee Ross, the red carpet host for the evening, approached Marisa, microphone in hand. "Marisa, your dress is simply darling. Who are you wearing?"

Simply darling. The word choice was not lost on Lauren, nor would it be lost on Marisa. These awards, more than most, were filled with ultra-sexy, barely there dresses worn by megastars who wanted to display all their assets to the absolute fullest. Marisa had left no doubt to anyone concerned that she did not want to go to this event looking like a little girl. Since Marisa was the up-and-coming star of the newest preteen television phenomenon, Marisa's handlers were obsessive about a squeaky-clean image for their protégée. Lauren understood their concern, given the fall of some of the previous bubblegum queens who had come before. Marisa, however, most certainly did not understand. In fact, she did everything in her power to thwart any and all efforts to make her appear young and innocent.

Her mother had brought her to *Deb Couture* and demanded a dress that demonstrated a clear awareness of high fashion but also an appropriate sense of modesty. Marisa had other ideas. The ensuing months had been little short of a blood-bath.

Now, Marisa smiled sweetly toward the camera. "I'm wearing *Deb Couture.*" She twisted and turned, showing off the dress to full effect. She spun with a little extra vigor in the direction that allowed the wrap to swing slightly open.

"You look absolutely adorable. Are you excited about your first awards show?"

There was no disguising the look of displeasure in Marisa's eyes, in spite of the perfectly white, toothy smile she displayed for the camera. "I'm thrilled. I'm just so humbled to be here among so many great artists whose work I admire."

"Yeah, right." Chloe at least had the wherewithal to whisper under her breath this time.

Marisa moved down the walkway toward the next stop, and Renee Ross looked toward the camera. "The amazing twin-sister duo of the fashion world strikes gold once again. Elyse and Rose Debowesky demonstrate their amazing versatility, from Rihanna's daring number to Marisa's sweeter-than-sugar pop confection."

"Woot! Woot! Did you hear that?" Chloe jumped up and pumped her fist. Lauren released the breath that she just now realized she'd been holding. "Too bad that reporter doesn't know who actually did all the work. The twin sisters are getting credit that should be pointed elsewhere."

While there was, once again, more than a little truth in what Chloe was saying, the fashion world didn't work that way, and everyone understood that fact. Someone like Lauren had to pay her dues, work hard, and pray that she would be given bigger and better chances along the way. "Chloe, I did not do everything."

"Most of it, then. You did the sketch. You did the last-minute details. You are the one who came up with that silver net sash when the powers that be decided the dress was too clingy and sexy. That swath of metallic glimmer around her waist was just the right touch to make sure she

10

still looked innocent, and the netted texture makes it look edgy at the same time." Chloe looked toward her mother. "Lauren's been putting in a massive amount of hours making sure this dress was perfect, and she was up all night last night working on last-minute details."

In fact, Lauren had been up most of last night steaming out anything that even looked like it might wrinkle, adding one more sequin here or there, and double-checking the hem stitching. Knowing that Marisa did not like the direction her handlers had chosen, Lauren had gone out of her way to make her as happy as possible.

"Well done, Lauren." Rhonda clapped her hands. "That dress is amazing. And to think that my heart-daughter was part of the process." Rhonda Inglehart was indeed a "mother-of-the-heart" to Lauren, and Lauren was so thankful to have her.

A commercial for the latest and greatest nationwide calling plan filled the screen, and Chloe said, "Mom, did Lauren tell you that they've already asked her to get started designing Marisa's dress for the next awards show?"

"No, she did not. Lauren, that is amazing."

"Actually, I was the only one left in the entire process that Marisa would speak to by the time it was all said and done. They're using me less because of my talent and more because I have managed to avoid offending Marisa." Lauren shook her head, thinking back to some of the all-out screamfests she'd witnessed between Marisa and her team.

Lauren had managed to stay in Marisa's good graces because she'd truly tried to help the teen star realize her own vision in a way that also stayed true to the aim of her handlers. The little things were what Marisa seemed to appreciate. Lauren could still remember her face when she'd shown her the little hidden pocket inside the sash. It was just the right size for the lucky penny Marisa carried with her everywhere. Marisa had hugged her and said, "I'm glad someone here actually cares what I think." That moment was when all the work became worth-while. All the sleepless nights. All the hours spent trying to get the exact right look to the dress. That little bit of appreciation had made it all bearable.

"Don't be so modest," Chloe told Lauren. "Her dress is beautiful, and you know it. That's why you got the next job."

"Exactly right." Rhonda stood up and made for the small kitchen in the apartment. "Time to bring out the banquet?" She pulled open the refrigerator, wafting the smell of hot salsa, quiche lorraine, and meatballs across the counter and into the tiny living room.

The three women had prepared several platters of finger foods to munch on while they watched the awards show. Lauren and Chloe walked into the kitchen to help put everything out, but Rhonda shooed them away.

"I'll get this. Why don't the two of you do whatever else you need to do to get ready for your guests?" She set a platter on the counter and swatted toward the girls. "Go on now, I've got it. I'll just put these in the microwave."

"Guests?" Lauren looked toward Chloe, eyebrows raised.

Chloe tapped her chin and stared just above Lauren's head, as if in deep thought. "Oh, didn't I mention it to you? Jasper's coming over." Jasper was Chloe's fiancé, and he stopped by Chloe and Lauren's apartment on his way home from work almost every night.

"Do we need to do something to get ready for Jasper?" Lauren looked at Rhonda, waiting for an explanation.

Rhonda's eyes had grown large. She looked toward Chloe with an obvious SOS expression.

Chloe picked up a mini quiche. "Well, he might have also invited Cody, the new guy at his work, to come join us." Her voice was as innocent as her actions were guilty. "Didn't I mention it?"

"No. No, you didn't mention it, as a matter of fact." Lauren glared at her friend. "Chloe, you did not just set me up with a blind date again, especially on tonight of all nights, did you? You promised after the last time that you'd stop meddling in my love life . . . remember?"

13

Chloe shrugged. "It's not a blind date. We just told him to come over and hang out with us, eat some food, and meet our soon-to-be-famous friend." There was a knock at the front door, and Chloe moved toward it, still turned toward Lauren. "The two of you just had to meet. I knew it the first time I saw him."

"Oh really? And how did you know that?"

"Come on, we needed a crowd here to celebrate your big night."

"You could have warned me."

"Oops." Chloe smiled and shrugged, both hands extended. "Must have slipped my mind." Somehow, Chloe could pull off that kind of insincere apology and come across as more lovable than annoying. It was hard to fault a girl who faced the world with such hope and exuberance.

Lauren looked around at the small living room, which was tidy enough but could use a good vacuuming and a round with a duster, the kinds of things she would have done if she'd known they were having company that wasn't "family." She looked down at her pink V-neck T-shirt and jeans, which were fine, but again, it would have been nice to know there were going to be strangers about, even if it wasn't a date.

Chloe led the two men into the living room while Rhonda arranged the platters on the Ikea coffee table. There was plenty of food, no doubt about that. At least they could just eat if the conversation got awkward.

Jasper came into Lauren's view, followed by a tall, broad-shouldered guy. His hair was short and brown, and he had just a hint of stubble across his jaw.

Jasper introduced him. "Lauren, meet Cody. Cody, Lauren."

"Pleased to meet you." Cody had a slight Southern drawl—not twangy country boy, but every word seemed extra slow and drawn out, as if he should be out on the veranda drinking sweet tea. His faded blue T-shirt and well-worn jeans looked more laid-back preppy than sloppy and seemed to confirm his Southern-boy status. Nothing about him appeared to fit with the uptight Los Angeles real estate agency where Jasper—and presumably Cody—worked. Of course, Jasper didn't seem to fit that mold, either.

"Nice to meet you, as well," Lauren said, suddenly wishing she had bothered just a little more with her hair that morning.

Chloe gestured toward the coffee table, which was rapidly filling with finger food under Rhonda's deft hands. "We're just planning to munch our way through the awards show, so eat whatever and whenever you like. The dress that Lauren designed has already made its way down the red carpet, but it will be on stage shortly."

"Your dress is presenting?" Cody's accent was charming.

Lauren laughed. "No. Marisa Remington is wearing a dress I did some work on. Somehow, Chloe has given that a bit more significance than it deserves."

"Lauren beat out over a thousand applicants for one of the three intern positions at *Deb Couture*. Then she was so good at what she does, she actually helped design Marisa's dress, and she was the one they had doing all the last-minute alterations."

Jasper looked toward Cody and shrugged. "I told you there might be a fair amount of girl talk."

"You saw one of the early pictures of the dress. It was beautiful, right? And that was before Lauren came up with the sash idea." Chloe folded her arms across her chest and waited for Jasper's response.

"It was beautiful, yeah"—he cast a nervous glance toward Chloe—"and . . . uh . . . that sash was a really nice touch."

Lauren rolled her eyes at him. "Like you even know what a sash is."

"Sure I do. It's a belt thingy. Kind of looks like a big ribbon or something."

Chloe giggled, then took Cody by the arm. "Let me tell you all about it." She began expounding in great detail the wonders of Lauren's dress.

"I'm going to kill her," Lauren whispered toward Jasper. "She didn't mention anything to me about you guys coming over."

Jasper leaned closer. "Don't be too mad. This one may be mostly my fault. Cody's new in town, plus I just thought an evening of fashion-watching might be a little more tolerable if there was another male in the room." His face was pure innocence.

Lauren burst out laughing. "For your sake, I'm going to acknowledge that there is probably some truth to that, and I will allow her to live. This time. Next time, no promises."

"What's happening next time?" Chloe was looking at them, still with a firm grip on Cody's arm.

"Lauren's going to make a dress for me. With a sash and everything." Jasper spread both hands wide and gestured around his waist.

Everyone in the room burst into laughter. Chloe turned her attention back to Cody. "Did I mention that Lauren made my wedding gown? Not many people have their dresses made by a world-famous designer."

"Especially people on our budget. Good thing we have an inside connection—it seems my fiancée knows the designer personally." Jasper nudged Lauren.

"Someday, when she's world famous, we'll be able to tell everyone that my wedding dress was her very first one." Chloe let go of Cody's arm but didn't move away. "You'll come, right? To the wedding, I mean. It's just a small affair, a couple dozen people and nothing fancy, but we'd love it if you could make it."

Cody reached up to rub the back of his neck. "I don't . . . I mean, it sounds pretty intimate. I'm sure you don't want someone you've just met . . ."

"Of course we do. Please, we would consider it an honor if you'd come. Four weeks from yesterday in Mom and Dad's backyard. Nothing too fancy—even my designer dress has purposely been made low-key."

"Well, I . . . I mean . . . sure. If you're sure."

"Of course I am. Now, let's eat."

They all gathered around the table, small paper plates in hand, and began piling on the meatballs, mini quiches, and other dishes that Chloe, Rhonda, and Lauren had spent the afternoon preparing.

Cody sat on the couch beside Lauren. "I don't know much about fashion, but I do know it is impressive that, as an intern, you were allowed to work on a dress for a big occasion like this. Good for you."

Lauren felt her cheeks heat. "It's mainly because they were so busy with the more established divas that no one had time for the newbie kid."

"Mom, we're needing one of your quotes here,"

Chloe called across the room. "Lauren is being entirely too modest. Help me out a little."

Rhonda squinted, nodded slowly, then said, " 'The secret of success in life is for a man to be ready for his opportunity when it comes.' Benjamin Disraeli."

"See. You had the opportunity, and you were ready for it. Now you're having success because of it." Chloe flipped her wavy blond hair over her shoulder in victory. "Quit belittling your achievement here."

Lauren would throttle Chloe later. For now, she decided just to continue the conversation as if this interruption hadn't happened. "My real interest is in fashion history, not the avant-garde stuff that's on the carpet tonight. Marisa's people wanted something sweeter, more old-fashioned, for lack of a better term, and no one else was particularly excited about doing it."

"I like sweet and old-fashioned." Cody looked straight into her eyes and smiled, causing the corners of his eyes to crinkle just slightly, then he popped a mini quiche into his mouth, still grinning as he chewed.

More stars made their way up the red carpet, with Renee Ross oohing and ahhing over each outfit. Lauren took a sip of Diet Coke and shook her head. "I'm glad I won't be spending tomorrow anywhere near Marisa. She's going to be livid over Renee's *darling* and *adorable* adjectives for her dress."

"I don't get it. That's what they asked for, right?" Jasper had leaned back against the couch, his arm across the back loosely, Chloe close by his side.

"It's exactly what her mother, her manager, and her agent asked for. She, however"—Lauren made an exaggerated shudder—"well, let's just say that she had other ideas."

"A regular femme fatale, huh?" Cody leaned just a little closer to Lauren, bringing the full effect of his handsome grin into close-up view.

"So she would like to believe." Lauren smiled back for just a moment, before turning her attention back to her plate, which was empty. She reached for a couple of strawberries.

On the screen, the lights went down in the auditorium and Taylor Swift opened the show with her newest single. Lauren put her plate on the coffee table and leaned forward. "Here we go. Marisa's the first presenter."

As the applause for Taylor Swift began to wind down, the voice-over announcer said, "To present the award for Best Female Video, please welcome Marisa Remington and Charles Baker, stars of the DTN Channel hit *Missy's World*."

The auditorium filled with applause once again as Marisa and Charles made their way to the podium. Marisa took a step, seemed to trip on the end of the silver sash, and suddenly, the wrapped portion of her dress pulled loose and fell open.

Wide open. As she was facing the camera. Directly. The screen filled with Marisa in her lacy black bra and bikini panties. She grabbed the loose sides of her dress and folded it closed. She looked toward Charles Baker and pulled one hand over her mouth, which was clearly open in shock. The entire room had gone silent. She finally pulled her hand away from her lips and began to fan her face. She said simply, "Oh my."

The crowd remained quiet as Charles put an arm around her, pulled her close in a protective way, and leaned over and kissed the top of her head. He edged toward the microphone. "On the bright side, I have to say that you've got some assets I never suspected." The crowd sort of laughed, still embarrassed for her, but they began to applaud in a show of support and solidarity.

Marisa gave a half smile. "Well, thanks, Charles. If I'm going to be embarrassed in front of the entire world, I'm glad to know that I meet your approval just the same." Everyone laughed outright and then applauded all the more, until it became a full-on standing ovation. Marisa nodded an acknowledgment to the crowd, then whispered something to Charles Baker.

He stepped back toward the microphone, and they continued on to present the award, Marisa holding her dress closed with her left arm snugged tight against her middle.

Lauren had no idea who won. She couldn't

breathe, couldn't think. Her cell phone vibrated on the table. It was a text from her boss at *Deb Couture.*

You needn't bother to show up tomorrow.

Or ever again.

"You know what? I've got a bit of a headache. I think I need to go lie down." Numbly, Lauren walked toward the back of the apartment before she remembered some semblance of her manners. She turned. "It was nice to have met you, Cody."

She closed the door behind her and sank to her knees. She didn't cry. She couldn't manage a single coherent thought. She just knelt. And prayed—or as close as she could get to a prayer. "Help. Please help."

two

"How bad is it?"

It was almost noon the next day by the time Lauren emerged from her room. She shuffled out to find Chloe sitting on the couch, leaning toward the barely audible television, elbows on her knees, remote in hand. In one swift movement, she jumped to her feet and powered off the TV. "It's . . . uh . . . not *that* bad."

"But yet you felt the need to hit the power button." Lauren leaned against the hallway door, thinking she didn't have the energy to move forward even one more inch.

Chloe just stood and stared for several seconds, clearly searching for something supportive to say. It was the first time in Lauren's memory that her friend had ever been speechless. Finally, Chloe gestured toward the kitchen bar. "Look what you just got." A small bouquet of fall-colored flowers sat on the counter.

"Who are those from?"

"I may be a lot of things, but a snoop is certainly not one of them." Chloe handed her the still-sealed envelope. "You tell me."

Lauren pulled open the flap and lifted out the card. *It was a pleasure to meet you. Cody.*

"They're from Cody." Lauren put the card back into the envelope. The words were kind but not one bit comforting. Everything was ruined, and kind words and pretty flowers would not change that. Light was glaring around the edges of the window shade and ricocheting off the framed prints of antique dress sketches that lined the living room walls, shining directly into her face. She closed her eyes against the pain of it. "Back to my earlier question—what are they saying on TV?"

Chloe wrapped her in a hug. "I can't believe them." She pulled back, shaking her head in the general direction of the television. "A bunch of preening house cats with a brand-new mouse in their claws. I've never understood the fascination with this kind of blood-in-the-water feeding frenzy." Chloe's long blond hair was poking out in all directions, and she was wearing her large black glasses, rarely seen after 7:00 a.m. Poor thing. Sensitive soul that she was, she seemed to be taking this disaster almost as hard as Lauren.

Lauren squeezed her friend's shoulder, determined to be strong in front of Chloe, even if she didn't feel like it. "I think you just mixed your animal metaphors again."

"They all apply, so why not?" Chloe managed somewhat of a grin, then followed Lauren toward the kitchen. "Can I make you some breakfast?"

"No thanks." Lauren pulled a Diet Coke from the fridge, popped the top, and took a long sip. "I just don't understand. I checked and rechecked every single stitch on that dress. For an entire seam to rip open like that . . . I'm stunned that I could have been so blind about what I was doing." She took another drink and nodded toward the television. "You might as well tell me. You know I'm going to hear it. Better to get it from a friend than those—what did you call them? Preening house cats on a feeding frenzy in the bloody water?"

Chloe shook her head. "You're not hearing anything from me. Not one word. Take my advice and don't turn on the TV for the next week or two."

Lauren walked across the room and picked up the remote, cast a hard glance in Chloe's direction, pointed the clicker toward the screen, and pressed. The E! channel lit up the screen with an entire segment devoted to a recap of last night's awards show—Taylor Swift with her latest boyfriend; JLo in her skintight, low-cut gown; Lady Gaga in her latest outlandish costume, which involved leather, feathers, and wings. Then, about every two minutes, the show reverted to what they were billing as the "wardrobe malfunction of the century." The scene replayed over and over again, slow motion, fast motion, regular motion, and then always ended with the freeze frame of Marisa's dress hanging open, revealing her bra and underwear. They were slightly blurring the area directly over Marisa's underwear—allegedly out of deference to her young age, but Lauren highly suspected it was more for dramatic effect. Either way, it left no doubt about what was being shown. Every bit of it. Then they'd play the audio of Marisa's breathless "Oh my," which served to bring the clip to an end.

"Marisa Remington's publicist expressed her outrage at what has happened," the show's host said. "The family is threatening legal action against *Deb Couture*."

Lauren dropped onto the couch and covered

her face with her right hand. "This is a disaster."

Chloe plopped down beside her, took a deep breath, and sighed. "Not com-plete-ly." Her words were long and drawn out, as if by stretching them a little farther they would somehow become true.

"Not completely? Really? How do you figure that? I honestly don't know how it could be any more complete." Lauren kept her head down but pivoted to look sideways at her roommate, hand still holding her forehead.

"Well . . ." Chloe flexed her fingers, took another deep breath, and stretched out her shoulders. "For one thing, I never really believed that you liked working at *Deb Couture*. The people were pretty cutthroat, and you were at someone else's beck and call. Tell the truth, you were looking forward to getting out of there."

"That job gave me opportunities that most people in my position would never even dream of. It gave me *experience* most people in my position would never even dream of. It moved me about ten steps closer to the place almost everyone in my position *does* dream of. Maybe I was looking forward to getting out of there eventually—like at the end of several years and complete with an I-did-an-internship-at-*Deb-Couture* line item in my résumé—" Lauren groaned. "My résumé. I'm sunk. How am I ever going to get another job in the industry again?" She turned her face back into her hand and moaned. "And truly, why should I? If I'm capable of making a mistake this huge, then maybe I shouldn't work in fashion."

And that truth, more than anything, had kept Lauren awake last night. How could she have overlooked something so crucial? It didn't seem possible. For the life of her, she couldn't figure out what had gone wrong.

"Okay, if there was ever anyone who was made to do what they are doing, it is you, so I don't want to hear another word about not belonging here. As my mother would say, let's think about this logically." Chloe paused, obviously trying to remember what kind of encouraging thing her level-headed mother would say. Or more likely, what kind of inspirational verse or quote she would give. "She would say . . . hmm . . . oh, I know—she would give you that Churchill quote she likes so much: 'Success is the ability to go from failure to failure without losing your enthusiasm.' That's what she would say." Chloe nodded her head, obviously quite pleased with herself. "You've just got to keep going forward."

"I don't know that I'll have the luxury of going on to another failure. This is more like a fatality, at least where my career is concerned." Lauren pulled her hand away from her face and slumped back against the sofa cushions. "My chances for another opportunity ripped apart with the tearing of that seam."

"Maybe you should just go ahead and go to work for yourself. A few years ahead of plan, but now might be the right time."

"Chloe, have I ever mentioned how naïve you are?"

"Am not. This is America. If you want to go into business, you are allowed that right. How can they stop you?"

"For one thing, it's very difficult to save and put aside money when you don't have a job, and lack of funding is an easy way this will stop me. And, even if I had a boatload of money, we get back to the main point—what woman in her right mind would come to me for a custom dress after this? Who wants to take the chance that they might flash everyone within viewing distance?"

"You are way overthinking this. It's not like most people are even going to know that you were involved in this whole ordeal. You're the nobody, remember?"

"At the beginning of last night, that was true. Now it's nothing more than wishful thinking. I know the Debowesky sisters' machine well enough to know that they will not bear the brunt of this. No. They will make sure it is universally known exactly who it was who messed this up. I can promise you that their names will be moved as far as possible from the whole debacle, and mine will be moved as close as possible."

Lauren had no sooner made the statement than

she heard the name Elyse Debowesky on the television. She looked up to see the glamorous Elyse standing before the camera, shaking her head. "Words just aren't enough for us to say how awful this is for us right now. Protecting that young woman's modesty was our utmost concern, and I have to confess, it was my fault."

"Ha! See there. She's taking the blame."

"Shhh!" Lauren waved her hand toward Chloe. "She's not done."

Elyse continued. "We made the mistake of allowing one of our interns to do some last-minute alterations. They were very simple modifications. Unfortunately, we didn't fully realize the degree of her incompetence."

"An intern?"

"Yes, Lauren Summers. She came to us very highly praised from the Fashion Institute, but apparently we put a little too much stock into someone else's word. That's a mistake we will not be making again, I can assure you."

"Is it safe to assume that Lauren Summers is no longer working at *Deb Couture*?"

"It is safe to assume not only that, but that she will never again work in the fashion industry in this town, if I have anything to say about it. We are all outraged over this."

Chloe put her arms around Lauren and drew her in for a hug. "Maybe this is a disaster."

"I'm pretty sure."

three

It felt good to be outside the apartment again. Lauren had been more or less locked in all week, trying to avoid the paparazzi who were loitering nearby.

Marisa, on the other hand, seemed to be made of stronger stuff, as she had been on the news almost every night this week, appearing at some public location or another. Lauren was grateful for that. At least she hadn't ruined Marisa's life as well as her own. She wanted so badly to apologize to her, but she had not been able to reach her. After multiple calls to Marisa's "people" remained unanswered, she'd finally left a message. "I am so sorry. For everything." There was not much else to say. All she could do was hope that someone would relay the message.

Now, as she drove north out of Los Angeles and onto the less-crowded sections of the 101, she actually began to enjoy the view—especially since the last twenty miles before Santa Barbara were mostly along the ocean. The sun glittered off the calm sea, where sailboats dotted the area between the mainland and the Channel Islands. She took a deep breath, relaxing for the first time in many days, and concentrated on the smell of salt and beach. Yes, she needed to get out of

LA more often, and here was her opportunity to do so.

As she drove into Santa Barbara, the ocean disappeared behind city streets, which were lined with businesses and restaurants. The mountains on her right became increasingly dotted by Mediterranean-style homes. She sighed deeply.

Santa Barbara. She loved this place. It would be a good place to start again, and thanks to a little help from Professor Navarro, her favorite prof from design school, she was perhaps about to get that chance.

Within two days of the wardrobe malfunction, Professor Navarro had called and said, "I have a couple of leads that I think would be beneficial to you."

"Really?" Lauren could still remember the desperation in her own voice. "I didn't know that was even possible at this point."

"I've done a little discreet asking around. No one is willing to publicly acknowledge this, but I've talked to a couple of places that—if you can manage to stay out of the news for the next several months—come spring or summer, they might be willing to quietly take you on."

"That sounds more encouraging than I'd dared to hope."

"It's not the caliber of job you could have gotten before all this, but it's a step in the right direction, and that's what we need at this point.

And, to be honest, staying out of the papers may not be as easy as you think, because it would be fairly lucrative to sell your picture to the gossip peddlers right now. And as long as there is money to be made, keeping yourself out of the public eye is going to be tricky."

"I already know that's true. My roommate has seen photographers loitering around our building night and day. I haven't stepped outside yet. I'm waiting for it to blow over."

"I think I have a solution for you, and it won't involve barricading yourself indoors. Actually, it comes with another piece of good news. Not only do I have a plan that will get you out of town for a while, but it will also have you doing design work in the meantime."

"How is that possible?"

"My oldest and dearest friend has a son who is a high school theater director at a large public school with one of the finest high school theatrical programs in the country. He called a few weeks back, because his school is about to launch a very ambitious rendition of *Camelot*. He wondered if I knew of any of my students who would be right for designing and fabricating a few high-end costumes. The pay is so small it's almost non-existent, but it is a rather prestigious program, and they have their reasons for needing this show to be excellent. Of course, we are talking about period clothing, which is why I immediately thought of you. At the time, you were at *Deb Couture*, so I didn't even mention it.

"Now, however, it presents itself as a good way for you to get out of town and out of the spotlight, as well as providing some in-the-business kind of work. If you do the amazing job I am certain that you will, it will help begin the process of restoring your credibility and give you a nice entry on your résumé, as well. I took the liberty of sending Theodore Rivers some photos of the Eliza Doolittle dress you designed last year for your costuming project. Of course, he saw at once that it was amazing, and he is itching to have you aboard. He said he has a lead on a place you can stay rent-free to help compensate for the lack of pay. I must warn you, though, if that place doesn't work out, the rents in that area are sky-high, and the pay won't come close to covering it."

Lauren felt something like hope—or at least the lack of despair—for the first time since the great malfunction. "And what area is that? With high rent?"

"Oh, I'm sorry, didn't I say? Santa Barbara."

"Santa Barbara?" Her voice squeaked just a little. Santa Barbara was far enough away to get her out of town, but close enough to allow her to still drive down for all the festivities for Chloe's upcoming wedding. "That's perfect. My lease is up here in another month because my roommate is getting married. I've been on the hunt for a new place but haven't found it yet, so the timing is good for a move."

"Almost like it's meant to be, isn't it?"

"Exactly."

"That's what I thought. Let me give you his contact information. He's waiting to hear from you." Professor Navarro gave her the information and hung up.

Lauren had immediately called Mr. Rivers. He was quick and to the point. "To be honest, there is a huge amount of pressure with this particular production. I do not have time to devote to overseeing costume work at all. Professor Navarro assures me that you can handle this with minimal input and supervision."

"Yes sir, I can."

"Wonderful. When can you start?"

"My only hold-up at this point is finding a place to live. Professor Navarro said you might know of something?"

"I do have a line on a place for you to stay, if you're interested. It's north of town, I'm told it's a bit of a fixer-upper, and the location is quite rural, so there's not much in the way of activity for someone your age. It would be night and day from Los Angeles, that much is certain."

"Believe me, that's a change I'm more than happy to make at this point."

"The location is lovely, or so I'm told. It's directly across the lane from some ocean cliffs.

One of our theater benefactors owns the place, but no one has lived in it for ages. It's about to undergo some renovation, so it's likely going to be a bit of a mess. Would that be a problem?"

"I'm sure it will be more than fine."

"Excellent. Let me call the owner and see if he can show you the house this weekend. Then I'll meet you at the theater on Monday to finalize plans. How's that?"

"Perfect. Thanks." Lauren hung up, pondering how quickly things seemed to have come together for this. And how quickly her life had fallen apart two days ago. As Rhonda liked to quote from the book of Job, *The Lord gave and the Lord has taken away; may the name of the Lord be praised.* One thing was for sure, Lauren was not going to take any of this for granted. If Job could give praise after all he went through, then Lauren most certainly could. And she'd be grateful for every single thing she received along the way. "Thank You, Father," she'd prayed after the phone call. "Whatever the outcome."

It was a few hours later when Mr. Rivers called back. "I have spoken with Ralph Edwards. He just needs to get final permission from the neighborhood manager, but he believes he will have it cleared in a couple of days. So, will Saturday work for you?"

"Permission from the neighborhood manager?"

"Yes. I suppose I should warn you. It sounds as

if the people who live on that little street are a bit strange. They're all fiercely private. If this gets approved, you'll likely have all sorts of rules you'll have to follow."

This did give Lauren pause. What kind of area would need so much privacy? She pictured a row of flop houses full of addicts and drug dealers. Still, what choice did she have? "It won't bother me. I enjoy my privacy, as well."

"Actually, those rules are working in your favor right now. One of the reasons the owner is so willing to have you there is that the regulations state that a contractor cannot be working in the neighborhood unless a resident is present at the home where the work is being done."

"So, I'm going to be the resident who babysits the contractor? Isn't that insulting to the contractor?"

"I would think so, and I can't promise that there won't be some resentment aimed at you because of that. Are you up for it?"

With a small bank account that was sure to evaporate in the coming months, did she have a choice? "Yes, I believe that I am."

And now she was about to find out. She made her way through Santa Barbara and out the other end, continuing north for several more miles. When she exited the freeway, she followed the directions toward the ocean. This area was mostly trees and hills and pastureland, hardly a building to be seen anywhere. Finally she came to a little pullout on the road, where a couple of cars were parked while their owners were snapping photos of the ocean far below, then about a hundred yards later, she found a nondescript brown fence flanking an offshoot road. On each side there were *Private Property, No Trespassing* signs. A few dozen yards inside the fence line, there was a small guardhouse. Lauren pulled up to the structure.

A gray-haired man in a blue uniform slid the window open. "May I help you?"

"I think I'm in the right place. Is this Hide Away Lane? I'm here to see the Edwardses' cottage."

"Your name?"

"Lauren Summers."

He didn't bother to look at anything, he simply nodded. "Yes, we've been expecting you. May I see some ID?"

"Sure." She dug through her purse and found her wallet, then pulled out her license.

He looked at it, looked back at Lauren, and nodded once. "Welcome to the neighborhood. We'll all recognize you and your car soon enough, so you won't have to stop here every time. I'm sure Mr. Edwards explained to you that this is an area where the residents value their privacy."

"Yes, I understand." In fact, Lauren had been given quite a list of rules. She was discouraged from having visitors at her cottage at all, but a few allowances might be made with advanced written notice and the approval of the neighborhood manager. It sounded like it would just be simpler to meet anyone she wanted to see in town—which seemed to be the point of the rules, anyway. "This is my first time in the area. It's the second one on the right, is that correct?" Looking ahead, she could see no sign of houses at all, only a treelined country lane that seemed in need of repair.

"Yes, it is. Just around the curve up ahead. I hope you like it here. My name's Sam, by the way, if you need anything." He offered a little salute, then opened the gate.

There were potholes every few feet, and the edges of the road were crumbling into the adjacent dirt. A dense thicket of ancient oak trees loomed ahead, creating a canopy all around. In her rear-view mirror, a cloud of dust billowed up behind her. Not the right home for a clean-car enthusiast, that much was sure.

After she rounded the left-hand curve and then another to the right, the first homes came into view. A large Tudor-style house on the right was offset from the large Mediterranean on the left, so that they didn't directly face each other. The Mediterranean was oceanside, although the blue water in the distance was well beneath this lane. Lauren felt hope begin to swell up inside her. This place was wonderful. She could still hear Rhonda's voice from last night. "Once you get into your own little quiet, secluded space, you need to spend some time and really go deep. Dig into the scriptures, pray, write in your journal. Most of life's distractions will be a nonissue when you're off on your own like that. This time is just what you need to emerge a stronger and deeper woman. A woman that God can use in a mighty way."

It seemed, as usual, that Rhonda was correct. This would be a wonderful place to relax and recharge and figure out some way to start rebuilding her career, which at this point was further back than when she'd first started. It was going to be a long climb.

When Lauren approached the second right-hand driveway, she could see a dust-covered white Lexus parked there. She pulled up behind it and looked toward the cottage in question. She simply sat in the driver's seat and took a deep breath. *"It needs some work"* had been an understatement.

Just then the screen door screeched open, hanging by the bottom hinge only and leaning at a precarious angle. A sixty-ish-year-old man in a gray suit walked toward her and extended his hand. "Lauren Summers?"

"Yes." She shook his offered hand.

"Ralph Edwards, nice to meet you." He gestured toward the cottage, which once had been a tiny, Craftsman-style-meets-surf-shack structure but now was mostly just a shack. In fact, it looked as if a strong wind might topple it. The pale gray paint was peeling in sheets, and the white shutters were peeling and moldy looking. The front porch ran the entire width of the house—which was not wide at all—and had a broken wooden step in the middle. In spite of the run-down condition, it was still adorable. Charming, even. One of those kinds of places that people drive by on vacation and stop to take a picture of just because they're so lovely. Rustic, they would call it, just before they kept driving.

"Why don't you come inside and check it out?" Ralph said.

Lauren nodded. "Thank you." She followed him inside, taking care to avoid the broken step. Once she entered, she held her breath and looked around.

"Sorry about the dust. No one has been here in several years."

The dust was indeed thick on everything. There was a combination kitchenette and living room as she first entered. Lime scale ran down the back of the sink, grime of an indeterminate nature stuck to the floors, and every bit of the upholstery looked as if it had gone through a dust storm that would have taken down John Wayne.

"We've had a little water leak in the bedroom," he said as he led her through the door to the back room, where a large portion of the ceiling was yellowed in a circular blob. "I'm afraid it's going to be a bit of a mess here until we get the new roof on and the rain damage repaired. You'll probably do best to sleep in the living room until they get this fixed."

"Don't worry. That will be fine with me. I'm happy and privileged to be here." And the truth was, there was a lot of good to be thankful for here. She had a place to live, out of the limelight and close enough to the ocean cliffs that she could hear the waves breaking from inside the cottage. She would take none of this for granted.

He nodded absentmindedly, as if he expected nothing less. "Listen, here's the deal. Our family has always supported the theater department at the local high school, and I have arranged all this as a favor to Theodore Rivers." He looked around and rubbed the back of his neck. "And it's a favor to me, as well. We've received several official notices that we need to get this place fixed up because neighborhood rules require a certain amount of upkeep. Those same rules, however, do not allow workers in a home unless a resident is present—and since we live on the far side of town, almost an hour away from here, that's not particularly workable for us. So, you need to be here when the workers are on-site."

He put his hand on a tattered window shade. "They'll be replacing the roof, the front porch, the bedroom ceiling, and some plumbing fixtures, but other than the exterior paint, not so much in the way of aesthetics. Feel free to do whatever you want to the interior of the place to make it more livable—paint, upholstery cleaning, new blinds, whatever—and I will reimburse you for the supplies if you keep the receipts."

"Do you want me to get your approval on colors and things?"

He shook his head. "Anything you do at this point can only be an improvement. No one has lived here in twenty years. I'm thinking of putting the place on the market soon, I'm just not sure I have the time to deal with all the hassle it would involve." He turned on the faucet, which sputtered a bit but then spit out a decent stream of water. "I had the utilities turned back on this week, just to be certain everything was in working order. You'll need to get them all changed to your name at the start of the week."

Lauren nodded. "I'll make those calls right away."

"Please remember that when the contractor is here, you must be here. He's already been cleared to be in the neighborhood, but you still can't leave him here alone."

"Got it."

"Also, don't bring in any friends whose names are not on the approved list—be sure to give them a list of names at the gate of people you expect, and please keep the list minimal. You might as well know, if any of your friends are in any way involved in the media, they will not be allowed in here.

"Do not, for any reason, wander into anyone else's yard, and don't take any pictures. Stay on the public paths only, especially when you are heading down to the beach." He pointed across the street to a path toward the ocean cliffs, which led through a wooded area directly across from the cottage. To the right of the path, an imposing Victorian rose up behind a wrought-iron fence. It and the surrounding landscape took up the entire end of the cul-de-sac. He nodded toward it. "In particular, stay away from anything to do with that house. The owner is very private. She has memorized every single landowner regulation ever committed to paper, and she would not hesitate to pursue legal action if she in any way thought that any of the rules were being violated."

"Avoid Victorian house and owner at all costs. Got it."

He smiled. "You'll do just fine."

"Sounds like there might be some mysterious characters around here."

"Not so much anymore. Most of the people who are here now are second generation, and most of them would like to see the rules eased up a little—my girls would have been thrilled to bring their high school friends here and make it sort of a beach camp. Miss Montgomery, the lady in the Victorian, is the only one who still holds tight to the pact made by the original landowners, and believe me, she doesn't budge even a little bit. But . . . we've all been spoiled by having our own little private beach without all the hassle of traffic and tourists, so most everyone sees some value in keeping things somewhat controlled."

Given his tone, Lauren suspected this declaration was more an attempt to be polite about a really irritating old lady, as opposed to a statement he truly believed.

"Why was it set up to be so secretive here?"

"All of the original owners were hiding from something. My father had somewhat of a colorful past involving bank fraud and loose women. He came from an upstanding New York family, so it was in everyone's best interest to give him a low profile for a while. This place fit the bill, so they sent him here to live while things cooled off. They intentionally made the place small so that he wouldn't get too comfortable during his exile.

"The man who built the Victorian"—he gestured toward the end of the lane—"built it for his mistress and their daughter, the current resident. He made sure he had the biggest and grandest place by far, because that's the kind of in-your-face guy he was. I gather there was quite the big brouhaha in Hollywood about their lack of marital arrangement. Now the daughter is just a grumpy old hermit in a big old house, and she likes to make sure no one else around her is enjoying themselves anywhere in her vicinity." He coughed, cleared his throat. "Sorry, that sounded bitter, didn't it. I just get rather frustrated about it sometimes."

"I'm surprised non-owner tenants are allowed to stay here, with things as rigid as they are."

"Technically, they're not. We were only able to get the approval for you to move in because the place had been unused for so long and has gotten run-down and become a bit of an eyesore. Plus, it's understood that you have your own reasons for wanting privacy right now." He looked at her evenly.

"Everyone here knows who I am?"

"Doubt it, actually. The homeowners' decisions now are mostly made by Neil Winston, the lawyer who is a paid neighborhood manager—his parents live in the Mediterranean house you passed on the way in. The residents don't want to be bothered with details like which contractor I've hired, so they pay a fee and let him deal with it."

"Sounds reasonable." Lauren looked around. "It's a beautiful location and a cute cottage. I'm surprised you don't use it more."

He shook his head. "Like I said, we live on the other side of town, close enough to the beach that there doesn't seem to be much point in driving all the way out here. Even when we do want some rest and quiet, my family is more of the go-to-a-hotel-and-get-a-massage-at-the-spa type. Having to arrive and spend the next day cleaning and stocking pantries doesn't really suit their style."

Lauren smiled and nodded, but inside she was thinking it was a waste of a beautiful place. "Well, I'm excited about spending time here."

"So remember, no violating privacy, no cutting through yards, and if you see someone who is nosing around, call security and have them sent on their way."

"Will do." Lauren couldn't imagine there were too many people who snooped around out here. The place was almost impossible to find, even with directions. Still, if the people who lived in the area were that paranoid, she wasn't going to complain. After all, part of the reason she was here was to get away from the prying eyes and wagging tongues of others.

He handed her a business card. "This is contact information for the contractor, in case you need to reach him."

With that, Ralph Edwards got in his car, drove away, and left Lauren in her filthy new home. She couldn't help but smile, though. The place was adorable, even in this sad state. A month from now it would be her dream place. She planned to get the work done as early as possible and then be able to spend some time enjoying the fruits of her labor. Yes, this was going to work out just fine.

She made a list of cleaning supplies, deciding she would start right now getting this place spic and span. When she was finished, it would be perfect.

Charlotte Montgomery drew back the velvet curtain of her third-story turret. She saw Ralph Edwards standing in his driveway, speaking to a young woman. She was dressed in jeans and a T-shirt, with wavy red hair—like a modern-day Maureen O'Hara. She looked innocent enough, but they all did at first glance.

She let the curtain fall closed, cloaking the room in the darkness she preferred. She walked across to the round table beside the doorway, lifted the phone off its cradle, and pressed the numbers she'd long since memorized. She walked back toward the window, extending the cord its full length across the room.

Neil Winston answered on the third ring. "Miss Montgomery, good morning."

"I don't like the looks of the girl who is moving in across the street."

He paused for a moment, then cleared his throat. "But we already agreed—"

"I've changed my mind. I don't want her here."

"I'm sorry, Miss Montgomery, we've already signed the agreement. You and I did discuss all this before, remember? You wanted the old place cleaned up a bit?" He was using his placating voice, as if his intentionally calm tone would somehow change the facts.

"Do not speak to me as if I'm an idiot. I know very well what I said about wanting that place cleaned up. I'm telling you I do not like the looks of that girl, and I do not want her here."

"Unfortunately, it's too late for that. There's nothing we can do at this point. Unless she breaks her end of the agreement, you're just going to be stuck with her until next summer. That is the duration of the agreement."

"Next summer? Ridiculous! That's far too long."

"But that was the agreement that was made, and the contract that was signed, nonetheless."

Charlotte watched the girl turn and go into the house as Ralph Edwards pulled out of the driveway. "We'll just have to see about that." She let the curtain fall closed.

four

Lauren made her way through the sprawling Home Depot parking lot. Her cart was loaded with buckets, bleach, and upholstery cleaner, and the handles of a broom and a mop stuck out beside her head, making it difficult to maneuver. She almost ran into a man loading some sort of pipe into the back of his truck.

As she approached her car, she noticed a woman leaning against the trunk of the blue BMW convertible in the parking stall beside hers. She steered a wide path, finally reaching her car without crashing into anyone.

"Excuse me." The woman at the BMW took a step toward her. "I'm wondering if you could help me."

"I will if I'm able." Lauren looked up at the woman, prepared to tell her that she, too, was new to town and didn't know the directions anywhere, nor did she have jumper cables, but she did have a cell phone and AAA on speed dial.

The woman wore black Lulu pants and an over-the-thumb black-and-white-striped yoga shirt. Something about her seemed vaguely familiar. "You're Lauren Summers, aren't you?" she said.

Ice-cold prickles ran from the back of Lauren's neck down to her fingertips. She began throwing the items from her cart into the cargo hold of her Ford Escape without giving any indication that she'd heard the question. She needed to get out of there fast. How could they possibly have found her? This soon?

"My name is Kendall Joiner. I work for the *Hollywood Reporter*."

That was why she looked familiar. Of course. "No comment." Lauren pushed her cart toward the return area, not looking back at all. How had this woman found her? And in the Home Depot parking lot, of all places.

"I'm not asking for a comment." Kendall Joiner was keeping pace, matching step for step. "Actually, I might have something for you."

"Oh really?" Lauren made certain her tone did nothing to hide her doubt about the truth in that statement. She shoved her cart into the queue and started back across the lot.

"Really." Kendall followed her back to their cars. Then Lauren realized the BMW looked familiar.

She stopped walking and truly looked at Kendall for the first time. "Are you following me? I saw you parked along the cliffs a little while ago, didn't I? Just outside that gated area?" At the time, she had chalked it up to a photo enthusiast looking for a peaceful shot just outside the restricted access. It had never entered her mind that it might be a reporter lying in wait. If this was reality, no wonder the people who lived on Hide Away Lane were so obsessive about unapproved visitors.

"Here's the thing." Kendall leaned against Lauren's car. "I know how it is when you're the scapegoat. Believe me, I've been in that position more than once."

Somehow Lauren doubted that Kendall had ever been humiliated on national TV, but then again, the entertainment world was cutthroat. She probably had experienced some unpleasantness. Regardless of her past, in the present she was a reporter looking for an angle to her story—likely some dirt on Marisa, who had already suffered enough. Lauren had no intention of feeding that beast. "I'm sorry for you, then. If you'll excuse me, I have things to—"

"Believe me, I understand why you don't want to talk to me. But I think if you'll listen for just a minute, I might have some information that you will find worth your while." Her brown ponytail stuck out from a pink ball cap, and in truth she looked more like she was ready for the gym than for researching her next big story. Maybe that was the idea.

Lauren folded her arms across her chest. "I am not giving you the inside scoop about Marisa Remington, her mother, her manager, or anything about the whole malfunction debacle. If that's what you're after, then you can just save us both a lot of time by getting out of my way."

Kendall smiled, and as she shook her head, her ponytail swung back and forth. "You've got it all wrong. It's not you giving a story to me, it's me giving a story to you."

"What do you mean?"

"I have a fairly major lead that the 'malfunction'"—she made air quotes around the word— "was staged."

"Staged? That's ridiculous."

"According to my source, Marisa Remington hated the squeaky-clean image they were always trying to douse her with. She wanted to be seen as grown-up and sexy—typical seventeen-year-old, right?"

So that was it. She needed Lauren to verify her sources about Marisa wanting to look sexier and, by doing so, to seemingly corroborate her invented story line. *Good luck with that.* Lauren wasn't talking.

She pressed the unlock button on her key fob and reached for the door handle. "I need you to move, please. You're in my way."

"Word is, her mother and agent were so over-bearing, Marisa decided there was nothing to do but take matters into her own hands." Kendall scooted out of the arc of the driver's-side door as Lauren swung it open. "In spite of the general outrage, if you've been anywhere near the internet recently, you have to have seen that there has been more than a little attention given to the fact that she does, indeed, have an amazing body."

"I've seen a little of the media coverage, and it's disgusting." Lauren pulled at the door, but Kendall held it.

"In fact, did you know that *Vivian's Unmentionables* has reported a run on the bra and panty set she was wearing? They completely sold out in a matter of hours after the awards show and are now reporting a backorder of several hundred thousand garments."

"That is just sick."

Kendall tilted her head to one side and offered a hard little grin. "That's the world we live in. I could tell you stories that would make this seem downright pure."

"No thanks."

"My point is, that kind of thing would be a dream ending for Marisa, if she did indeed plan the whole thing, wouldn't it?"

That statement knocked the breath right out of Lauren. In spite of how utterly absurd the story sounded, it also just slightly rang true. A successful ending . . . for Marisa. Never mind that it had ruined Lauren's career before it even had the chance to begin—a career she'd worked hard to even have the hope of achieving. And now, *poof.* She thought of all the laughs she and Marisa had shared together during fittings. The comments that Marisa had made about having "at least one person around here who gets me." She wouldn't have set this up knowing it would destroy Lauren. Would she?

Lauren had spent many sleepless nights worrying about Marisa since the mishap, and she'd been so proud of her being brave enough to immediately go back out into public. It couldn't all have been planned out. Surely not.

Lauren held the car door. "If what you're saying is true, and I don't believe that it is, but if it were, then I *really* wish I could help you, because I could get my career back. But even if it is, I don't know anything about it, so I'm afraid I won't be able to help you."

"I know. Let's go grab a quick cup of coffee, shall we?" She gestured toward the Starbucks on the far side of the parking lot.

Lauren wanted to go back to the cottage. But somehow, what Kendall was saying intrigued her enough that she just couldn't do that until she'd heard it all. A few minutes later, she was sipping a flat white, doubt mixed with hope mixed with anger rising inside her. "So, I'm still not clear on what you want from me. Like I told you, this is all news to me."

"Exactly as I expected. I don't have cold, hard proof yet, but I'm working on getting it. When I do, I would like to come to you for an official interview. We'll do some sort of piece where we break the story wide open, giving your side of it. We'll make a big point of how her selfish ambition destroyed what you'd worked long and hard—and honestly—for. It will be a contrast that our readers will eat up. You'll suddenly be seen as the innocent victim of a wild child's scheme to get some publicity. You'll go from being a scapegoat to a martyr in one fell swoop. People are going to love you."

"That sounds almost too good to be true." And too awful. She still couldn't begin to believe that Marisa would have done this to her.

Kendall shrugged. "And yet . . . it is true. It will take a little work to get the absolute proof—and believe me, no one would touch this story without some strong evidence behind it—but when I pitch the story to my editor, I just want your word that you will give me exclusive access until the story has broken wide open."

"If you can clear my name in all this, I'll grant you exclusive access for as long as you want." Lauren hadn't even realized the weight of the burden that had pressed against her until some of it was suddenly and unexpectedly removed. Maybe she hadn't made a mistake, after all. Maybe this really wasn't her fault in any way. She felt so . . . free. "Sounds like a dream come true."

"Great. I was hoping you would say that."

"I can't believe it." Lauren took another sip, her imagination already daring to picture a second chance at everything. She could get her life back due to one little article. For now, she would keep her head down and spend the next few months keeping her word and doing some interesting work for the local theater. Kendall could continue to research her story until she found proof. At the end of it all, Lauren would be hardly any worse for wear.

"Listen, I do have a little favor to ask in return."

Here it came. She'd known it was too good to be true. "I already told you, I don't know any-thing about Marisa or her personal life."

Kendall made a dismissive gesture. "Nothing like that. In fact, it has nothing to do with Marisa at all."

"Really? What then?"

"I know you are moving into the Edwards family's house right now, next door to an old Victorian." Kendall looked directly at her, her gaze unwavering.

"How do you know that?" Lauren rubbed her finger around a circular stain on the wooden table, hoping to hear a logical and nonthreatening explanation, although she couldn't think of what that might be. The silence continued until Lauren finally looked up to find Kendall's attention still locked on her.

"The lady who lives in that old Victorian is Charlotte Montgomery, a wannabe movie star from the late 1940s and early '50s. I'd be interested to know about any interaction you have with her."

"Interaction? I doubt seriously I'll have any. I'm told she keeps to herself."

"Definitely true, which is why I'd be happy to have any and all information."

"There is a very strict privacy policy in the neighborhood."

"Don't I know that. And I'm not asking you to break that agreement in any way. No pictures or roaming through private areas. All I'm asking is for some general information if you should run across her."

"What kind of information?"

"Anything at all. How she looks now, what she

might be wearing, any jewelry you might see. I'm working on an article about her. She left Hollywood sixty years ago—right after a high-profile and very suspicious murder. No one was ever arrested. I've been doing some investigative journalism, just for fun, and I've come across some things that have led me to believe that she might have been more than a little involved. There are a couple of gowns and one particular piece of jewelry I would love to know if she still owns. So . . . if you ever see her, I'd be most interested in what she's wearing."

"Why don't you interview her?"

"As you said, she keeps to herself. Basically, she's little more than a hermit. Receives very few visitors, and if she even gets a hint that there is press around, she goes into all-out lockdown mode. Most people have assumed she's just a rich, eccentric old lady. I'm wondering if there might be more to it. Google it when you get home— the Randall Edgar Blake murder case. I think you'll find it interesting. Anyway, I'm not asking for you to spy on her, just if you see her out in the open, let me know." She reached into her jacket pocket and pulled out a business card. "Here's my number if you have anything to tell me. Other-wise, I will keep in touch and keep you updated on anything I find out about Marisa and the malfunction."

"Okay." Lauren put the card in her back pocket.

"Well, I need to get back to my new home and get to work."

Kendall stood up and offered her hand. "It was nice meeting you."

As Lauren drove back toward the cottage, she tried to wrap her mind around what she'd just learned. *Marisa may have set the whole thing up?*

She called Chloe and told her everything.

"That little brat," Chloe said. "Remember how you were so convinced that she was actually nice deep down? A classic case of the wolf in sheep's clothing, only the wolf turns out to be a peacock— one with nudist and flashing tendencies."

Lauren couldn't help but laugh at the mish-mash comparison. "If it's true, and I still don't think it is, but if it is, I hope Kendall is able to find some concrete proof."

"Just think how this will sound to the public when they read this story. *Wronged design intern doing amazing work for high school theater, for a pittance, after spoiled, scheming star ruins her life to serve her own evil purposes.* You will come out the victorious hero in the end, and everyone will know it."

Lauren was trying hard not to get her hopes up. Anger was battling with betrayal, which battled with disbelief. Where was the truth here? She had no idea. "I hope you're right."

"Of course I am. It's going to be wonderful."

"Speaking of wonderful, my new living arrangement needs a little work before it reaches that lofty distinction. I'm going to stay and do some cleanup today and will probably just crash here tonight. I'll drive back down tomorrow and get some clothes and things."

"So you're going to move in there right away?"

"I'm going to start working on it immediately, trying to get it livable while I've got the time. I have a meeting with the theater director on Monday and will need to start work rather quickly. It's too much driving if I don't stay here most of the time."

"You'll still make it to tea on the sixteenth, right?" Chloe and Jasper were planning a very small wedding, but they had arranged several creative events during the weeks before, and even after, the wedding. Something to satisfy Chloe's quirky, creative nature. A week from Wednesday, Chloe's mother was hosting the girls for high tea at a local Danish bakery.

"Chloe, I may be moving a hundred miles north, but I am still your best friend and maid of honor. I've never been to high tea before and have always wanted to try it, and there's no possible way I would miss spending a few hours with your mother and her words of wisdom. Of course I'll be there. Not to mention, I want to do one last fitting of your dress."

"That's what I was hoping you'd say. And speaking of my mother and her words of wisdom,

I'm trying to make a list of some of her more memorable quotes. I'm making her a keepsake for her fiftieth birthday that will include a bunch of them. Can you help me think of some and maybe text or email 'em to me?"

"You got it. See you sometime tomorrow."

Lauren hung up just as she drove through the entry gate. She was busy thinking through all the quotes and verses Rhonda Inglehart had bestowed on them over the years as she glanced toward the Victorian house at the end of the lane. She thought about what Kendall Joiner had told her and found herself glancing to see if Charlotte Montgomery might be outside, maybe carrying some sort of sixty-year-old murder weapon. Lauren shook her head and laughed. Ridiculous.

There was no sign of movement anywhere near the Victorian. *Sorry, Kendall, I tried.*

One of Rhonda's quotes popped into her memory. She laughed when she thought about the random Bible verse Rhonda used to quote whenever she felt that Chloe or Lauren was being drawn in by a bad crowd. *Be careful not to make a treaty with those who live in the land where you are going, or they will be a snare among you.*

The words kept rolling over and over in her mind, getting louder and louder and louder. *Be careful not to make a treaty with those who live in the land where you are going, or they will be a snare among you.* Weird. She did not plan to have anything to do with Charlotte Montgomery, much less make a treaty with her. It was time to move on to a new quote.

She carried her supplies into the house, and still the words nagged at her. Well, it was time to get to work, so there was only one thing to do in this situation.

She pulled out her iPod, put in her earbuds, and turned up the music.

five

The sink was scrubbed to a color that was as near white as it was going to get, the countertops were spotless, and the cabinets were cleaned and polished as the daylight began to fade. Lauren felt her strength draining with the fading light. The place was coming along, but dirt that went as deep as this required more than a little effort to clean.

She'd hauled the mattress and box spring out onto the back porch to air out and had thumped them with a broom like she'd seen people do in old movies. Nothing visible flew out of them, which she found somewhat comforting. Her plan was to fix the place up as nice as possible. Not just to make it livable, but to make it nice. It was the best way she could think of to show her appreciation to the Edwards family. Even if they didn't use this place, they would certainly be able to see that she appreciated getting to live here for several months rent-free.

There were three wooden cupboards in the kitchen. The front panel was cracked down the middle of one of them, and the other two were badly scarred. She didn't know much about refinishing but thought maybe she would give it a try. Her phone rang. "Hello?"

"I've gone and done it again." The sound of her best friend's frazzled voice quickly brought a smile to her face.

"Oh really, Chloe? What have you gone and done?"

"My usual. I was so caught up in the details of your story about that brat Marisa's little trick, and then of course worried about my own pre-wedding plans, that I didn't even ask you the details about your new place. So . . . what's up with it?"

"It's charming, truly charming. Needs some elbow grease, which I've already started applying, and even now it is beginning to show its potential. Say, what do you know about refinishing cabinetry?"

"That would be a big zilch. But Jasper knows how to do it. I've heard him talk about it. Why? Are you thinking of trying it?"

"I'm thinking about it. The kitchen cabinets here are pretty rough looking. Thing is, I don't want to do it if I'm going to mess it up and make it look worse than it was in the beginning. You know what I mean?"

"Maybe we can drive up and have a refinishing party sometime soon. Jasper could lend his expertise, and you know Mom would be all over it. Between all of us, I'm sure we could make it look nice."

"You don't have to do that. You've got plenty of other things going on in your life right now."

"Of course we don't have to, we want to. You know we're all dying to see the new place."

"I better make sure I get your names on my approved visitor list, then. Don't be alarmed if some FBI agents show up at the apartment asking a bunch of personal questions."

"Approved visitor list? Are you kidding me?"

"Apparently not. Everyone has to be cleared before they are allowed through the gate. I was being sarcastic about the FBI, obviously, but it's still pretty intense."

"Well, make sure you add me, and Mom and Dad, and Jasper, and probably you should add Cody, too, just so you're prepared."

"Somehow I doubt that will be necessary."

"Oh, I think it will. Jasper says he keeps asking about you. I'm surprised he hasn't called you himself, or has he and you're just not telling?"

"No, he has not."

"He has your number, right?"

"Not that I'm aware of."

"You didn't give it to him? When you sent that thank-you for the flowers?"

"No. Why would I? That seems rather pushy, don't you think?"

"No, I don't think it's pushy." She paused. "Okay, well maybe a little pushy, but not much. Tell me the truth, what's your problem with him?"

"I don't have a problem with him at all. I have a problem with me. It's all just so embarrassing. The one and only time he ever sees me is when I'm humiliated in front of the entire world. And then I just walk out of the room and leave, which I know was so rude, but honestly, I just don't think I could have done it any differently."

"Apparently he still thinks you're worth getting to know. And besides, supposedly he has a little workbench in his garage. I'm guessing he would be just the man to help with your cupboards. What?" Chloe's voice trailed away from the phone. "Listen, I gotta run. I'll talk to you soon." The phone line clicked, and Chloe was off and running to her next event. That girl lived in a swirl of chaos and activity that never calmed down. It was one of the things Lauren was going to miss while she was out here all by herself.

She went to her car and removed an insulated bag of snacks she'd brought with her just in case. Tomorrow evening she would buy some groceries on her way back with her clothes and things. Given the distance from this place to anywhere she might want to go, grocery store included, living here would definitely require advanced planning. For tonight, she would eat the apple and yogurt she'd bought and call it dinner.

First, though, it seemed like a good time to walk down to the beach. Just the thought of putting her toes in the ocean revived her energy. Nothing like the cold spray of the Pacific to wake a girl up, and the prospect of watching the sun set above the water on a regular basis was enough incentive to make her all the more determined to get this place spiffed up.

She stepped down from her porch and took a good look at the home at the end of the lane. It had a wrought-iron fence around the expansive lawn. The area just outside the gates and fence was simply a patch of dirt between the fence and the street curb. It looked drab in comparison to the lawn area, which was mowed and had neatly trimmed interior shrubs. The landscaping, even inside the fence, was manicured, but it by no means had the appearance of being tended with the loving care Aunt Nell, her great-aunt, would have shown it.

The large Victorian home was painted a medium green with dark green trim. It was two stories tall, with a turret that went up to a third level, offering what Lauren could only imagine to be breathtaking views of the ocean on one side and the mountains on the other. The home was striking in its beauty and quite an unusual sight in this part of the central coast, where the homes tended toward the Mediterranean or Craftsman styles. On this little lane it stood out in both size and style, but she suspected that had been the builder's intent. To stand out.

She crossed the cul-de-sac and started down the dirt path, which ran adjacent to the Victorian home. Farther back, there was a clear view of the backyard through the fence. The back side of the home had an expansive back porch and gazebo. The yard eventually dropped off, leaving nothing but clear ocean views. What an amazing place.

A movement caught her eye, and she noticed an elderly woman walking slowly across the back porch. She was shading her eyes from the sun and looking directly at Lauren. "This is a private area!" she yelled across the lawn. "You must leave here immediately." Her ash-blond hair was pulled back in a rather formal twist, and she wore a full-length evening gown.

"I've just moved into the cottage across the street. I was told that I am allowed to use this trail to walk down to the ocean."

"You don't say." The woman leaned on the rail surrounding her raised back porch. "You might be allowed to walk to the beach, but you most certainly are not allowed to snoop around my place. We all live here because we want to be left alone and in peace. I was assured by Mr. Winston that you would understand that very clearly."

"Yes, I do. I'm sorry. I didn't mean to pry."

"Mean to or not, that's what you were doing. Either abide by that principle or find yourself somewhere else to live, because I absolutely will not tolerate it." A short necklace glinted at the base of her neck in the fading evening light. It appeared to be blue in color, but from this distance it was hard to tell. She swept around in a half circle and glided back toward her house. The dark blue silk gown she wore trailed behind her.

Lauren was almost certain the dress was an Angelina Browning—the Los Angeles designer famous for her elegant dresses dating back to the mid-1940s. Lauren adored fashion history, especially that particular era, and Browning was among the very best.

An elderly woman in a Browning gown who valued her privacy to the point that she was willing to strictly enforce the already strict neighborhood code, all for the sake of extreme privacy? What was she hiding? Lauren thought about Kendall's story of a decades-old murder and wondered if her neighbor was indeed involved in some way.

She turned and made her way down the steps toward the ocean. This was going to make for an interesting place to live, that much was certain.

When she got back to the cottage later, she sent a quick email to Kendall.

Just saw my elusive neighbor. She is not exactly warm and fuzzy, I'll say that much about her. Not much to report, but I can verify that she does exist and was wearing a blue evening-type gown. That's all I can say for sure.

Since she didn't know if the gown really was a Browning, and couldn't see any detail at all about the necklace, she chose not to mention them.

That night Lauren dreamed about Aunt Nell. Scenes of them hiking together, going to town for ice cream, and working in the garden. Unfortunately, the dream morphed into her strongest memory from after the funeral—looking in the rearview mirror down Aunt Nell's long driveway and seeing the weeds and shriveled flowers in the flower bed. Even in the midst of the dream, she felt nauseous.

She awoke filled again with regret for the disrepair Aunt Nell's yard and garden had fallen into when she'd gotten sick. It should have been an immediate tip-off to the neighbors that something wasn't right when her pristine lawn and flower beds suddenly became overgrown and weed filled. However, Aunt Nell was always such a quiet, unassuming person, apparently most people never even thought to check and see if something might be wrong.

Since all her kids lived in other states, and since

Lauren had been in LA at school, no one in the family had known about Nell's diagnosis because she had decided not to "bother" anyone. None of them had realized that she had gotten so sick that she could barely take care of herself—she certainly never alluded to it in phone calls or her trademark handwritten letters that were more like novels. She had died alone and in pain, and while she had done so for purely unselfish reasons, Lauren wished very much that her aunt could have understood that they all needed to help her. That doing so would have made their good-bye less painful. Less guilt-ridden.

She shook her head and got out of bed, wondering what had prompted that particular dream. She hadn't had it for a couple of years now. Maybe it had something to do with Miss Montgomery. She was roughly Aunt Nell's age. Although that was probably the closest thing to a commonality the two women would ever share.

six

On Monday morning, Lauren woke up shivering. The cottage was drafty, and with the wind coming from the general direction of the cool Pacific waters, it made for a frigid morning. She knew that it would be warm by noon, but she chided herself for not bringing some flannel pajamas and warm fuzzy socks from her apartment yesterday. She reached to the bedside table for her phone to check the time. 6:45 a.m. The contractor would be here in less than two hours, so she needed to get moving. She climbed out of bed, heated some water for a cup of tea, and planned to take full advantage of what Rhonda referred to as a time to go deep.

Tea in hand, she wrapped up in a quilt and sat down on the sofa with her Bible and journal. Now was the time to tell the absolute truth—to herself and to God. But where did she want to start? She finally scratched out her first line. *I like it here, even in the draft, even in the cold. No one can see me here. There's no one to laugh at me.*

She shook her head and closed the journal. Feeling sorry for herself on paper wasn't going to help anything. She picked up her Bible and dropped to her knees, then fell forward on her face and just poured out what was inside her. "God, help me. Lead me. Use me. Don't let this time be wasted, whatever Your purpose." She turned randomly to the book of Philippians and read. *I want you to know, brothers, that what has happened to me has really served to advance the gospel, so that it has become known throughout the whole imperial guard and to all the rest that my imprisonment is for Christ. And most of the brothers, having become confident in the Lord by my imprisonment, are*

much more bold to speak the word without fear.
Those verses gave her pause. Most people would
not think of prison as a great thing to advance the
kingdom of God.

How could God use Marisa's wardrobe malfunction to advance His kingdom? Lauren didn't
know the answer to that one, but she did believe
He was in ultimate control of everything and He
did have a plan. It was hard to fathom how what
had happened could possibly be a good thing for
anyone, though. She read a little more, then
decided to walk down to the beach and pray.
Maybe standing on the shore, where she could
clearly see God's majesty on display, she would
find the answers she sought. She pulled on a
knit cap and gloves and picked up her tea.

As she made her way down the steep stairway to
the shore, she continued to mull over her dream.
There was a vague idea in the back of her mind
that maybe this Charlotte Montgomery might be
the person who needed her help—the way Aunt
Nell had needed help—and it was up to Lauren
to find a way to get to her. That hardly seemed
likely, though, did it? "Well, God, if that's what
You want me to do, then You're going to have to
make it obvious and make a way for it to happen,
because it doesn't make sense to me, and I don't
want to get a tongue-lashing every day unless
You are behind it somehow." She dug her toes
into the sand and looked out over the ocean,

wondering what the plan for her life could possibly be. Nothing seemed certain anymore.

It was over an hour later when she began the climb back up along the sea wall and toward the cottage. She had not in any way "felt" God's presence as she'd hoped to, but she did somehow feel just a wee bit stronger. She would fight the good fight. Give it her all. She just wasn't sure what her fight might lead her to.

Her cell phone buzzed in her pocket as she was reaching the top of the cliff. When she pulled it out, she noticed a couple of missed calls from the same unidentified number. "Hello?"

"Good morning, Miss Summers, it's Sam here at the gate. Got your contractor here, and I wanted to make sure you are home and expecting him."

"Oh, well, yes . . . he's a little earlier than expected, but yes . . . I'm walking up from the beach now. Send him on back."

When she reached the cul-de-sac, she saw a white work truck pulling into her driveway. She looked at her watch in alarm. 7:45. No, she wasn't late. The contractor was supposed to meet her here at 8:30. She made her way to the cottage and found him on his knees beside the broken porch step. He saw her coming and immediately stood up and extended his hand. "You must be Lauren. I'm Derek Allen." He was in his late forties, slightly heavyset, wearing Carhartt pants, a Carhartt jacket, and a faded yellow baseball cap with an embroidered bee and the word *Bumblebees* on the front and *Coach Derek* in white thread on the side.

"I'm sorry to have kept you waiting." Lauren shook his hand.

He made a dismissive gesture. "Not your fault at all, I'm almost an hour early. It's just that my daughter left this morning for sixth grade camp. We had to meet at the school at six. I got her sent off, went and got some breakfast, made a stop at the hardware store, and I couldn't think of even one more thing to do to kill time, so I thought I'd take a chance and drive on out here."

"Sixth grade camp, huh? Where are they going?"

"Catalina Island Science Camp. Doesn't seem quite fair to me because I've never been to Catalina myself, and believe me, I'd love to go. But now all three of my kids will have spent a week there. What I want to know is, when do we get parents' camp?"

"Sounds like a reasonable question." She immediately knew she and Derek were going to get along just fine.

"This step is rotted out, obviously." He gestured toward it. "I suspect there's dry rot in a lot of this front porch. We'll replace it ASAP—don't want anyone falling through on my watch."

"I appreciate that."

"And I've got the roofing crew starting this morning. They should be here by nine."

"Perfect. Remember that I have a meeting this afternoon. I'm sorry to disrupt your flow like this, but today couldn't be helped."

"Not a problem. We understood the situation when we signed up for the job, and everyone is going to work around your schedule as best they can. Don't you worry about a thing. It's a real treat to get to work in such a beautiful area."

An hour later there was a trio of men up on the roof, ripping off shingles at an impressive rate. Derek was inside the cottage cutting out parts of the ceiling that clearly needed to be replaced, sending white dust flying all across the room. It was going to be a challenge to find a clean place to do her work for the next few weeks, that much was clear.

Later that afternoon, Lauren pulled into the high school parking lot. The brand-new theater was the only building on campus taller than a single story, so it was easy enough to find. The words *Ralph Edwards Performing Arts Center* were lettered across the top of the building. Ralph Edwards? Only at that moment did Lauren begin to realize exactly how much of a theater booster the Edwards family was.

The side door was unlocked, just as she'd been told it would be, and she made her way down the glass-block-lined outer hallway until she came to the backstage area. She turned the corner to find a tall, painfully thin man flipping through a stack of papers.

"Hello, I'm looking for Mr. Rivers?"

He set the papers by his feet, smiled, and walked toward her. "I'm Theodore Rivers." He looked to be in his early thirties, he had thinning red-brown hair, and his skin was so pale it appeared he never stepped outside into the California sunshine. He wore the serious, rectangular black glasses that seemed to be in favor among the artsy crowd these days. "So pleased to meet you." His handshake was warmer and firmer than she would have guessed. "I can't tell you how important this play is to our school. We are being considered as one of the fifteen schools nationwide that will be allowed to premiere the theatrical version of Disney's latest movie-to-theater extravaganza. Our fall production will be one of the deciding factors as to whether or not we are chosen."

"Sounds amazing. I'm glad to be a part of it."

"I'm glad to have someone with your talent and experience."

Lauren felt her face heat. She had been up-front about her most recent endeavors. "*Most* of my experience, anyway."

He smiled and shook his head. "We all make mistakes, all have our own version of a complete disaster somewhere back in our careers. Some of us have it in more public ways than others, that's all."

"I definitely got the public part."

"Yes, you did." He laughed. "Remind me some-time to tell you about my time on Broadway. I have a story or two of my own, but that's for another day. Come back here and let me show you what we've got on hand."

A loud bell rang, and soon teenage voices filled the outer edge of the auditorium with laughter, shouts, and giggles. Theodore Rivers ignored them and led her toward the back corner of the stage, where there were several rolling racks of costumes and random pieces such as pirate hats, feather boas, satin jackets, and prairie dresses. He gestured toward the clutter. "Our budget is a bit higher than usual. One of the parents this year has donated a nice sum to be used for costuming and staging, and she is friendly with the owner of one of the large fabric shops down in the Fashion District in LA and has finagled us a discount. Some things we have on hand, obviously, but especially when it comes to the scenes with Guinevere, I really want her to shine. I don't want it to be the usual assortment of moth-eaten, reused hand-me-downs that we usually see in high school plays."

As more and more kids entered the audi-torium, it was getting increasingly difficult to hear him. He finally turned toward the front and shouted, "Quiet, everyone! I'll be with you in just a moment. I need you all to take a seat and keep the racket to a minimum in the meanwhile."

Lauren looked up to see a group of girls staring at her and whispering. They turned the other direction as soon as she glanced their way.

Theodore focused his attention back toward Lauren, gesturing toward the racks. "We have several old gowns that might work, but the truth is, they are all worn out. The men's jackets are falling apart, and it is imperative that everything about this show be top-notch."

She nodded. "I will do my absolute best for you. I love working with old-fashioned costumes." She walked the length of one of the racks, stopping at a brown satin dress with faux fur trim. She picked it up and turned it around. "This is rather nice. With just a bit of freshening up, it should be usable."

He nodded. "Agreed. It is probably the nicest piece we have. There are a couple more pieces over here." He led her around to another row and pulled out a green dress. It was worn, with a significant amount of fraying at the hemline, but Lauren felt it had potential.

"We could turn up the hem a bit and make this usable, I think." Then a cobalt-blue fabric caught her eye. She reached for it and picked up a crushed-velvet dress with white spatters all over the sleeves and a large white blob at the bottom.

"I'm afraid there was an accident with that gown a few years back. One of the props fell over, the paint can was sitting on top of it, and well, this is what we got." He sighed. "These things happen. My wife talked me into not completely trashing it, saying the fabric might be useful someday."

Lauren turned it around. "This fabric is still in wonderful condition, and it would be a shame not to use it. I'll see what I can come up with."

"Whatever you can salvage would be great. I can't tell you what a relief it is to have this part of it off my hands. We're in the final callbacks for tryouts right now, and then we are going to be moving forward at lightning pace. You will, of course, have the student costume crew, and they will be able to help you with some sewing and mending."

Lauren nodded. "I was on the costume crew back in my high school days. I will enjoy the chance to work with them." In fact, she'd been the head seamstress for every show her high school had done during her years there, but there was no reason to say so—hopefully her work would speak for itself. She intended to make certain it would.

The bell rang again, signaling the beginning of the period, Lauren supposed.

"Well, that's it, then," Theodore told her. "Feel free to look around and see what we have that you might need. I've got to get back to auditions." He turned to walk away. "Our cast should be fully assembled by the end of the week. You'll be able to figure out what fits who and get measurements then."

"When do I officially get started?"

"Yesterday. I want you to start getting your ideas together. I'm particularly concerned about the wedding dress and Arthur's wedding jacket. They need to be superb."

Wedding dress.

Lauren felt a little rush at the idea of designing another wedding dress. And it would be the old-fashioned, glamorous kind she'd always loved. While she might not be making much in the way of money with this job, there wasn't a single thing she could think of that she'd rather do. These kids were going to get her very best. "I'll get to work on some sketches right away."

"I look forward to seeing them."

Theodore Rivers went to the front of the stage. "Okay, everyone, we've got lots to do."

Lauren walked down each of the three racks of clothes, pulling out the occasional garment and turning it over in her hands. She slid the clothes away from one edge and began to form three distinct groupings. Things they could use with minimal modification, which she would leave to the crew. Things that might work if she got really creative with repairs. And things that needed to be trashed but that she would keep, in case things got desperate. The latter group far exceeded the rest, and she realized then just how much work she had before her.

As she was walking out of the auditorium, she

noticed the group of girls looking toward her again. She heard one of them say, "If she's doing costumes then we're all in trouble. Better stop eating carbs and start training a lot harder, because the whole school will be checking us out pretty soon."

"Maybe that'll help me get a date to the winter formal."

They all were laughing as the door closed behind her.

Maybe she wasn't going to be quite as hidden here as she had hoped.

seven

Charlotte watched the small blue SUV pull into the cottage's driveway. That girl was trouble, no doubt about it. She drove in and out of the neighborhood all the time. If she was truly here for the peace and quiet she supposedly needed, why did she feel the need to run around so much?

The girl walked around to the back of her car and pulled out . . . what appeared to be . . . they were gowns! One was a bright blue, the other brown. Looked like there was fur on the brown one. What in the world was she up to?

"I brought your afternoon tea." Frances's voice came from somewhere behind her.

"That girl across the street. She is removing evening gowns from her car. Does she think that she is going to sell those to me, is that what she was planning when she moved here? Ridiculous. Where's the phone? I'm calling Neil Winston right now, because this type of thing will not be tolerated."

Frances set the tea tray on the table beside her. "I believe that those are theater costumes, ma'am."

"Theater costumes?" Charlotte looked up at her housekeeper, furious that she had not been apprised of this information before now. "She's from Hollywood? How dare Neil Winston not let me know this—"

"No, they are costumes from the local high school."

"What?"

"From what I understand, she is doing the costumes for their upcoming production of *Camelot*. I believe that's how she came to live in the Edwardses' place. They are big supporters of the theater here, you know."

"Hmmph. We'll just see about that. There is more to this story, and I know it, and I am going to get to the bottom of it. I do not like this. I don't like it one little bit."

After the construction workers left for the day on Wednesday, Lauren drove into town. She'd spent most of the past two days shut in the little cottage, repairing costumes to the incessant thrum of saws and hammers and inhaling more dust than she cared to think about. Derek had very graciously made her a sort of thick plastic tent to encase the living room—which was also her workroom and bedroom for the next week or so. It kept the dust to a minimum in that area. The men all took great care to leave everything clean each night so that the place was usable after they were gone. Still, she didn't want to pull out her sewing machine or any of the nicer garments until this part of the work was over.

As of that afternoon, she had finished most of the preliminary work. Since the cast list wouldn't be finalized until Friday, she vowed to spend tomorrow working in the cottage's yard. To begin with, she'd plant a few things around the fence line, the one area of the yard that was not currently being trampled by workers coming and going.

At the nursery, she made her way through the rows of seasonal vegetation. She hadn't heard back from Kendall and was desperate to hear about any new developments in regard to Marisa. She pulled Kendall's card out of her wallet and punched the number into her phone.

"Hi, Kendall. It's Lauren Summers. We haven't spoken since the other day, and I wanted to check in."

"I'm so glad you did. I've been following some

leads on my end that are looking quite fruitful."

"Really?"

"Really. For instance, did you see the pictures on the front page of yesterday's tabloids, showing Marisa in a teeny little bikini?"

"I haven't seen the tabloids, but I did read something about it online. Those pictures were sneaked over a backyard fence, right? Why are the paparazzi allowed to do that? It seems so wrong."

"I *might* agree with you . . . except . . . maybe not in this particular case. How is it, do you think, that a photographer just happened to be there at the right time to catch Marisa in next to nothing?"

"You're saying it was planned?"

"You've seen that girl's ivory skin, and you know how they are with her. They protect her from UV rays like she's the Mona Lisa. The only tan she's ever had in her life is a spray tan. Now, all of a sudden, she gets the urge to lie around and sunbathe on the pool deck, and a photographer just happens to be there? Of course it was planned."

"Surely not."

"Don't be so gullible. And it's not just a theory. I have it on good authority that the photographer was tipped off by someone deep on the inside."

"Like Marisa herself?"

"It's pretty clear she was the ringleader, I'll put it that way."

The row of petunias blurred. How dare Marisa,

how dare she do this? If she set up the wardrobe debacle, then she likely set up the photographs, too. At least the bikini photo wasn't hurting anyone else. If she had indeed set up the wardrobe incident, she had to have known that it would ruin Lauren's entire career. Did the girl not think of anyone other than herself?

"So, you're getting closer to proving"—Lauren looked around to make certain no one else was nearby, then intentionally walked toward the corner of the yard for increased privacy—"that the other thing might have been intentional?"

"There is a very good chance that I will be able to confirm just that, but I can't say with utter certainty yet. There is a photo that I'm trying to get my hands on that should prove very helpful." She paused for a long time, as if expecting Lauren to respond. Finally she said, "How about you? Have you seen your reclusive neighbor again?"

"No, just that once."

"You said she's not exactly warm and fuzzy. Did you actually interact with her?"

"More like she interacted with me. She reminded me of the neighborhood privacy policy and basically told me to move along and quit looking her way."

"Neighborhood . . . privacy . . . pol-i-cy . . ." Kendall said each word slowly, as if she were writing them down on a piece of paper. "What was she wearing again?"

"I couldn't really see much about it."

"What could you see? I'm not asking for personal information or anything, just background information. These kinds of details merely provide depth and texture to the final story."

She did have a point. It was just conversation, that's all. Background information. "It was a blue evening gown. Looked vintage, but I was a fair distance away."

"That sounds right. Rumor is that she dresses for dinner every night, always in her antique gowns from the old days. Anything else you can tell me about what she was wearing?"

"Not really."

"Well, that's too bad. Keep your eyes open there, and I'll keep my ears open here, and hopefully the next time we talk, we'll have some new and helpful information for each other. Don't you think?"

"I hope so."

"So do I, Lauren. So do I."

eight

By the time Derek and his crew arrived, Lauren was already working some fertilizer into the soil around the fence line. Last night she'd bought a sack of bulbs and a large flat of pink and yellow pansies. Her great-aunt had taught her to bury the bulbs, then to plant the pansies right over the top of them. It would keep the ground colorful and beautiful now while waiting for the bulbs to work their magic and bloom in the spring.

The ocean breeze was brisk, but the sun was warm on her back as Lauren spent the day digging in the sorely neglected ground. It felt good to be working in the yard again. It had been several years since she'd had a lawn to tend, and only now did she realize how much she'd missed it.

As she worked, her mind kept wandering back to the conversation with Kendall. Something about her made Lauren uneasy. Maybe she really was overthinking everything because of Marisa's betrayal. Now she was having trouble trusting other people. Kendall could help her get her life back, a life that had been wrecked through no fault of her own, and it wouldn't hurt anything for Lauren to tell Kendall about what she'd seen her grumpy old neighbor wearing. It wasn't like she was spying on her personal life or anything, and Kendall already knew the woman dressed for dinner each night, so it wasn't like this was all hush-hush.

She turned her attention back to the flowers and reminiscences of working in the garden with Aunt Nell. Most of Lauren's happy memories from her childhood were of time spent with Chloe and her family, or in Santa Maria with Aunt Nell. A familiar pang pulled at her. She stood up to stretch out her legs and to clear her mind, her eyes wandering toward the large house at the end of the lane.

She still had several bulbs and quite a few pansies left over after she'd done what she'd planned to do at the cottage. What if she went across the street and planted these outside the fence? It wouldn't be violating the rules, as the area outside the fence was considered neighborhood property. It would make for a cohesive look around the cul-de-sac and would be something nice for Miss Montgomery to look at every day when, or if, she ventured outside the fence of her compound. Since Lauren had never seen her anywhere but on her own back porch, she wondered if Miss Montgomery ever came out front. Even if she didn't, it would be nice for the rest of the area residents to have flowers to look at. That was, after all, the reason they'd agreed to let her stay here for the next few months—to improve the upkeep on this place.

In the past several days, Lauren had met all the other neighbors. There was the middle-aged couple from the Tudor house, Christi and Elliott, who only lived here on the weekends. During the week they stayed in their downtown condo for convenience. They arrived every Friday evening, along with their pugs, Artoo and Detoo, whom they walked several times a day. And there was George from the oceanside Mediterranean, a seventy-something man who jogged by Lauren's cottage in the early-morning hours. His wife, Edna, kept to herself, but she still walked the lane occasionally. George and Edna were the parents of the mysterious neighborhood manager. Surely they, too, would appreciate a little sprucing up. But somehow Lauren knew that neighborhood appreciation had nothing to do with her reason for wanting to plant the flowers.

She hadn't been able to get her mind off the woman she'd encountered on the back porch of the Victorian. Maybe it was because of the repeated dreams she'd had since that encounter. Sometimes she dreamed of Aunt Nell's deteriorated planters, other times she dreamed of Aunt Nell walking with her along a rocky shore. Suddenly, Nell would be wearing a gorgeous antique ball gown, with jewels glittering around her throat. Then she wasn't Aunt Nell at all anymore, she was Charlotte Montgomery, and a large wave was coming in behind her. Lauren would scream at her to run, but she never did. She always stood perfectly still while the salt water slammed against her body, soaking her dress and drenching her hair. Then Lauren would wake up.

She'd puzzled over the dreams. Why would her subconscious keep lumping her grumpy neighbor into a dream with the one true and faithful person from Lauren's childhood? Perhaps it was because they were roughly the same age. Maybe it was because Charlotte Montgomery had been wearing the most gorgeous antique gown Lauren had ever seen—so much so that she was even dreaming about it?

Enough of this self-examination. Time for action. Lauren took over a bag of topsoil and spent the next few hours pulling weeds and getting the ground ready. Then she planted the bulbs and very carefully laid the pansies over the top. She stood back to admire her work. Yes. It looked satisfactory. Quite satisfactory, in fact. Hopefully this would bring a little bit of cheer to Miss Montgomery's day.

"That looks really nice. I hope the recipient appreciates it, although somehow I kind of doubt it." Derek Allen was loading some tools in his truck when she returned to the cottage.

"We'll see."

"Just remember, the gift is no less thoughtful, whether or not the receiver understands its value."

Lauren looked at him and smiled. "That is very profound." She needed to write that one down for Rhonda. Just the thought of that dear woman brought a twinge of something like being home-sick.

Derek adjusted his ball cap. "I'm a philosopher at heart. Doesn't do much in the way of paying bills, though." He nodded toward the house. "Roof will be finished up tomorrow. Starting next week we'll be working on the deck and the exterior painting, but it should be a lot less mess and a lot fewer people inside and in your way."

"Perfect. Next week is when I'll be sewing full blast, so it will be nice to have a clean work space."

"You've been a good sport about your tent."

"You were a good sport to make it for me."

He tipped his hat and climbed into his truck. "Enjoy your evening. See you in the morning at eight."

"Good night." Lauren made her way back to the cottage and rewarded herself for all her hard work with a nice hot shower, followed by a bowl of popcorn and an old black-and-white movie on TV. She watched Bette Davis saunter across the screen as Margo Channing, watched the story unfold of the young girl named Eve, who was trying to take over Margo's place as the high queen of the theater. But mostly, she watched the costumes. The clothes of that period were nothing short of divine. Even in black and white, the beauty shone through. Glamorous, yet not pretentious. And classy—which certainly wasn't a word that could be applied to most of today's fashions. Certainly not those worn by most of the stars on the red carpet.

Her phone rang. "Hello."

"Good news, earthling. I come bearing good news." Chloe's voice was as perky as ever.

"I'm glad to hear that, my non-earthling friend.

What might the news be which you are purveying to our little planet?"

Chloe laughed. "To put it in earth terms, due to some issue or other, Jasper has tomorrow afternoon off. We're hauling ourselves up to Santa Barbara. Prepare for some cabinet refinishing tomorrow evening."

"Oh, Chloe, I can't have you spending a free afternoon two weeks before your wedding working on my little rental cottage."

" 'Course you can. We all want to see that place. Even Mom is coming. Make sure we're all on your list, because otherwise we'll be picketing just outside the gate."

"Your names are on the list already, all three of you. In fact, your names are the only ones on the list. What time are you planning to hit the road?"

"Probably just after two."

"Perfect. I've got a fitting at the high school at two, so I should easily be back here by four."

"And we'll be arriving somewhere close to five, I imagine. Works great. I look forward to seeing you and to checking out your new beach pad. By the way, Mom says she'll bring a burrito casserole and a salad with her. She says there is no way that someone should be expected to provide food for self-invited friends less than a week after moving into a new place."

"Your mother is the best."

"Don't I know it. Oh, and by the way, Cody

looked at the picture of the cracked wood and says he's pretty sure he can devise a new piece that will work. What?" Her voice trailed off, and Lauren heard other voices in the background. "Oh, sorry, I gotta run. Late as usual. Love ya. See ya tomorrow. Bye."

And that was that. Nothing else to do but watch the credits roll across her screen. She sank down onto a chair and took a deep breath as she watched the names of Bette Davis, Celeste Holm, and then Marilyn Monroe roll up the screen. In later years those names would rearrange in importance. She smiled as she watched the rest of them, until a name at the very bottom caught her attention. Charlotte Montgomery as the second autograph seeker.

What? Miss Montgomery, her neighbor, was in *All About Eve*? Surely it was a different Charlotte Montgomery. It had to be. What she wouldn't give to be able to hit rewind right now.

She promised herself she'd research her highly private neighbor later and see what IMDb would tell her. For now, well, if she was going to have a houseful of people tomorrow afternoon, she'd best get busy doing a bit more unpacking and fixing up around the cottage.

Charlotte had been giddy with excitement. Her father had secured her a spot in the new Bette Davis movie. It was a tiny spot. Only a couple of lines, lines that were shouted at the same time that several other people were shouting out their lines—"Miss Channing, Miss Channing" while holding out a piece of paper for an autograph.

Up until that point, Charlotte had been doing what her father called "paying her dues." Taking midsized parts in small productions. This one, though—this one was different. This one had a level of prestige that none of her other films had carried. In spite of the fact that her part was almost nonexistent, she would get listed in the credits. It was the next step up in her career, and she couldn't wait to keep moving.

Charlotte could still smell the cigarette smoke that hung like a cloud around the set. On screen, off screen, everyone smoked back then. One of the cameramen would sneak her the occasional Chesterfield, in spite of the fact that her mother had told her she wasn't allowed to smoke until she turned eighteen. But that didn't stop the shots of bourbon that showed up in her glass, either. It was a free-for-all on set. They were the elite, the privileged, and rules for other people simply did not apply to them. Everyone seemed to know and understand this.

She remembered walking into Schwab's Pharmacy one evening with her new friend Juliette. They had gone to the shop under the pretense of getting a soda, but the truth was, they wanted to see who might be in there. It was the

Sunset Boulevard stop for so many actors and directors, not to mention Sidney Skolsky, the Hollywood gossip columnist for the *New York Post*. He had long since made the pharmacy counter his "office."

As the two of them approached the counter, they saw Sidney Skolsky right away. He was sitting beside a woman who had her back to them. This made it easier for them to gawk at the sable coat she wore. It was unlike anything Charlotte had ever seen, and her mother had more than a couple of nice furs. This coat, though, was on a whole different level of luxury, one that even most of the "mink crowd" would not have been able to afford.

Just then, the owner of the coat turned toward Charlotte.

"Hello there, darling. Nice work on the set today." She inhaled deeply from her cigarette and turned back to face Sidney, conversation over.

Juliette's mouth had dropped open and remained there. "That is Bette Davis."

They were still new in their friendship, so Charlotte tried to play it cool. She shrugged nonchalantly, trying to pretend it wasn't the huge, gigantic deal that it was. "Yes, I know. We're working on the same film."

Of course, Charlotte knew that Bette Davis did not know her name, and the use of *darling* had been less an endearment and more of a cover-up.

She also knew that Bette only recognized her because they had done Charlotte's one-and-only scene at the very end of the day. During a scene break, Anne Baxter had nodded toward Charlotte and said, "You're Collin Montgomery's daughter, aren't you?"

"Yes, ma'am."

"Is that so?" Bette Davis had said, looking Charlotte up and down. "Nice to have you here, dear." And then she'd turned and walked off. Just like that.

Charlotte had vowed that she would become a big enough star that she would someday be able to walk up to a total stranger and completely make her day by acknowledging that she existed in the same world. It was a laughable goal. She just didn't know it back then.

nine

"This is Priscilla. She'll be playing the role of Guinevere." Theodore Rivers gestured toward a beautiful blond teenager. She was tall and thin, and the slight tilt of her nose and lift of her chin gave her a regal bearing that did indeed make her appear to be a perfect Guinevere.

"Hello, Priscilla. I'm Lauren, and I just need to take some measurements."

Priscilla nodded and stepped closer. "What do you need me to do?"

"Extend your arms first." Lauren pulled out her tape measure and began making notes.

"You used to work in LA, huh?" There was an edge of excitement in her voice.

"Yes, I did." No need for further comment. She didn't want to encourage this conversation.

"It must be thrilling to be there, in the middle of all the action. Better than being bored to death around here."

Lauren couldn't help but smile. She remembered her own dreams at this age. "Sometimes it is really exciting. Most of the time, though, it's just plain hard work, with loads of added stress. Still, I have to admit, there are times when it is magical."

Priscilla turned to regard her. "I hope that you are going to be more careful about your work on our costumes than you were back there. We are one of the top-performing high schools in the country, you know, and we only accept excellence. Sloppy work doesn't cut it here. We won't stand for it."

Her expression and voice did not change as she said it. Simply stating a fact, as if she were a far superior professional giving the ground rules to a novice. Everything inside of Lauren wanted to snap back at this rude little twit, or at least to defend herself. But she decided to keep her mouth shut for now, and when Kendall revealed the truth to the world—that it wasn't Lauren's mistake at all—it would be that much sweeter. For now, head down, mouth shut, she would wait for vindication. "I'll try to keep that in mind."

"Good." Priscilla tossed her hair over her shoulder and said nothing else.

Lauren managed to make it to her car before she burst into tears. She knew that she should not let the words of a teenager she'd never met before hit her so hard, but she was still so raw about all that had happened.

She had pulled herself together by the time she reached the neighborhood gate. She was glad that Chloe and gang were coming up tonight. It would help keep her mind too busy to stew and fret over the words of a teenage beauty queen.

"Good afternoon, Lauren. Are you still expecting your guests this evening? I'm looking forward to seeing some young people around here." Sam always had a smile on his face, always just so happy to see whoever pulled up to the gate.

"Yes. I believe they should be here in the next hour or so."

"I look forward to meeting them." Sam saluted as he opened the gate for her.

As she drove up the street, Lauren saw two people standing outside Miss Montgomery's fence. To their left was a smear of something brown, and beside that lay a large black trash bag. Lauren wondered if a neighborhood dog had been digging in the new flowers, which would definitely be a bummer. As she got closer, she saw that Miss Montgomery was standing out in the road beside a man who was kneeling at the fence —ripping out the flowers and tossing them into the bag.

Miss Montgomery gestured wildly with her arms, leaving no doubt that she expected Lauren to drive over to her immediately. Lauren pulled up beside them and rolled down her window. Miss Montgomery put both hands on her hips. "What is it, exactly, you are hoping to accomplish by attempting to commandeer the plot of land in front of my house?" She gestured toward the man and the pile of recently uprooted flowers beside him. "I had to pay Richard overtime to pull this all out."

Richard, a gray-haired man in tan coveralls, didn't look up. He dug his hand into the soil and tossed a flower toward the bag without looking.

"I'm not attempting to commandeer anything. It's just that I have been planting flowers over at the cottage, and there were some left that I was going to have to throw into the trash. Instead of wasting them, and since there was nothing growing out here, I thought I would plant them outside your fence. I was simply trying to be nice."

"I've encountered your kind of nice before. What that means is, you do what you perceive as a favor for me, and then soon enough you are asking for favors in return. No one does anything for free, I've lived long enough to know that." She was wearing a beautiful silk dress of the sort that wealthy women would have worn in the daytime back in the 1940s. It was white, with little blue flowers dotting the fabric, and quite stunning in its simplicity. Lauren would have asked about the fabric if she were speaking to Miss Montgomery under different circumstances—and if Miss Montgomery were a more pleasant person.

"You may have lived long enough, but you clearly have not lived around the right kind of people. I do apologize if my kindhearted gesture has offended you." Lauren had several more sarcastic words ready to spill out, but as she took a breath to continue, she remembered this morning's quiet time. Paul had been severely beaten after his arrival in Jerusalem. The Roman soldiers had to carry him out to keep the crowd from killing him, and they took Paul back to the barracks for his own safety. Yet he requested to speak. He then attempted to preach to the very people who had beaten him, the same ones who were still trying to kill him. He didn't ask God to avenge him, and he didn't defend himself in any way. He simply looked at the people for who they were—people who were lost, afraid, and in need of love. At the time, she had prayed for that kind of love. Now, in the heat of the moment, she wondered why she'd wanted it.

She noticed a glint at Miss Montgomery's neck and caught sight of a gigantic sapphire and diamond necklace, barely longer than choker length. Lauren was certain it was the same necklace she'd seen across the way during her previous encounter with Miss Montgomery. It glistened in the fading sunlight, demonstrating its full brilliance against the drabness of everything around it. Kendall would be more than happy to know about this, Lauren was sure. She drew in a deep breath and used every bit of her strength to keep her voice calm and even. "If you prefer, in the future I will throw my leftover flowers in the recycling. Again, I apologize for upsetting you. I can assure you that was not my intention."

This time Richard did look up. He offered a half smile, winked at her, then turned his attention back to the task at hand. Lauren was pretty sure she saw Miss Montgomery's mouth hanging open as she turned her car toward home.

Once parked, and still shaking from the encounter, Lauren removed a couple of costume pieces from the back of her SUV, then cast a glance back toward the road. Miss Montgomery whipped her head around, pretending that she hadn't been watching, when clearly she had been. She shook her head as if in disgust, said something else to Richard, then pushed open the wrought-iron gates and hurried up the walk to her house. What an unpleasant and unkind woman.

Lauren carried the pieces inside and put them in her bedroom, where she'd finally been able to set up a sewing station. Tonight's cabinet-refinishing project shouldn't cause any problems back here. She paced around the cottage, still worked up by the way Miss Montgomery had treated her. Priscilla had been rude, but at least she had the excuse of being a teenager. Miss Montgomery, on the other hand . . . How could anyone be so mean? It seemed that no one considered Lauren good enough to do anything anymore. A little question niggling inside her wondered whether so many people could be wrong about her.

She shook off the thought. Aunt Nell would call it a pity party. Time to text Kendall with a description of the necklace. She had said she was particularly interested in a couple of pieces of jewelry and some gowns. Surely that spectacular necklace Lauren had seen today had to be at the top of the list—especially since it seemed to be a favorite. If Miss Montgomery was really a murderer, the sooner she was exposed, the better.

Be careful not to make a treaty with those who live in the land where you are going, or they will be a snare among you. Rhonda's verse ran through Lauren's mind once again. Lauren had no plans to make a treaty with Miss Montgomery. She didn't know why that verse kept coming to her mind.

Lauren picked up her cell phone, but something

inside her made her pause. Why? She was not breaking any of the privacy rules of the neighborhood—she had encountered Miss Montgomery on the street, not on her private property. Besides, Miss Montgomery did not deserve her loyalty, that much was certain. Lauren simply was giving a few details about a piece of jewelry she'd seen her neighbor wearing while standing in the street.

She opened her contacts list and scrolled to Kendall's name. She typed out a brief description, but for a reason she still did not understand, she underplayed what she had seen.

Saw CM on the street today. She was wearing what appeared to be a sapphire and diamond necklace. Quite large, but I didn't get a great look. Will continue to watch for more details.

She pressed Send and went on with her day.

ten

Charlotte Montgomery went in search of a good book. Her mind was crowded by memories she did not want to entertain. She'd put all those things far behind her, and now this new girl had moved in across the road and stirred up everything again.

In particular, shadows of Juliette Richards kept popping into her mind unbidden and would not be removed. Much as the real Juliette had done long ago. Charlotte could still see her face, remember her close-cut blond curls. She had been one of the prettiest and most popular girls in high school. She could choose any boy she wanted to date, and every girl wanted to be her friend. And Juliette had chosen Charlotte.

This friendship brought Charlotte a new level of acceptance from the other kids at school. The people at the studio had always been polite to her, of course. They didn't dare do otherwise, as her father could have them fired. But teenagers worked on an entirely different hierarchy of importance, and Juliette was at the top. Charlotte had always been somewhere near the bottom, partly due to the fact that she was not one of the prettier girls, and partly due to the fact that other kids' parents did not approve of her mother and father's living arrangement and forbade their kids to hang out with her. They seemed to believe that adultery and having children out of wedlock were not only passed down genetically to the child involved but also contagious for their own kids. It was certainly a disease that no one wanted to catch.

One day Charlotte had been heading toward the library during lunch—she often sat in there and pretended to study to avoid the cafeteria. It was too humiliating to sit at the losers' table, and she wasn't welcome anywhere else.

"Charlotte, hi. How's it going?" Juliette had come right up to her, smiling like they were old friends.

"Fine." Charlotte hadn't been able to think of one other thing to say.

"Hey, listen, I was planning to walk down to Jerry's Place after school. You want to come get a soda with me? We can talk about our history project."

"Uh . . . well . . . sure. That sounds great."

"Super. Why don't you come sit with me at lunch? I'm getting so tired of the same old people and the same old conversations. Know what I mean?"

From that day on, the two of them had been inseparable. Juliette invited her over after school, they went to the movies together on weekends, and they spent warm afternoons at the beach. Those months were among the happiest of Charlotte's life.

It had taken some time before Juliette's true intentions made themselves clear. First it was just small statements, little hints. "Wouldn't it be fun if I went with you to the Hearst Ranch sometime?" Which grew into "Do you think I could come watch you on the set?" Which then became "Do you think your father might give me a small part?"

Charlotte had worked up every bit of her courage and approached her father about it. "Just a little part. Just for fun."

When Juliette stopped by the house later that night, Charlotte's father was still there. He sat Juliette down and told her that if she really wanted to be in the movies, she was going to have to be willing to do the work, and there were no free rides where he was concerned. She smiled and nodded. "Of course, of course, thank you so much for the advice." Moments later she had developed a headache and left for the evening.

Charlotte went to school the next day, excited about the weekend ahead. She waited at the usual place outside the cafeteria for Juliette, but Juliette never showed up. Charlotte began to wonder if her friend was sick—maybe last night's headache had been the start of something. And then, in her second-period class, Suzette Lemons leaned forward and whispered, "Big crush on Cary Grant, huh? I heard you practically stalked him at Mr. Hearst's home in San Simeon. So much so, they had to ask you to leave him alone." She then leaned back and roared with laughter.

Charlotte sat completely stunned. There was one person and one person only who knew that story. Why would Juliette have told it? By the time lunch rolled around, it was abundantly clear that other stories had been shared, as well. Charlotte was the laughingstock of the entire school.

When she went to the lunch table to confront her best friend, Juliette looked up coldly and said, "This table is reserved. You need to go sit among your own kind. My days of charity work are done."

Lauren pulled out her iPad and Googled the name Charlotte Montgomery. There wasn't much information. Most of Charlotte Montgomery's public life had happened well before the computer age, but Lauren did dig up a little bit about Charlotte Montgomery's father. His name was Collin Montgomery, and he had apparently been something of a big-deal producer back in Hollywood's golden era. He had been married to a socialite from New York, who had one son. There had apparently been multiple affairs, including one with an aspiring actress named Jean. She became pregnant, and in spite of the fact that Collin Montgomery's wife did not give him a divorce—nor did it appear he'd even attempted to get one—Jean had her last name legally changed to Montgomery, and Collin openly kept her as his mistress and supported the child. A daughter named Charlotte.

Jean seemed to have given up any attempt at acting after the birth of her illegitimate child, but at an early age, little Charlotte was making regular appearances on screen. In Charlotte's early teens Jean pushed hard to get her daughter an established acting career, but it was troublesome. It seemed that Charlotte was not quite the beauty that producers and directors were vying for. Still, when Collin Montgomery bought a large share in one of the major studios, and when up-and-coming actors found out that their chances of getting into a Collin Montgomery film were greatly enhanced by being photographed squiring Charlotte Montgomery out on the town, well, she quickly became the darling of Hollywood social life. Aspiring actresses all befriended her, the men all dated her, and they all gave every indication of loving her. There were rumors of affairs with the likes of Errol Flynn and Clark Gable, among others.

Then, in 1954, Collin Montgomery died unexpectedly after a heart attack, and the truth became heartrendingly clear. In his will, he left his share of the studio and most of his Los Angeles holdings to his wife and son; he left a significant sum of money, a small LA bungalow, and a large Victorian home near the Santa Barbara coast to his mistress and daughter. Charlotte Montgomery was immediately blackballed by the studio and, by all indications, was never in a studio film again. Just as suddenly, paparazzi photos of her sitting at the Brown Derby with Deborah Kerr or Cary Grant, or even the lesser-known B actors, seemed to disappear. Louella Parsons and Hedda Hopper both made mention in their columns of her pariah status, and then her name went completely out of mention.

Lauren went to IMDb and looked for Charlotte Montgomery. Sure enough, there was a glamour shot from 1953, along with a fairly impressive list of movies Charlotte had appeared in. She seemed to have moved from big parts in minor movies to smaller parts in big movies. All part of climbing her way up the ladder, Lauren supposed. After 1954, there were no further entries. It was as if Charlotte Montgomery had ceased to exist.

Lauren rushed outside as soon as she received a call from Chloe that they were approaching the gate. Jasper's red pickup soon pulled into the driveway. It hadn't even stopped rolling before Chloe was out the door and hugging Lauren. "I've missed you so much."

"It's only been a week." Lauren knew she needed to say the words, to throw Chloe off the scent of her terrible, awful day. Sarcastic humor was the best camouflage for this kind of pain.

"A week is a long time." Chloe squeezed tight, then let go. "Dad says to tell you he's sorry he couldn't make it. His knee is all swollen again, so the doctor has him lying down and icing it. You know Dad, he's put off a knee replacement for far too long."

"Sounds like he should get it looked at."

"Sounds like he should get it looked at? Hello?

It's not like you to fail to join in the campaign for Dad to have the surgery and take better care of himself." She stood and observed Lauren for a couple of seconds. "You are preoccupied. What's up?"

Lauren shook her head and looked away from the scattered dirt on the edge of the cul-de-sac. "I agree that Jim needs to get that knee replacement, and I'm thinking that maybe Rhonda is wrong about some things."

Rhonda, who had climbed out of the truck by now, hugged her and said, "That can't be true. I'm sure that has never, ever happened." She playfully flipped Lauren's hair back. "What could I possibly be wrong about?"

"You, my darling and wise heart-mother, said that best efforts always pay off."

"And you're trying to tell me now that this is not correct? Is that what I'm hearing?"

Lauren gestured toward the cul-de-sac. "I planted some leftover flowers outside the fence across the street, thinking it would be a nice surprise for the elderly woman who lives there. When I got home just now, I found her having them all ripped out. So much for the nice surprise, huh?"

"You're kidding me. What kind of person would rip out flowers? What kind of person would make light of something so obviously considerately done?" Chloe's face glowed red with indignation. Even Rhonda's face turned pink.

Lauren shrugged. "Apparently the kind of person my neighbor is."

"Mom, can you imagine anything so rude? That is so awful. Why would someone do something like that?" Chloe was getting worked up now.

Rhonda kept one hand on Lauren's arm, squeezed, and reached out the other to put it around Chloe as all three of them looked toward the dirt in the road. "Eric Hoffer once said that rudeness is the weak person's imitation of strength."

"Yeah. Exactly." Chloe nodded her head vigorously, then paused and looked toward her mother. "Wait, what?"

"Weak people, they try to appear strong by being rude. Sometimes it's all they've got in the way of self-defense."

"Hmm. Well, maybe . . . but it still really makes me mad. I'd like to . . ." Chloe's attention shifted toward the truck. "What's taking you two so long?"

"You *two?*" Lauren looked at her friend.

"I told you, Cody's good with wood. He says he thinks he can replace that split panel without too much of a problem."

"Cody? You brought Cody?"

"I told you that I might."

"No you didn't. You said that he thought he could make a new panel. You didn't say you were bringing him here. How did you even get him through the gate?"

"Well, I told everyone that I might have forgotten to tell you he was coming, so when we got close to the gate, he lay on the floor and Mom covered him with some of the old rags we brought for the refinishing. The guard at the gate never had a clue."

"I can't believe you sometimes."

"Oh yes you can. It's not like this is the first time I've surprised you. Won't be the last. Come to think of it, I'm not really sure why anything I do surprises you anymore."

"That's true enough." She leaned closer to whisper. "You know I'm not ready for any kind of relationship right now. Not in the middle of all this chaos."

"I know that, and so does he. We just brought him along because he's a friend of Jasper's, and because he's good with wood. Okay?"

"That better be what it is."

"It is. I promise." She looked toward the guys emerging from the truck. "Come here, you two. Let me show you what Lauren's neighbor did." Chloe grabbed both men and dragged them out into the street, pointing toward the scattered dirt.

Lauren saw a curtain flutter up in the third-floor turret. Perhaps Miss Montgomery was enjoying the little scene she had created. Well, Lauren wasn't going to give her any more satisfaction.

"All right, all you looky-loos. Enough gawking at my humbling rejection." She glanced toward Cody, who was grinning at her. "I think we all know it is not my greatest humiliation in recent history. Let's forget all about it and move on, shall we?"

Cody walked up to her and tipped his Atlanta Braves cap. "I'll bet they were nice flowers, too. Don't let an old crank keep you from doing nice things. People who do nice things are getting fewer and farther between. The rest of us need as many of you as we can keep in circulation."

"Says the man who just rode for hours to do work in the kitchen of someone he's barely even met."

He nodded. "Come to think of it, you're right. We nice people have to stick together. It's a cold, cruel world out there. Where's this piece of cabinet I need to replace?"

eleven

Charlotte Montgomery picked up her phone and punched in the usual numbers. "Mr. Winston, we simply must do something about this girl who has come to live here."

"Miss Montgomery. So nice to hear from you. I trust you are feeling well."

"I would feel a lot better if the neighborhood was back in its right order."

"Yes, so you've told me several times. And each of those several times I have done my best to reassure you. What causes you to continue to feel this way?"

Charlotte looked out her window toward the front gate. "I just know, that's all. I need you to find out everything you can about her."

"Already done. I checked her background thoroughly before I granted the permission for her to come into the neighborhood."

"Oh really? What is it that you know, then? What about her family? Where does she come from?"

"She comes from the Los Angeles area. Her mother was a bit actress."

"See. Exactly the kind of person who would have an interest in making trouble around here."

"I did say *was* a bit actress. She died of an overdose some fifteen years ago. After that, Lauren lived with her father and his various girlfriends and wives until he and the newest wife moved out of state during Lauren's high school years. She apparently moved in with her best friend and her family at that point. She spent summers in Santa Maria with her great-aunt, who worked as a bookkeeper for one of the larger farms up there. Lauren just completed her courses at the Fashion Institute of LA with the assistance of their largest and most prestigious scholarship."

"Fashion Institute? Then what is she doing here in the middle of nowhere if she wants to work in fashion?"

Neil Winston went on to explain the wardrobe malfunction, the story of which Charlotte had actually seen on the evening news. She had never made the connection, though, between the paparazzi videos and the girl who was living across the street.

"She has basically been blackballed from any sort of job in fashion or Hollywood."

Blackballed.

The word struck a nerve where Charlotte would have sworn there was nothing left to feel. But now she did feel—a twinge of something long forgotten. Sympathy, was it? She shook her head. Those kinds of thoughts could skew what a person saw, make it easier to overlook the truth, thereby rendering one weak. Charlotte did not have room in her life for weakness.

"Well, I want you to put an investigator on her now and see what she is up to. She planted some flowers outside my fence yesterday afternoon. For some reason she seems to have it in her mind that she wants to get on my good side. There is an ulterior motive there somewhere."

"Maybe that's just the sort of person she is. Did I mention she's done mission trips to South Africa, Micronesia, and Kenya, not to mention parts of LA and San Francisco that most people would never bother to go into? I think she's just a really nice girl."

"I'm glad you think so. Now, find an investigator and see if you can prove it. And make sure the four people who just went into her house have been cleared at the gate."

As was her custom, when she'd said all she needed to say and didn't care to listen to anything else, Charlotte hung up the phone.

Then she had an idea. If no one else was going to do the job and find out what was up with this girl, she would have to do it herself.

Early Saturday morning Lauren was up and going, in spite of the fact that Chloe and the others had been there until well past midnight. The cabinets looked amazing. So did the grout in the bathroom, and the heating ducts had been deep cleaned and the filters changed. Yes, there was quite a bit of satisfaction in what they'd accomplished. Lauren was certain she had the best, best friend in the world. And her mother, too. And her fiancé. And her . . . well, and Cody, too.

Over the past week, her dwelling place had cleaned up nicely and was significantly less ramshackle. She had spent more money than she had intended on her spruce-up projects, but with the free rent, her conscience would not let her do otherwise. In spite of the fact that her savings account was shrinking at an alarming rate, she felt compelled to repay generosity with generosity. She felt good knowing that she would return this place to the Edwards family in much better condition than she'd received it— not only because of Derek Allen's work, but because of her own. She was glad for that.

Rhonda's words of wisdom from last night had hit home as always. She'd had two very good pieces of advice. The first was that God's good opinion mattered and what anyone else thought or believed was less important, even if they ripped out flowers. The second was her insistence that Lauren was there for a reason and Charlotte Montgomery was part of that reason.

"Part of the reason, how?" Lauren had asked.

"I have no idea, but I'm telling you, there's a reason you're here." Was that reason to give Kendall enough info to help her catch a murderer? Or was it because Charlotte Montgomery needed Lauren's help? That hardly seemed likely, given yesterday's flower incident.

Lauren poured a cup of coffee and began her digging-deep time. Soon after finishing her coffee, she started across the street, but instead of walking directly toward the dirt path through the trees, she couldn't help but detour to examine the freshly turned soil outside Miss Montgomery's fence. The blow felt almost physical, it was so strong. How could anyone make such an insult out of an attempt at friendliness? She knelt beside what was left of her gift, picked up the stray pink petal of a pansy, and rubbed it gently between her fingers.

So this was what happened to people who made an effort at good will toward Miss Montgomery. Miss Montgomery fended it off with raised fists and ripped-up roots. Aunt Nell had died alone and in pain, having to watch as the landscape that she so highly prized deteriorated along with her health. Miss Montgomery, on the other hand, deliberately insulted the very person who'd tried to help her. Sounded like something a coldhearted killer might do, didn't it? The kind who deserved to be found out.

As Lauren made her way down the stairs to the beach, the air was crisp with a breeze that blew cold against her skin. She found her favorite boulder, pulled her knees up under her chin, and looked out to the horizon. A freighter was making its way far out in the channel, visible as a low rectangle against San Miguel Island. "God, I feel so lost right now. I keep trying to do my best, but I keep messing things up more and more. People in the fashion world mock me, the high school girls, and Miss Montgomery—it's like I'm not good enough for anyone. I'm going to go completely broke on my current salary, even without paying rent. Am I supposed to get a second job? Will I be able to do the costuming work when it gets to be crunch time if I'm occupied elsewhere?

Won't you lead me, Father? I feel as though I have done the very best I could do with the things I was given, and none of them are enough."

Another of Rhonda's quotes came to mind. "A ship is safe in harbor, but that is not what ships are built for." While Lauren knew there was truth in the quote, the idea of a harbor—somewhere safe—sounded highly appealing to her right now. "Give me the strength I need. Thank You for providing a job and place to live. Help me to keep sailing out into the waves, and please point me in the right direction."

By the time she climbed back up the steps, she found her attitude changed enough that she was feeling somewhat sorry for the bitter old woman who occupied the giant mansion all alone, in spite of the fact that she still wanted to go over and ring the doorbell and give her a piece of her mind.

She glanced toward the yard, determined to hold her head high regardless of what had happened yesterday. A woman in a black dress and white apron was sweeping the back porch. When she saw Lauren, she gestured toward her, dropped her broom, and hurried across the lawn. Lauren stopped her forward progress and took a step toward the fence. The woman was almost running, but not quite.

"Good morning." She was out of breath by the time she came to stand across from Lauren. "I'm Frances Brown, Miss Montgomery's housekeeper."

Frances Brown looked to be about sixty and had short, curly brown hair with just a hint of gray mixed in. She was quite lovely, with a square jaw and a full chin, reminding Lauren very much of Bette Davis in the movie she'd watched recently. Smaller eyes, but whose eyes weren't smaller than Bette Davis's?

"Good morning. I'm Lauren Summers, the new neighbor across the road."

"Yes, I know." She took a couple of deep breaths and fanned herself. "Not as young as I used to be." She sort of smiled but kept gasping for air. She looked to be in good shape for her age, in spite of her currently winded state. "I have something of a favor to ask, I'm afraid."

"Okay . . ." Lauren braced herself for what was to come. She suspected this "favor" involved a request to not plant flowers and basically to stay away from this place as much as possible.

"First of all, let me apologize on Miss Montgomery's behalf. The flowers you planted were lovely, and the sentiment behind them was lovely."

An apology offered through a maid? That was certainly a new one. Still, Lauren supposed it was a start.

"No problem." Then Lauren thought about the woman she was speaking to and decided perhaps a more formal answer was in order. "Apology accepted." She smiled at the woman and bowed her head slightly. "Now, Ms. Brown, I believe you said that you wanted to ask a favor."

She waved a dismissive hand. "Please, call me Frances. And yes I do. I understand from Mr. Edwards that you are working on the costumes for the local high school and that you know a fair amount about sewing."

"That's true, yes."

"Well, here's the thing. Miss Montgomery has a number of older dresses, a couple of which need some work done on them. I called our usual tailor in town, and he told me that he is booked up for several weeks. Miss Montgomery has one particular gown that she absolutely insists on wearing tomorrow. It needs the hem brought up just a bit, and there's another dress with a waist seam that needs repair. Is that something you could fix?"

"I'd have to take a look at the dresses to say for sure, but if I'm able, I'd love to help out."

Frances Brown nodded. "I'm so glad. I will go get them right now and bring them to your house."

Lauren walked toward her cottage, amazed that one of her prayers seemed to have already netted a positive response. "Thank You, Father."

twelve

Frances stood at the door smiling, a trio of dresses folded over her forearm. "Thank you so much for being willing to help me with these. The white dress in particular she wants to wear tomorrow night, and the blue-green tulle has pulled apart at the waist seam—which is a problem, as you can see, because of several layers of fabric. The gray chiffon has a rip and is ruined, so she actually sends it as a donation for the theater, if you think you'll be able to use it."

Lauren took the dresses. She held up the white one. "This one she just wants hemmed?"

"Yes. Three-quarters of an inch should suffice. She doesn't wear heels now like she used to."

"When do you need it back?"

"Tomorrow before dinnertime."

Lauren looked more closely. "I can definitely have it hemmed by then. I'll have it done by early afternoon in case it needs any further adjustments." There were some loose stitches around the neckline, but otherwise the gown was in amazing shape considering its age. She knew before she saw the label that it was a vintage Balmain.

"Don't worry, Miss Montgomery will pay you a fair price for your work."

Lauren looked at her. "That's not necessary. For one, we are neighbors. For two, working on a garment like this is a privilege. I wouldn't charge anything."

"Miss Montgomery does not like to feel as though she owes anyone a debt. She will pay. She always pays the going rate, never more, never less."

Lauren set the white dress aside and picked up the aqua one. "I can fix this seam, as well, but it will take a little extra time, because I'd want to proceed with great care with these fabrics."

"She understands that will likely be the case. Just do it as soon as you can."

"All right." Lauren held up the gray chiffon for inspection. She felt that fluttering bittersweet ache she sometimes got when faced with an amazing work of art. The entire skirt was hand embroidered and hand beaded with a floral design. She saw the tear at the bottom of the skirt and pulled it closer. "Wow, this is an amazingly intricate design. This whole dress is gorgeous." She looked closely, noting the unusual pattern. She saw the label at the neck. *Angelina Browning*.

Angelina Browning had been the "it" designer of the late 1940s and early 1950s. Then she mostly stopped designing for the public, serving only a few select private accounts before ceasing altogether. Her pieces were considered works of art, and almost all were collector's items.

"She doesn't want to send this out for repair?"

"It's all done by hand. We made inquiries at some of the bigger fashion houses, because they do have a few in-house people who could do this, but none were interested in repairing someone else's design. We managed to get one quote, but it was outrageous."

Lauren nodded. "I'm sure that's true, but what a shame. This is incredible."

"Yes. She thought maybe you could do some sort of border on the bottom that would make this usable in the theater."

"I'm sure that would work, but I'd hate to see something so beautiful used in a school play. I could make a border and return it to her, as well."

Frances shook her head. "She doesn't want to feel as though she settled. Top quality or nothing is her motto."

"All right, then. Tell her thank you for the donation." She motioned toward the other two dresses. "I will bring these over as soon as I get them done."

"That would be nice. I will see you then."

And with that, Lauren watched Frances walk across the street toward the enigmatic woman who lived next door.

Charlotte watched until her housekeeper made her way back across the street empty-handed. In a world full of crooks and frauds, Frances was the exception. One of the few people she'd ever known who had proven to be just as good as her word. And while it was true that Charlotte Montgomery had once picked up Frances's mother from the sidewalk, that had been long ago. The memory of it still angered Charlotte, but as it had happened before Frances was born, that could not be her reason for staying. All these years later, the only thing that kept her here now was utter and complete loyalty. Something that was very rare indeed.

Charlotte hurried for the stairs and waited on the landing as she heard Frances climbing toward her. "Well, what did she say?"

"She said she would have the white dress hemmed by early afternoon tomorrow so that you will have plenty of time to make sure it meets your satisfaction before dinner."

"And the other ones?"

"You should have seen her face when she saw the Browning gown. That is a girl who knows quality work when she sees it. She just kept looking at the embroidered skirt, talking about what fine work it was. There were actual tears in her eyes."

"Those were tears of joy, thinking how much money she'll be able to get when she sells it on eBay."

"She asked a couple of times if you were certain you wanted to part with it, flaw or no. She said it seemed too beautiful to become a prop in a school play."

"Of course it is. Not too beautiful to sell for a profit, though, you just wait and see."

"I really don't think so. I think you're going to be surprised by this girl."

"Neil Winston has promised me he will be monitoring the situation very closely. As soon as that dress shows up for sale, he'll file the paper work with Ralph Edwards to get her evicted from that cottage. If you ask me, it can't come soon enough."

thirteen

Lauren hemmed Miss Montgomery's white wool dress in no time. She hung it up and admired the beautiful simplicity of it. White wool, fitted waistline, V-neck, and long sleeves. It looked as though it belonged in *Casablanca* or some other such film, probably with a jeweled brooch glistening on one side. She looked again at the loose stitching around the neckline. It would be simple enough to fix and would prevent problems later on. She pulled the dress down and went back to work.

After she finished the first she studied the aqua dress more carefully. She could fix it, but it was going to be tedious. She decided to save it for another day. Then she picked up the gray chiffon again. She spun around in a circle, with it flying by her side, imagining how this gown must have looked in a ballroom. It was so beautiful she just couldn't find the words for it. She looked again at the tear and the pulled embroidery and beading on the bottom. The gash was a good six inches long, making it impossible to just hem the skirt a little shorter and make it work. In her wildest thoughts, she could not feel right about tossing this piece of art into the bin with the pirate hats and boas of the theater department. She shook her head, sad but also thankful that Miss Montgomery had given her this fine garment. Surely she could make something useful of it.

She turned on the black-and-white movie currently running on the classic movie station. This one was set back in the days of Henry VIII. She found the style of these costumes close enough to *Camelot* that they inspired her as she sketched out a couple new design ideas. At one point Deborah Kerr walked onto the screen wearing a gorgeous gown with huge bell sleeves made entirely of fur. While Lauren studied the garment, she finally realized what to do about the blue crushed-velvet dress from the school. What if she cut the ruined sleeves off at the elbow and made bell sleeves out of faux fur? Since another dress already in the theater had fur trim, it would be cohesive with one of the other costumes.

But that still left the problem of the skirt. The

bottom twelve inches of it were ruined, and twelve inches of fur on the hemline would be difficult to pull off without it looking like what it was—a patch job. But if she shortened the fur and added some heavy lace cutouts above to cover parts of the damage, sort of Imperial Russian Court style, it just might work. In fact, if she found the right lace design, it would actually help the gown look all the more regal.

She glanced again at Miss Montgomery's beautiful gray chiffon dress. There had to be some sort of solution for it, too. She pulled out one of her books on couture sewing techniques and began to thumb through it. Perhaps a silk charmeuse edging around the bottom? That would definitely work for the purposes of the theater. Still, for the dress itself, it seemed like such a loss.

Just for the fun of it, she pulled out a needle, found a spool of gray thread, and took a stab at redoing the work herself. Professor Navarro had taught her some of the finer points of couture embroidery and hand beading, but it was mostly a lost art. The women who did it in the high-fashion houses had fingers that were incredibly strong after years and years of it, and few people were willing to spend the money or wait the time required for this type of work anymore.

Her cell phone vibrated from the kitchen counter. Reluctantly, she got up and followed the sound. "Hello?"

"Hi, it's Kendall. How are things going?"

"Pretty well."

"They are about to get even better. I've got some good news for you."

"Oh really? What is it?"

"It's better if I show it to you. Meet me tomorrow at the same coffee shop as last time. Ten o'clock."

"How about a little later in the afternoon? I'm planning on going to church tomorrow morning." Easy as it would be to forgo church in a new place, and this far out of town, she had concluded in her morning digging-deep times that these were the exact reasons she needed to make the effort to go. It would be too easy to isolate herself out here. She needed to push herself a little, even if it would be more comfortable to stay inside and safe.

"All right, then. How about one o'clock?"

"I'll be there." Lauren hung up the phone. That small feeling of hope began to grown a bit larger and then a bit larger still. Was it possible that she would be vindicated soon? "Thank You, God, for sending me justice."

She turned her attention to repairing the embroidery on the gray gown. The work was coming together more seamlessly than she would have guessed given her lack of experience. Yes, this just might be repairable. In fact, maybe everything was going to work out all right, starting with this beautiful gown.

fourteen

Lauren had stayed up late last night, hand embroidering Miss Montgomery's dress, stitch by stitch. Once she'd started the process, she had trouble making herself stop. She seriously doubted she would be able to repair it to a professional standard in the end, and it would certainly take many hours even if she could, but it gave her a thrill to have the chance to try. If she had to give up all hope, then she would figure out a lesser repair method for the theater.

As a result of her late night, she woke later than she'd intended to on Sunday morning and had to rush to get to church. The closest one she'd found was still almost a half hour drive from the cottage. She managed to slide into a back row just as the service got started. Still groggy from lack of sleep, it took her a while to get plugged in, but after she did, she was thankful she'd made the effort to come. The sermon was on seeking the approval of God rather than man's approval, which dovetailed exactly with what Rhonda had been telling her lately. There seemed to be a theme in her life right now.

When the service was over, she drove to Goleta Beach and watched families picnicking and paddle boarders and kayakers enjoying the warm weather. It made her grateful for Chloe and Rhonda and Jim and Aunt Nell—and it made her miss them just a little bit more. Finally, she started her car and drove toward her meeting with Kendall.

She was still twenty minutes early when she arrived at Starbucks, so she was surprised to see Kendall already there waiting for her. She had procured a little round table in the corner, and she waved Lauren over. "Check this out." She passed a 5x7 photo across the table.

The picture showed Marisa Remington in the VMAs dress pushing open a door marked *Ladies Room*. Another woman was following close behind, although her back was to the camera. Lauren looked up. "I don't understand."

"Not yet." Kendall handed over another picture, this one taken as Marisa was leaving, alone this time.

Lauren looked back at her. "I still don't understand."

"You will. Here's a blowup of the first photo. Notice the waistline of the gown." Lauren studied it, and it looked just as she expected it to.

"Okay."

"Now look at a blowup of the second one. Check out the waistline in particular." Lauren leaned forward for a closer inspection. In this very large blowup, it became clear that an entire row of thread, one that held the dress together, was gone. "The stitching is gone."

"Exactly. Unfortunately, this picture alone is not enough evidence to run a story like this. We need to find out who the other woman is, and we need to find some witnesses."

"So . . . is this the end, then?"

"Not by a long shot. A couple of other people went into the bathroom while the two of them were in there. Including one who supposedly saw Marisa Remington 'making a last-minute repair' on her gown. The woman helping her had a small pair of scissors in her hand."

"So your next goal is to find this woman?"

"Yep. That's the plan."

"I can't tell you what a relief this is. Your work is making it possible for me to get my life back."

Kendall nodded and smiled slightly. "That's my job." She put the pictures back in an envelope. "Speaking of my job, how are things going with Charlotte Montgomery? Any recent sightings?"

"I've spoken with her housekeeper a couple of times." Lauren's answer was true, if not complete. She was growing increasingly uneasy about sharing information with Kendall. If she was truly where she was now in order to help Miss Montgomery, then reporting back to Kendall about her neighbor hardly seemed like the right thing to do. She did know that Kendall would be very interested in the gowns currently in Lauren's cottage, but should she tell her about them? What could beautiful old gowns possibly have to do with a sixty-year-old murder?

"Her housekeeper? What did you speak to her about?"

"Um . . . she had a dress she asked me to hem." Lauren didn't mention the other two, feeling especially protective about the Browning original.

"Really? One of Charlotte Montgomery's gowns? Do tell." Her eyes gleamed as she lifted pen to paper, ready to take down every word.

"It's just a plain white wool number. Nothing special."

"Who is the designer?"

"I . . . didn't notice."

"You know, Lauren"—Kendall looked up, clearly annoyed—"I'm going out of my way to help you here. No one else would spend the time and expense that I have in order to show what really happened to Marisa's dress. Don't you think that, in return, you should be going out of your way a little bit to help me?"

"I know, and I appreciate what you are doing. It's just that she values her privacy."

"Of course she does. So did Al Capone. When she ends up in court some day, you'll find out exactly why she valued her privacy so much. Here, I brought you an article that you might find interesting." She handed Lauren several printed pages. The top one had a headline that read *Who Killed Randall Edgar Blake?* There were several black-and-white photos on the front page, one of a distinguished-looking man and one of a mansion set on a pristine lawn. "Read the article. Of course, Charlotte Montgomery's name is barely men-tioned, because the person who wrote this article did not have the kind of information I have. Very few people see the smaller clues in things that I do—like those missing stitches at Marisa's waist, for instance."

Lauren nodded. "I can't fault your attention to detail."

"Do you really want to protect a murderer?" She stood. "I'll call next week for another meeting. At that time, I expect that you will have some sort of information for me. Like I said, particularly concerning gowns or jewels. If you don't, it may be that I find out I have less time for further research into the Marisa Remington debacle." She walked out of the Starbucks without looking back.

After arriving back at the cottage, Lauren double-checked her work on the white dress and then carried it across the street. She was surprised to see a red Mercedes parked in Miss Montgomery's driveway. Somehow she had assumed that Miss Montgomery did not receive visitors. She tried to be glad for the woman, that there were indeed other people involved in her life, but Lauren's own wounds were still so fresh that she found it difficult.

The wrought-iron gates opened with a squeak. The lawn was well maintained and green, but she couldn't help but feel again it was missing the TLC of someone who really enjoyed working in the garden. Considering what had happened to her pansies, she considered the blame for this lack to rest squarely on Charlotte Montgomery.

She climbed the four steps up to the wrap-around front porch and pressed the button in the brass encasement. A deep, melodious sound, like bells in a church steeple, came from somewhere inside. The thumping of footsteps caused Lauren to pre-pare to greet Frances as the door began to open. Instead she was met by a young woman. She appeared to be about Lauren's age, a stunning brunette with short, stylish hair, tall and lithe, and wearing very little makeup, though certainly none was needed.

"Can I help you?" the girl asked.

"Yes, I'm bringing back Miss Montgomery's gown."

"And you are?"

"The neighbor next door." Lauren pointed back over her shoulder toward the cottage.

"I see." The woman reached out to take the dress from Lauren's hand. Something about returning the dress to someone other than Frances or Miss Montgomery made her uncomfortable, but this woman was apparently welcome in Miss Montgomery's home. There shouldn't be any harm here, in spite of her gut feeling.

Just then, much to Lauren's relief, Frances walked up from somewhere behind the younger woman. "Oh, Lauren, you finished with the hem. Thank you so much."

"You're welcome. I was happy to do it."

Frances gestured toward the younger woman. "May I present Miss Montgomery's niece, Willow Montgomery. Meet Lauren Summers."

"Nice to meet you." Lauren extended her right hand.

"Pleasure." Willow shook her hand while clearly sizing her up.

Frances waited until they finished, then asked, "And the blue-green one? You are going to be able to repair it?"

"Yes. It is a little tricky, but I should have it back to you by the end of the week."

"Very good." Frances moved forward and took the garment from Lauren, pulling the bodice closer for inspection. "You fixed the loose stitching around the neck."

"Yes. It really didn't require much work, and I just thought as long as I had it anyway . . ."

"I'm sure Miss Montgomery will be delighted. It's not often I see someone going above and beyond like this."

"It was simple, really. I'm glad I was able to help. Please let me know if Miss Montgomery has any concerns about the work."

"It appears as though it is quite exceptional," Frances said. "I'm sure she'll be pleased."

Lauren nodded toward Willow. "Nice to have met you."

Willow folded her arms across her chest. "You, too."

As Lauren turned to go, something about Willow bothered her. She couldn't quite put her finger on what it was. Maybe it was just that she reminded her too much of her old world—a young, beautiful woman with plenty of money and no regard for anyone. But what did she know of Willow and her regard for others? Not one thing.

"Sorry, Willow, it won't happen again," she whispered to herself as she walked up the steps to the cottage. She turned for one last look over her shoulder and saw Willow standing at the front window, watching her.

Maybe she was bored. Or maybe she just needed a friend. Something inside told Lauren it was much more sinister . . . but there she went jumping to conclusions again.

Who Killed Randall Edgar Blake?

Lauren read the article, which had been written just last year as a review of the six-decades-old mystery. Randall Edgar Blake had apparently been a director in Hollywood, a bit on the shady side. He was known for seducing women, drinking excessively, and cheating most anyone he could manage to cheat.

The article told of how one of his more "usual" female companions, a Lina Orbaker, had left his home around seven at night. She stormed out because he had told her that she was no longer slated for a supporting role in his next movie project, *The Power of Love*. The entire project, in fact, had been revamped because he'd decided to take the movie "in another direction." This other direction seemed to involve the Playmate of the Month, who also happened to be his most recent conquest.

Lina left in a fit of anger, got into her car, and drove to a friend's house, where she spent the evening drinking heavily and telling anyone and everyone who would listen that Randall was a scumbag. At approximately ten that night, the police found her sitting on the pool steps, fully clothed and completely inebriated. They informed her that Randall Edgar Blake was dead, shot in his own driveway and left faceup on the ground.

Lina's purse had been found near the murder scene, and given their most recent interaction—overheard by neighbors all up and down the block—she was the obvious first suspect. It didn't take the police long, however, to learn that there were plenty of witnesses as to Lina's whereabouts for the past few hours, and it was nowhere near Randall Edgar Blake.

The original theory had been that she killed him first, then came to her friend's house, started drinking due to the guilt, and got into the pool to wash away any evidence there might have been on her clothing. Except the neighbors reported hearing gunshots at nine o'clock, some two hours after she'd left his house and arrived elsewhere.

A second theory still involved Lina Orbaker, but this time as a murder-for-hire. Until the day she died, Lina Orbaker was the chief suspect in the murder, but there was never enough proof to bring anything to trial.

At the very end of the article, the writer had thrown out a couple of other theories. One of them came from Mr. Blake's shady business dealings with known members of the mafia. There was no shortage of people who had a grudge against Randall Edgar Blake. The final theory, barely mentioned in passing, was that several other people had also been displaced from *The Power of Love*, and all of them were angry. The author named three of the possible suspects and their special reasons for wanting Mr. Blake dead.

Charlotte Montgomery's name was last on that list. There was no confirming evidence at all, other than her association with and then removal from *The Power of Love*. Lauren assumed that this particular author did not give much credence to Kendall's theory. But still . . . here it was in black and white. The theory was out there. Who knew how much truth was behind it?

fifteen

Aunt Nell was wearing the gray dress and whispering something so quietly Lauren couldn't understand her, in spite of the fact that she was kneeling on the floor beside the couch and helping with the hand beading. "What are you saying, Aunt Nell?" Lauren asked as she sank the needle into the fabric again and again.

Finally, her aunt leaned forward, close enough to be heard. "Help me."

Lauren woke up gasping for air. What was it with all these dreams? She shook her head and made for the shower. The sooner she got on with her day, the sooner she could forget about this latest iteration. Or so she hoped.

Once again her devotional centered around serving others, even when they didn't seem to deserve it. It was a theme that she liked in theory, but at this point in her life, it was a little too close for comfort.

When Derek arrived, he knocked on the door. "Brought you something."

"Really? What?"

"Creeper roses. My wife bought three flats of them this weekend, had almost a whole flat left over. I knew that you had a knack for growing things and thought you might want some of them. They would make for cute ground cover, and the lady at the store said they would hold up rather well in this climate."

Something about the fact that he'd thought enough of her to bring these made her feel really good. A much-needed boost. "I'd love them, thanks."

Soon enough she was working the soil, enjoying the feel of the earth softening and churning beneath her touch. She would place these roses around the cottage itself, since the repainting was complete. Once again the activity conjured up memories of Aunt Nell and the happy times Lauren had spent with her. And even though she tried not to go there again, inevitably the memories led to guilt over having not driven out to visit her great-aunt more often, in spite of a heavy workload at school and a job.

When she had finished all her planting around the cottage, she looked toward the Victorian. There were still several plants left. Quite a lot, actually. Still, it was not helpful to force something on someone who clearly did not want it.

She dumped the remaining plants in the green recycling can and went inside. Because of the nagging questions still haunting her, Lauren returned to the computer to find more information about Charlotte Montgomery.

Without Charlotte's father there to buy her way into the movies, and with her father's bitter wife holding all the power, Charlotte's time in Hollywood was finished. Thankfully for Charlotte and Jean, however, Collin Montgomery had left them his huge estate just north of Santa Barbara and a sizable stock portfolio, with specific instructions that Charlotte receive an income from his estate to pay living expenses plus thousands of dollars a year for designer gowns.

When Collin's wife found out about that final stipulation, it was rumored that she sent word to all the major designers that if they wanted to continue to work with her movie studio, they had better think twice about making anything for Charlotte Montgomery. This seemed to work completely, until Angelina Browning, the most celebrated designer of the era, declared that she would not allow others to dictate her work. She would design gowns for whomever she wanted. In fact, she declared Charlotte Montgomery would be her primary client.

Wow. This information alone was thrilling. One of the greatest designers of all time had worked closely with Lauren's next-door neighbor. What were the odds of that? She kept reading.

While this could have been the kiss of death for Angelina Browning's career, the fact that she was willing to walk away from everyone else began something of a stampede. Suddenly the A-list ladies were all clamoring for a Browning gown. Angelina Browning was a wise enough business-woman to greatly limit her output, keeping the demand—and the prices—sky-high. Elizabeth Taylor, Audrey Hepburn, and crowned heads all across Europe were constantly on a waiting list for the next Browning gown. Yet Charlotte Montgomery remained her number one client until the day Angelina Browning died in a boating accident just off the island of Catalina in 1959.

Jean Montgomery had committed suicide three years after Collin Montgomery's death, leaving twenty-one-year-old Charlotte to fend for herself. There were rumors of an engagement to the son of a mafia boss. He was never named, and it was never confirmed.

Eventually, Charlotte disappeared from public life completely. It was later reported that she was living on the Santa Barbara estate, with a maid, a cook, and a gardener being the only people allowed to come and go from the property.

The story brought up a deep sadness in Lauren. She wanted to help the woman, she really did. Her mind returned to the roses just outside in the recycle bin, but how could planting flowers that were only going to be torn out again be helpful? It couldn't.

She pulled out the gray dress from the closet

and put it on her dress form. She spent the next few hours working on the beading, thinking through all that she knew and didn't know about Charlotte Montgomery. Finally, she decided there was nothing for her to do but pick up the phone and make the call she knew she needed to make. She reached over and grabbed her cell.

sixteen

"So, I guess what I'm asking is . . . what am I supposed to do?" Lauren had spent the last few minutes pouring out everything to Rhonda. Everything from her dreams to what she'd learned on the internet.

"I, for one, am hoping that you two become great friends." Rhonda's voice had an excited edge to it.

"Great friends? I don't think that's very likely."

"Not likely, but possible." She paused, as she always did when gathering her thoughts to make a point. "Think of it as your very own Good Samaritan assignment."

"Yes, but the Good Samaritan helped a man who had been beaten and robbed, left penniless and broken. In all likelihood he was a perfectly nice man and was grateful for the help, and he didn't have the ability to help himself. Miss Montgomery, however, is not a very nice woman.

It may not be her fault what happened to her in her childhood, but it is most definitely her fault that she doesn't have any friends now, and she likely has more money than all of us combined will ever see in our lifetimes."

"None of that means she's not alone and in need of someone who cares. Sometimes it's the ones who seem like they are most in charge who really are the ones who need the most help. They're just too proud to ask for it. Think of Zacchaeus."

"He's the short guy who climbed the tree to see Jesus?"

"Yes, but he was also a tax collector and rich. The fact that he was so short meant people had probably made him a bit of an outcast from an early age. The fact that he was a tax collector definitely made him an outcast as an adult. But somehow I doubt very much that he was walking around with his head down, you know what I mean? I'll bet he was going around in fine clothes and jewels and rubbing it in everyone's faces that he was rich and powerful, and they weren't."

Lauren had never considered this point before. But quickly another thought came to mind. "And probably there were people who tried to be his friend. Some of them probably even did it because they thought they felt compassion for him, but their true motivation might have been to have a rich and powerful friend. What if my motive in befriending Miss Montgomery is to get a look at her Angelina Browning gowns? I mean, I think I want to be nice to her for niceness's sake, but I wouldn't be honest if I didn't say I would kill to see her dress collection. I don't want to be a user. What if I do it by accident?"

"The fact that you're aware of those feelings is a good thing. You need to pray for right motives with every single interaction you have with her. But I am convinced you are supposed to interact with her."

"She doesn't want that, though."

"Zacchaeus didn't even call out to Jesus for help, he just climbed up to get a peek. Jesus had to call out to him first. He was up in that tree and would likely have watched the crowds go by, climbed down feeling even lonelier than he was in the beginning, and acted all the more obnoxious because of his pain. If Jesus hadn't seen him and taken the time to call him down, it could have ended very differently. Hurting people who hide behind their pride can't ask for help; it makes them vulnerable. Zacchaeus remained hidden in the tree, his way of protecting himself. Just like Miss Montgomery's way might be closing herself inside that gigantic home and tearing out flowers that people who are trying to be nice might plant."

"Maybe you're right. I'd never really thought of it that way."

"I think maybe it's time you do."

• • •

Once again, Lauren worked on the Browning gown until late in the night. Finally she made herself set it aside and begin the work on repairing the aqua gown. The gray dress was simply an experiment, and she knew she shouldn't allow it to take up all her time. In spite of this knowledge, as soon as she finished the aqua gown, she went right back to the gray and worked until the night sky began to lighten and the stars faded into nothingness with the dawning of a new day. She finally went to bed to get at least a little rest.

A few hours later, she definitely felt the effects of staying up most of the night hunched over fine needlework. She did a few minutes of stretching before she stepped out of the cottage to do her beach walk.

On her way back from the beach to the cottage, she glanced toward the Victorian house. "I do want to help her. Please test my heart for the right motives. Always."

There was no sign of movement. She looked at the empty dirt out in front—all that was left of her previous attempt at kindness. Would a restitched gown fare any better? Could she bear the thought of doing all this work and having it ripped out and thrown away? She resolved that yes, she would indeed take that chance. She went back to the cottage and went back to work on the beading.

Many hours later, she made her way across the

street. When Frances opened the door, she seemed surprised when she saw both dresses in Lauren's hand. "What's this? Miss Montgomery donated this one, remember?"

"Yes, she did. But the thing is, this dress is so beautiful, and then I had an idea about how to fix it, and I did. She may not like it, and if that's the case, then I will take the repaired dress to the school and donate it, as per the original intention. To tell you the truth, it just hurts my heart to think of throwing this beautiful piece of art into the mix of pirate hats and feather boas."

"We were led to believe that no one could do this kind of work these days."

"It is definitely a dying art, but one of my favorite professors had a fondness for this type of work. Since I was interested, she taught me the basics. My skill is not to the level of the original, but I believe that I have been able to repair it so that it is not obvious."

Frances held out the dress at arm's length. "This is amazing. It looks as good as new. I'm sure Miss Montgomery will be thrilled."

"As I said, if she doesn't like it, I will take it to the school. You can just let me know, and I'll come get it."

"Wait just one moment, I'll go check with her. She's still in her room and not ready to receive guests, but I will speak with her about it."

Frances closed the door, leaving Lauren alone on the porch.

seventeen

Charlotte was sitting in her bed, reading a leather-bound copy of *Jane Eyre*. Again. How she loved the classics. Yet why was it, she wondered, that these old stories always involved some beautiful, poor girl falling in love with a rich man who would take care of her and love her and protect her? Why was there never a wealthy heroine who found a man who adored her for who she was, not what she had or what power she did or didn't possess? She supposed that was too outlandish, even for a work of fiction. In real life, wealthy women were stepping-stones to be used and then discarded when the goal was reached.

She heard the sound of approaching footsteps followed by a quick knock and the turn of the knob. Charlotte set the green satin ribbon book-mark into place and looked up, wondering what had prompted this disturbance.

Frances entered the room, a huge smile on her face, swinging the gray Browning gown around her as if she were doing some sort of flamenco dance. "You're not going to believe this. Look what Lauren did with your dress."

Charlotte grabbed the dress as soon as it was close enough to reach. The ridiculous way Frances was swinging it around meant she couldn't see anything. She held it at arm's length, stunned by what she saw, then pulled it closer. She reached down into the basket beside her chair, pulled out her magnifying glass, and examined the newly repaired beading and embroidery. "But this can't be. Every reputable tailor I've ever taken this to has said that this type of dress could not be mended."

"When she brought it back, Lauren did say that it was a technique that wasn't really taught anymore. She learned it from a teacher who had studied the dying arts and thought she'd try her hand at it."

"But why? This dress was worth a fortune, even in its previous condition. It's worth even more now. You told her that I was donating it and she was under no obligation to return it to me. Why would she go to all this trouble?"

"I can't say, ma'am, but I will say that she has done a beautiful job." Frances cleared her throat.

Charlotte continued to look through the magnifying glass. Except for the fact that she'd looked at it so many times that she knew it all by heart, she would have sworn this dress was in its original condition. "How much did she charge for this?"

"I can't say for sure. When she brought back the white wool she said that there wouldn't be a charge because it was such a privilege to work on such amazing clothes. I told her that you wouldn't see it that way. She didn't really fight me on it, but when she brought this back today, she asked me to see if you liked it. She said that she will donate it to the school as per the original plan if you are not pleased with the work."

"What do you think she is hoping to get out of this? This intricate work. She must have some sort of angle she is playing. What is it?"

"Maybe she's just a very nice girl. Have you ever thought of that?"

"Thought of it and dismissed it out of hand." Charlotte gave the dress back to Frances so she could hang it in the closet. Then she had another thought. "Frances, will you please pay her for the repair work she has done on my gowns—at whatever rate we were paying that other tailor."

"Yes, ma'am."

"Also, please tell her . . . tell her that Richard is planting some purple sage around the house for me next week. Tell her that she may use any remaining for herself—and that she is welcome to plant some outside my fence, if she would like to, as long as she uses my supplies. I don't want to be left owing her anything."

"Richard is planting purple sage? Next week? I thought you told him no when he suggested purple sage."

Charlotte frowned at Frances, owing her no explanation and not planning to give one. "Give her a key to the potting shed and tell her . . ."

"Tell her?"

"Reiterate again that she must use my supplies for any work she does on my property. Give her the key and show her around the potting shed. Go right now and do it. Make sure she understands that I do not want to be beholden to her."

"Yes, ma'am. I'll go right away."

Frances was smiling when she left the room. So was Charlotte. Perhaps they were smiling for the same reason. Then again, perhaps not.

Lauren had begun to wonder if she had been forgotten by the time Frances returned to the front door. Her smile was wide, excited almost.

"Miss Montgomery is quite pleased with your work. She sends her thanks and insists that I pay you for the work you have done." Frances handed her a check. "This is for the first two. I paid you at the same rate we pay the other tailor. With the gray dress, I had no idea how much the rate should be, so I need you to give me a number— either the fair price for the work or the number of hours you put into it."

"Really, it was done just for the thrill of working on something so magnificent. I couldn't possibly accept pay for that one."

"We'll see about that." Frances folded her arms. "In the meantime, I have a message for you." She went on to explain that Lauren could use the extra purple sage and was allowed to plant outside the fence, then said, "Here, I've brought you the key. Let me walk you around and show you the potting shed." She seemed almost giddy as she led Lauren around the side of the house.

The two women followed the hedge line to a little shed in the side yard. Frances unlocked the door, which squeaked as they opened it. Once they stepped inside, Frances flipped on a switch, and pale light brightened the space. There were several rows of shelves full of every kind of pot and vase, bags of various plant foods and topsoil, and a neatly aligned row of smaller hand tools.

"Miss Montgomery said you may use anything in here as long as you are using it for the property adjacent to her fence."

"Okay." Lauren really didn't have time to play the plant-and-rip-out game again. But for some reason, she couldn't bring herself to give up without another try. "I'll check back in a couple of days."

Frances smiled. "Good. As much as it may not appear that way, I do believe your gesture meant a lot to Miss Montgomery. It's been a long time since someone did something nice for her who didn't want a favor in return."

"Then I'm glad I did it." And she meant it. Maybe she really was here for a purpose, after all.

eighteen

On Wednesday morning, Lauren woke up with a sense of dread. Mr. Rivers had arranged a special deal with one of the fabric stores in the LA Fashion District, but it felt much too soon and too raw for her to return to that area now. Until the dress debacle, those few blocks had been almost a second home to her. Now . . . it was a place she'd rather avoid for a long while. But she needed to finalize her concept for the wedding-dress costume, and she needed the fabric in order to do that. Since she would be in the general area for Chloe's tea this afternoon, it was obviously the right time to do her shopping.

Simply because it gave her a feeling of anonymity, she wore a baseball cap and large sunglasses. She shouldn't have to stay long, and the truth was the area was so crowded, the chance of running into someone she knew was very small indeed. Once she'd survived the Fashion District, the rest of the day would be a happy one. Lauren brought along her dress for the afternoon tea in the back of her SUV. Just the thought of that dress brought a smile.

As she made her way down the 101, she thought that, for once, she wouldn't mind some heavy traffic. Anything to delay the inevitable. Of course, it was the clearest she'd seen the road in years, all the way through to LA. She pulled into the parking garage closest to *Leah Rae's Fabrics*, hoping for a quick in and out.

As Lauren made her way through several blocks of the fabric and notions stores in The District, the smell of the hot dog and burrito food trucks, the cacophony of many different languages being spoken, and the crowded and dirty sidewalk all reminded her so much of her former life that it was physically painful to be right in the middle of it.

At least now she had hope that she would eventually be cleared of wrongdoing and would be able to return to her life here. Kendall seemed to be moving closer to the proof she needed. It was just a matter of time.

As with many of the fabric stores in the Fashion District, *Leah Rae's* was packed to capacity with inventory. There were bolts and bolts of fabric standing upright in the middle of the store, with barely a walkway cleared around the perimeter, while the walls were lined by side stacks of some of the more popular fabrics. Lauren knew that the heavier satins and laces were in the very back, so she made her way through the tunnel of fabric, which was packed so tight she had to turn her shoulders at an angle to walk through. She found some beautiful silks, but most were well beyond the school's budget, even at a deep discount. She did find the dove-gray silk charmeuse she was seeking and some faux fur for her patch job on the blue dress. She walked over to check the remnants racks, hoping she might find just the right thing for Guinevere's wedding dress.

The smell and feel of the fabrics had always given her such a feeling of joy, a quirk that she fully acknowledged as odd but embraced nonetheless. She smiled at the memories from previous trips here and was just getting ready to walk away when the most gorgeous white-and-gold brocade satin caught her eye. It was of the very highest quality, thick and lustrous. The kind of fabric that actually brought tears to her eyes—something Chloe teased her about mercilessly. "Only girl I know who can sit dry-eyed through a tearjerker but gets downright weepy over a well-done textile."

Lauren rubbed the fabric between her fingers, remembering that sensation from many years ago when she'd gone to see her very first show at the theater. *The Phantom of the Opera.* Her mother had managed to land a background part, a real coup, and they had celebrated it with every bit of joy imaginable. And when Lauren had sat out in the audience, when she had seen the amazing dresses that the lead character, Christine, wore, she had cried with happiness. Maybe even back then it had been the sheer beauty of the costumes, although she suspected most therapists would tell her it had more to do with the fact that her mother had a paying job that would keep their rent and electric bill paid and keep her too busy to be out partying and using drugs with her friends in the meantime.

Although that didn't turn out to be completely true, it was the closest thing to security Lauren ever felt when she was with her mother, and it was a memory she cherished. This fabric—well, it provoked the same kind of emotion.

This could work perfectly as the fabric for Guinevere's wedding dress. She checked the price. Since it was marked way down, it was something they could afford. There was enough on the bolt for a full costume and probably even a second. A cape, perhaps? There was a similar fabric beside it—a midnight-blue silk with just a hint of brocade. It, too, was beautiful. Lauren thought of the costumes yet to be made for the show and could not come up with one logical place she might use this, but she couldn't imagine leaving it behind. And then she had a thought. What if she made something for Miss Montgomery?

This fabric would work brilliantly in her collection of antique dresses. Lauren shook her head. Just the thought was ridiculous. Why would Miss Montgomery want to wear something Lauren had made when she had a closet full of the top designers' best work, including Angelina Brownings and Balmains, among others?

For whatever reason, sentimentality or the beauty of the fabric, Lauren picked it up. She tried to make her way up the narrow passage while carrying three different bolts, having somewhat comical results. One roll would get caught up, she'd have to maneuver sideways, and then a second roll would get caught on the other side. Step by step, she moved slowly forward. She had reached just about the halfway point when she saw someone rounding the corner. There was no choice in this situation but for the other person to back all the way out. She looked up, smiling apologetically, prepared to make a plea, but then she saw the person's face.

Marsha Flanigan.

Marsha had been in her class at the Fashion Institute. In fact, Marsha had been second in the class—behind only Lauren. She'd never shown anything other than a strong dislike of Lauren and had stated she felt Lauren's talent was overrated. It had only gotten worse when Marsha also applied for one of the internships at *Deb Couture* and was passed over. When she found out that Lauren had gotten one of the jobs, she was livid—and very loud about how flawed the selection process had been and how Lauren's "teacher's pet" status with Professor Navarro and a couple of other professors had allowed her to unfairly move ahead of others who were more deserving. *Others* meaning Marsha.

"Well, well, well." Marsha planted herself in the middle of the aisle and just looked at Lauren. "I must say, I'm surprised to see you here buying fabric. I didn't think there was anyone left in Southern California, or the entire country for that matter, who would want you sewing on a button, much less creating a piece of clothing." She looked at the fabric and touched it. "I remember this fabric from a few years ago—back when it was on trend."

"Can you please move out of my way, Marsha? I've got places I need to be."

"Somehow I doubt that." She rubbed a piece of the blue silk between her fingers. "Some lucky person who doesn't mind three-year-out-of-date fabric is going to really love this, I'm sure."

"I'm sure you're right. Now please move." Lauren had no plans to try to defend herself to Marsha. It was not like she could change Marsha's opinion, anyway.

Marsha did turn and make her way slowly back up toward the front of the store. She seemed to be making a point of walking slowly, stopping occasionally and pretending to check out a fabric or two. "You know, I got a call from *Deb Couture*. It seems they have realized they made a mistake—not only in who they hired, which is obvious, but also in who they didn't hire. Which, come to think of it, is obvious, too. Suffice it to say, the job is now being handled by the right person."

"Well, congratulations, then."

"When I get back to the workroom this afternoon, I'll be sure to give everyone your best regards."

"Please do." By now they had reached the end of the aisle, and Lauren was free to move up to the counter. She did so without looking back.

She set the fabric on the table, had the charmeuse cut, and pointed toward the blue fabric. "Ring this up separately, please. It's for my own personal use." She waited until she was leaving the store before she glanced behind her, but Marsha had disappeared into the back of the store. Lauren let out a deep breath and hurried toward her car, praying there would be no more encounters| ahead of her.

Thankfully, the drive to her old apartment took long enough for her to calm down from the interaction. She began to review her mental list of next steps for the theater costumes, especially the grand wedding dress. She pictured the fabric draped across the dress form, the placement of the draping tape to mark the neckline, how she wanted the waistline to fall. By the time she made it up the stairs, she had mostly refocused and calmed herself sufficiently to enjoy the afternoon.

Chloe and Rhonda were both in the apartment waiting, and they both jumped up and hugged her as if they had not seen her in years. It felt so good to be with them. It felt like home.

Half an hour later, she was in a significantly better emotional place as she hurried to finish getting ready. She touched up her hair and makeup, then hurried out of the bathroom.

"Look at you. I love your dress." Rhonda looked up from her mother-of-the-bride to-do list as Lauren made her way into the living room. "Twirl around and let me see this beautiful ensemble. Did you make it?"

Lauren spun around in a circle, then curtsied before her best friend's mother. "I made it a couple of years ago. Your daughter threw one of her famous themed parties—this one was for Audrey Hepburn night." Lauren couldn't help but smile at the memories of all the crazy things Chloe had come up with over the years. Jasper was in for an adventure, that much was certain.

Her dress was made from a pale green chiffon with black polka-dots—yet another fabric Lauren had found on the remainder rack. She had made a wide sash out of black taffeta to go with it and trimmed the neck and armholes in black taffeta piping. The skirt was full and fell down to just above her ankles. She had to admit, she did feel a bit fabulous wearing it. Once again, she was reminded why she preferred fashion history to today's couture.

"Ready for some tea, girls?" Rhonda asked.

Lauren followed Rhonda and Chloe in her own car so she could head back to Santa Barbara after today's event. She pulled into the parking lot, looking forward to the afternoon ahead. The Great Dane, a small Danish bakery, had a special upstairs room just for their high teas. The white wicker furniture, glass tabletops, and floral wallpaper gave the room an old Victorian feel. Lauren wondered if the inside of Charlotte Montgomery's home was anything like this. Somehow she doubted there was anything warm or cozy where that woman was concerned.

It was just the three of them, plus Zandy, another friend of Chloe's, who met them there. "Isn't this fun?" Rhonda said as they took their seats. "This is the nice thing about a small wedding. You can afford to do some little extra things like this."

Soon the waitress brought over a variety of teas for them to sample, as well as a three-tiered tray of food. On the top layer was a variety of scones, the middle layer held various kinds of finger sandwiches, and the bottom layer held all sorts of sweets and treats. "This looks amazing," Lauren gushed. Soon the four of them were laughing, sipping tea, and eating little bites of all sorts of deliciousness.

"I wonder why this tradition stopped. Tea time, I mean." Chloe looked around the sparsely filled room rather dreamily.

"Well, I suppose it's because we're all so rushed these days. No one has the time to sit around and relax over tea, sandwiches, and cakes anymore," Rhonda said.

Zandy patted her stomach and sighed. "Not to mention the fact that no one can afford the calories."

"Well, I still think it's a shame that it stopped." Chloe shook her head sadly, then turned toward Lauren. "Speaking of shame, how are things going with your neighbor?" Chloe took a sip of tea, her pinky finger extended for effect.

"About the same. Although she has condescended to allowing her maid to ask me if I could do a little work on a couple of her gowns. She insists on paying market rate and will not accept anything that might be regarded in any way as a favor or gift. But her maid did inform me yesterday that there will be some leftover purple sage later in the week. I will be allowed to plant this outside her fence, if I so choose, as long as I use only her own gardening materials."

"Really? I'd say that's progress, then." Rhonda leaned forward and squeezed Lauren's arm. "I knew you'd break through that barrier."

"I hope so." Lauren started to take a bite of scone but then added, "Her maid told me she thought that I've been a good thing for Miss Montgomery, although I certainly don't see it yet."

"I told you that you were there for a reason." Rhonda's face beamed with happiness. "I actually thought of you during my quiet time this morning.

I'm reading the book of Galatians. Did you know it was written because of a mishap? Paul said sickness had brought him to them, and that sickness had been a burden to them, but they had not treated him that way. You know that he was a go-go-go kind of man, so you can only believe that his getting sick and having to stop and have people take care of him would not have been something he sought. Somehow, Lauren, that whole thing with Marisa Remington, it was supposed to happen, and I believe that a big part of the reason might be your new next-door neighbor. That woman is your mission field, I feel it with every fiber of my being."

"I'm not there with every fiber yet, but I will say that I'm beginning to believe that you may be right."

"Aren't I always?" Rhonda offered a cheeky grin and took another sip of tea.

Lauren got back to the cottage late Wednesday night with both her heart and her stomach full from the afternoon tea event. She carried in her fabric and spread the wedding silk across the couch. It would be beautiful, and the gold brocade would bring out the golden highlights in Priscilla's hair. Not that the girl needed any sort of encouragement about how beautiful she was, but Lauren's job was to make her as beautiful as possible.

She looked at the sketch she'd made and began draping muslin across the dress form to create a pattern. Her phone buzzed that she had a text, and she walked over and saw that it was from Chloe.

Saw Cody tonight. He keeps asking about you. He is great, don't you think?

As I've said before, Cody's very nice, but I'm just not there right now. There are too many other things I've got to work out before I even think about seeing someone.

Party pooper.

Lauren returned to her work, thankful that Chloe had backed down so easily. That girl was nothing if not persistent, and sometimes it took a little work to get her to drop an issue.

Lauren had completely lost herself in the work and was surprised when her cell phone buzzed again. She picked it up, ready to see what counter-argument Chloe might have dreamed up. Kendall's name appeared at the top of the message.

Any more sightings of your neighbor?

I haven't seen her. I've been out of town.

That, at least, was the truth.

Anything at all you want to share?

She decided a quick yet truthful answer might work well here.

No.

That truly is unfortunate.

Her phone went silent then.

nineteen

The next morning, Lauren was still troubled about Kendall. More and more, she seemed to be implying that she was only willing to help Lauren bring out the truth if Lauren was willing to give up information on Miss Montgomery. Surely not, though. The Marisa incident would be a big news story. Surely any reporter would want to be the one to break it. Lauren had just grown suspicious because of all that had happened to her recently.

As she made her way back up from her morning beach walk, she glanced toward the Victorian and saw Miss Montgomery herself on the back porch. Lauren waved briefly, then made a point of turning her attention in the other direction. No need for a confrontation about snooping this morning.

When she glanced back toward the house a few seconds later, Miss Montgomery was gesturing toward her. Lauren walked over closer to the fence, and Miss Montgomery slowly made her way across the lawn. She wore medium-height heels and a lovely dress. It was coral in color, just below knee length, with a flowing skirt and a knit top with white flowers.

"Good morning." Miss Montgomery walked up to the fence, her face almost showing a smile, but not quite.

"Good morning." Lauren made a point of smiling all the more brightly. "How are you?"

"I wanted to say thank you for the work you did to repair that dress. It was rather remarkable."

"You're welcome. It was a privilege to spend time with that gown. It is a true work of art." Lauren stopped herself from gushing on and on about it, even though she easily could have. She simply concluded with a shrug and said, "I couldn't stand the thought of throwing it into the bin at the high school theater."

Miss Montgomery nodded once, appearing thoughtful. "You could have sold it."

"Sold it? It wasn't mine to sell."

Miss Montgomery stared at Lauren, hard, for the course of several seconds before she continued. "The reason I called to you is that I seem to have lost a necklace. I wear it quite a lot, and the last time I remember having it was during dinner a couple of nights ago. I did a little walk-about that night, and I'm concerned it might have landed in the grass or the landscaping. When you're walking along the path there, or if you do some more planting, will you please keep an eye out for it?"

"Of course I will." Lauren glanced down around her feet. "I'm usually pretty good at finding things—my roommate used to always call on me when she dropped the back of an earring."

"Good, we could use a little bit of that talent right now. That necklace holds great sentimental value. It's worth more to me than any cash value attached to it."

"Don't worry, I'll keep my eyes open. What does it look like?"

"It's short, not much more than a choker really. The entire length is sapphires encircled by diamonds."

"Yes, I think I've seen you wearing that one." Actually, she *knew* she'd seen it but didn't want to sound like a snoop. "Where might you have walked on the path? I'll go search for it now, before the workers arrive."

"Mostly right around where you are. I went out on the road in front of the house and down to the end of the lane. Richard has already walked all those places looking, but since you do walk around a fair amount, I'm just asking you to be on the lookout."

"Of course I will." Lauren knew that she would walk all through those paths before returning home.

"Good," Miss Montgomery said. "Thank you." She started back toward her house, then paused and turned. "By the way, Richard brought the sage earlier. He said you'd find the leftovers in the potting shed, if you want them."

"Sounds great. Thank you."

Lauren walked slowly all around the dirt path, to the end of the lane, closely examining every place she believed a necklace could have fallen. She found nothing, but she had trouble giving up.

Finally, she returned to her cottage, disappointed and troubled. She hoped that the necklace had been located inside the house by now. Probably it had. Why couldn't she rest easy about it?

"Look at you, Aunt Charlotte, trying something new for a change."

Charlotte glanced over at her niece. "You make it sound like I always eat the same thing when we come here. That's not true. Last time I had the spinach salad with grilled lamb sausage, and the time before that it was the farmers' market salad." She looked at the half papaya with Dungeness crab and curry sauce that currently graced her plate. "What would make you say that?"

"I suppose you do eat different dishes, but you always insist on lunching at the exact same place every time we come to The Village. You need to expand your horizons a little." Willow tossed back the remainder of her chardonnay and held up the empty wine glass toward the waitress.

Charlotte looked away and offered no further explanation. She would not tell her niece that, while the food here was excellent, the food was not what kept bringing her back.

It was her father.

When he had first purchased the land on the far side of Santa Barbara, they would journey up here every few weeks to check on the progress as the house was being built. They always stayed at "Charlie Chaplin's place," as her father called the Montecito Inn, because Mr. Chaplin and some investors had built it. The rooms were beautifully appointed and looked right over Montecito Village. It was also a perfect stopping place for the trendy crowd as they made their way from Hollywood up the coast to William Randolph Hearst's palatial estate in San Simeon.

Smart and interesting people were always staying at the inn, and when Charlotte was with her father, they all treated her as though they thought she was just as wonderful as they. Sometimes, when the party would move the hundred miles north to Mr. Hearst's, Charlotte and her father would go along. Charlotte lived for those times.

The people at the castle were so gay all the time. There was never a dull moment, never a frowning face. What fun they had, sitting in the great hall at the table that held dozens and dozens of people, with bottles of ketchup and mustard placed every few feet up and down the table. The East Coasters always made fun of this, but Charlotte liked it. She vowed that someday when she was a big, rich star, the people at her table were going to have ketchup straight from the bottle, too.

She could still remember sitting out by the pool one day, wearing the same white silk dress with little blue flowers that she wore this very day, when Gloria Vanderbilt had walked over and declared her outfit "divine." Charlotte had thought she might actually melt with happiness.

Sixty-three years later, she could only sit here in the Montecito Cafe in the same old dress and relive the same old memories. It was the closest she ever came to feeling like she was touching her father. She cherished these memories so. They were all she had left.

Lauren had enough work to keep her busy late into the day and did not have the time to do any gardening. But on Friday morning, she decided that she couldn't hold back any longer. She was going to plant that sage in front of Miss Montgomery's house. Now that she had permission, it was just too tempting to ignore.

She made her way to the potting shed and walked to the back counter, where there was indeed some purple sage lined up and waiting for her. Since the soil at the fence line had been recently turned and fertilized, she supposed she wouldn't need to add anything to it, so she left those bags alone. She picked up a trowel and a hand cultivator from the end of the shelf. Just then, the glint of something caught her eye. She did a double take.

There, lying on the floor against the back wall, doubled over on itself, was the necklace. Lauren picked it up and turned it over in her hands. It was surprisingly heavy. The sapphires were huge and round, each surrounded by diamonds that were by no means small. There were eight sapphires, each as big around as a quarter. She could only imagine what something like this was worth. Sentimental value or not, it was no wonder Miss Montgomery was so desperate to find it.

She carried it around to the front door and rang the bell. The chimes sounded from somewhere inside, but there was no resulting movement.

Lauren glanced down at the necklace again. Never in her life had she dreamed of holding something so amazing. What was she supposed to do with it until Miss Montgomery returned home? She didn't want to put it back in the potting shed, it was too damp in there. Leaving it on the front porch was not a good option, in spite of the rural location. The only thing that made sense was to take it to the cottage.

She walked across the way, looking down the lane, hoping to see Miss Montgomery returning. She was going to be so happy to have this back. But the only movement came from the seagulls overhead. Lauren went inside and set the necklace on her kitchen table.

No, she couldn't leave it there, it felt too exposed. In spite of the fact that she was the only one who came in here now that all the repair work had shifted to the outside, and though the workmen all seemed completely trustworthy, she still felt the urge to get the necklace out of sight. She settled on her sock drawer, where she gently placed it, then covered it completely before returning outside to finish her work with the sage.

Lauren spent a couple of happy hours planting around Miss Montgomery's place. When she was finished, and still no one was home, she cleaned up her tools and made her way back to the cottage.

Once inside, she checked the necklace to be certain all was well, then took a shower and went back to work on the costumes. She was starting to piece together the wedding dress and was loving the process. It reinforced her dream of making beautiful gowns of her own design someday.

Kendall would love to know all about the necklace in her sock drawer, there was no doubt about that. But in this particular case, it didn't feel right to share the information with her. She had, after all, picked this up on Miss Montgomery's property. Still, Lauren stopped what she was doing, walked to the drawer, and picked up the necklace. In the brighter light of her cottage, it sparkled from every angle. It was amazing in every respect. She turned it over and noticed an engraving on the clasp. *To the one who owns my heart. REB.*

REB? Lauren thought about the many possible combinations of names with those initials, but one name stuck out in her mind. Randall Edgar Blake. The man who had been murdered. Had Miss Montgomery been having an affair with Blake and then killed him in a jealous rage?

Maybe Kendall's theories were not that farfetched, after all. Maybe she was indeed on the trail of a cold-blooded killer. Maybe it would be okay to share what she knew with Kendall. Maybe it would help bring justice.

Lauren pulled out a piece of paper and wrote down the words. *To the one who owns my heart. REB.* Then she photographed the necklace front and back. She wasn't going to send the photos to Kendall, but she was definitely going to give it a little consideration. Maybe revealing this information was truly the correct thing to do. Again she found herself pondering that same verse: *Be careful not to make a treaty with those who live in the land where you are going, or they will be a snare among you.*

twenty

Lauren decided she would hand bead the bodice of the wedding dress with faux pearls. Not a full-blown couture embroidery job, but something special. At *Deb Couture* she had worked on a couple of dresses with genuine pearls sewn in. Well, this was going to be just as fabulous, and she doubted there would be any jewelers in the audience who would notice the difference. The point was to look beautiful, not be the most expensive. She stitched together the pieces of the bodice. On Monday she would take it by the theater for a fitting with Priscilla and make any changes necessary before the final seams and beading.

It was after dinner when she noticed headlights coming down the road. She stood up to stretch and watched the taillights disappear down Miss Montgomery's driveway. She went immediately to the drawer and took out the necklace. With something this special, the sooner she got it back into the hands of its rightful owner, the better. As she started out the door, she put her hand inside the pocket of her jacket. On the rare chance that someone else was out and about, she didn't want them seeing what she carried.

On the walk over, she glanced toward the new

purple sage outside the fence. It looked nice. She was smiling as she pushed the doorbell.

Lauren heard the sound of approaching footsteps and was ready to give Frances the good news. She pulled the necklace out of her pocket and was just starting to extend it when the door pulled open to reveal Willow standing there.

"Well, look who's back." Willow folded her arms across her chest. "It's the laundry lady."

"Is Frances here? Or your aunt?"

Willow looked down at Lauren's hand. "What do we have here?" Her eyes lit with interest.

"I'd like to see Frances, please, or your aunt."

"They're upstairs. Aunt Charlotte has spent the whole day having medical tests. She is exhausted. Frances has taken her up to draw a bath."

"Medical tests?" Lauren glanced toward the stairs. "Is she okay?"

"I'd say that's none of your business." She tilted her chin back and looked down at Lauren. "Why do you have my aunt's necklace?"

Lauren could not mistake the condescension in Willow's expression. She had the urge to give her a nice hard shove but managed to control it. Just barely. "I'd say that's none of *your* business."

"Oh, I would disagree. I'm guessing this is the very piece that my aunt has been looking for. I would say that is very much my business." Willow focused in on the jewelry.

Oh, this was ridiculous. What did Lauren care

about what this girl thought? The important thing was that Miss Montgomery's missing treasure had been located, and that would make her very happy. "I found it in the potting shed this morning."

"The potting shed?" Willow looked toward Lauren and yawned. Lauren knew without a doubt that Willow was making an effort to appear less interested in the necklace than she actually was. She leaned up against the doorframe in a slouched posture, but the action moved her several inches closer to Lauren. "Good for you, then. Thanks for returning it. I'll take it up to my aunt right away."

"I will come back over in half an hour. Surely Frances will be available by then."

"I get it. This is yet another of your ploys to gain my aunt's favor, and you want to make sure that you, and you alone, get the credit for finding this. You and I both know there is an underlying motive, the way you keep kissing up to her. I'm telling you now, you may as well save your energy, because you're not getting one cent of her money."

"My goals are closer to a friendly neighborhood hello than a piece of her bank account. Your sense of reality seems to be a bit warped."

"Right. If you expect me to believe you ar truly that naïve, then you are the one with a warped sense of reality." She looked down toward

Lauren's hand, which still held the necklace.

It was very rare that Lauren truly disliked anyone. Willow, however, had been added to that very short list.

Willow sighed and extended her own hand. "Just give it to me. I will make sure she gets it."

"That's all right. I'll come back." Lauren turned to leave.

"Give that to me. It belongs here." Willow reached out and grabbed the part of the necklace edge that was hanging out of Lauren's hand.

Lauren clamped down firmly, but Willow pulled hard and continued to do so. Lauren became afraid that the necklace was going to break, so she released her grip.

Willow looked up at her victoriously. "Now, why don't you run on back to your little freeloader's shack and leave us alone."

"Just make sure she gets it." Lauren walked off the front porch, feeling very uneasy about leaving the necklace with Willow.

She went home and sent a text to Kendall, hoping even as she did that it wasn't a mistake.

What do you know about Willow Montgomery?

The call came before Lauren was even certain her text had gone through. Kendall's voice was high-pitched and excited. "Willow Montgomery? What makes you ask about her?"

"She is visiting her aunt right now. Something about her just doesn't seem right to me." *And I really, really dislike her, too, but maybe I shouldn't go there.*

"Wait, she's visiting her aunt?" Kendall's voice squeaked with excitement on the last word. She paused for a second, as if trying to collect herself. In truth, when she spoke next, her voice had gained a measure of control and sounded very professional and businesslike. "And you know that how?"

"I just saw her. I went to . . ." Lauren stopped herself before she blurted out more than she'd intended. "I went to return something to them, and Willow was there. I've seen her there before, and something about her bothers me."

"I'd say you're a good judge of character, then. Something about her bothers a lot of people. Her father was Collin Montgomery's one legitimate heir. He had—still has, actually—quite the reputation as a playboy. He's burned through a pile of his daddy's money, from what I can tell, on wine, women, and song. There are five kids, all by different wives and girlfriends. Willow is the youngest of his children. Her mother was an Italian supermodel. He's been through a couple of wives since then but has managed to avoid producing any more offspring, which is a good thing, because he can't afford them anymore.

"Willow is known for being a socialite party

girl, as are most of Eduardo's spawn. Rumor is, he cut every single one of them out of the will a few years back. They all have an allowance from the trust fund that he's not allowed to touch, but rumor has it, that fund is dwindling at a fairly rapid rate. Supposedly he declared his offspring and their mothers a bunch of ingrates. He set up his will so that anything he has left when he dies goes directly to charity. Needless to say, there have been lawyers working full-time on both sides of this issue since the first announcement of Eduardo Montgomery's intentions."

"There is something to be said about coming from a family that is flat broke. At least I've never had to deal with this kind of drama."

"True enough." Kendall paused a moment. "So, what was it you were returning to Miss Montgomery's house?"

"It was . . . I did some gardening for her, and I found a couple of misplaced items in her potting shed. I just returned them so they could be put in the right place."

"That's a dreadfully dull answer. Next time, look for something a bit more exciting. Okay?" Kendall laughed as she said it.

You have no idea. "Yes, I sure will."

Charlotte had hurried through the house and out back the moment they'd arrived home. All day long she had been thinking about that necklace, wondering what Lauren might decide to do with it. When they'd pulled up tonight and she'd seen that the sage had indeed been planted, she knew that Lauren had been there.

Without bothering to explain to anyone where she was going, she had grabbed a flashlight and rushed out the side door toward the potting shed. Once inside, she flipped on the light and hurried over to where she had so carefully dropped the necklace. She felt her heart begin to race when she saw that it was indeed gone.

Lauren's true nature was about to be revealed, and there would be no second-guessing it. She couldn't wait to see the results. She hurried back into the house. "Frances? Frances?"

"Yes, ma'am." Frances appeared at the top of the steps. She had been turning down the bed in Charlotte's room.

"Were there any messages when we arrived home? On the phone, I mean? Or at the door?"

"No, ma'am. I did hear Willow speaking to someone, though. You might want to check with her."

Willow came around the corner just then. "That girl from next door stopped by. She wanted to make sure that you saw that she'd planted the sage out front. It seemed important to her that you know that she was the one who did it."

"Well of course I know she did it. Who else would have? Did she say anything else?"

"Nope, not a thing." Willow started up the stairs. "By the way, I think I'm going to head back to LA tonight. I've got a job interview in the morning."

"A job interview? Well, good for you, then." Charlotte was proud that her niece was taking the initiative to improve her life.

twenty-one

Charlotte watched out her window as Lauren made her usual morning trek down to the beach. She stopped to speak with Frances through the backyard fence, but Frances didn't go near her. She clearly didn't hand her anything. Charlotte's heart squeezed within her. Why had she allowed herself to get her hopes up? She made her way down the stairs. "Frances? Frances."

She went to the back door, where she found her maid sweeping the porch. "What did Lauren want?"

"Oh nothing, she just said good morning. I was asking her how the play was coming along."

"She didn't give you anything? Or mention the necklace?"

"No. Not at all."

"That's what I thought." Charlotte turned toward the front of the house, her legs feeling extra heavy with the exertion. Of course that girl would not return the necklace—what would have made her think differently? By now, she should know better than to hope for such things. Anger rose up to help her drown the pain. She welcomed the relief.

She made her way out the front door and through the gate, then looked at the recently planted sage. The work of a fake and a conniver. She wouldn't have it near her house. She knelt down and ripped one out. Then another. And another. She didn't stop until the entire two rows were pulled out and lying in a pile. Her back and fingers ached from the exertion. To her horror, she realized that she did not have enough strength left to push herself back up to stand. What was she going to do? It would certainly ruin the effect if Lauren came back up and found her sprawled and helpless on the sidewalk.

She crawled closer to the fence. By gripping the rungs she could manage enough leverage to pull herself upward. With a huge amount of effort, she finally got her right foot flat on the ground and then her left. She managed one last pull and was finally upright again. Rage always seemed to strengthen her, and, as usual, that seemed to work in her favor.

Her face was covered in sweat from the exertion, and it was difficult to breathe deeply enough. Finally, after a moment, she felt quite improved. She leaned down, still holding the fence with her right hand, and used her left to dust the dirt off her crepe de chine robe and gown. Likely they were ruined, as was her manicure, but it had been worth it. She looked up just in time to see Lauren round the corner and witness the destruction. The look on her face was as if she'd just been slapped. Hard.

"Frances said if I used your materials it would be okay for me to plant these out here." There were tears pooling in her eyes, the little faker.

Charlotte wanted to tell her that liars were not welcome here, and neither were their fake acts of kindness. What she said instead was, "I assumed that it would be understood that it would need to be planted properly." Charlotte gestured toward the pile of dirt and plant roots. "Those things were much too close together. It looked like a cluttered mess." She turned and walked back inside the gate without looking to see if her words had found their mark. She concentrated very hard on walking, not hobbling. She wanted to project the right image.

Now to make some calls and make certain that little thief was punished for her crime.

Lauren walked back into her cottage, dropped onto the sofa, and burst into tears. "God, I don't get it. I've gone out of my way to be nice to that woman. I've tried to be the Good Samaritan, even though she seems to neither want nor deserve such treatment. I've done everything she's ever asked, and yet she is still nasty to me. I just don't get it."

She thought about Rhonda's words, but this wasn't the same. Zacchaeus came down from the tree when called. He accepted Jesus' invitation and changed his life. The wounded man accepted the Good Samaritan's help. He didn't treat him badly in exchange for his consideration.

Maybe Miss Montgomery truly was just a bad person. Maybe she was a murderer, come to think of it. Maybe Kendall was right, and maybe the person who needed a Good Samaritan in her life was the reporter trying to get to the bottom of a man's murder.

Lauren walked over and picked up her cell phone. She started a text to Kendall and attached the pictures of the necklace, front and back. She let her finger rest over the Send button. She wanted so badly to press it, but her insides screamed against it. Finally, in frustration, she tossed her phone onto the sofa.

A couple of hours later, Lauren saw Frances out cleaning up the mess from the planting. She walked over and began to help her pick up the pieces. "I don't understand. I thought this would make her happy."

Frances shrugged. "She's just so upset this week." She looked at Lauren, a disapproving expression crossing her face.

"Hopefully she's at least a little cheered up now that she has her necklace back."

"What?" Frances looked alarmed, then leaned closer and whispered, "What do you mean?"

"Miss Montgomery's necklace. I brought it back last night."

Frances reached out and grabbed her arm. Tight. "What did you do with it?"

A cold and sharp sensation worked its way through Lauren. "I left it with Willow."

"Why does that not surprise me?" Frances dropped her grasp and glanced back toward the house, shaking her head. "That girl, she is trouble, that's what she is."

"You mean to tell me that she didn't give it to you or Miss Montgomery?"

Frances shook her head. "No. And she left late last night. She never said a word about it."

"Maybe she left it in her room, since Miss Montgomery was so worn out last night."

"What do you mean, worn out? That woman is a night owl if ever one existed, and a little outing does nothing if not perk her up."

"Willow told me she'd been in medical tests all day and was too exhausted for either you or her to come to the door."

Frances shook her head. "Of course that's what she said." She wrapped her hands around the wrought-iron rungs of the fence and rested her chin on her left arm. "The three of us spent the day window shopping in Santa Barbara proper and then Montecito. There are some artists there whose work Miss Montgomery admires." She sighed. "Poor Miss Montgomery. It will just crush her if she finds out that Willow has made off with her favorite piece of jewelry."

"She has to know that Willow is not exactly a loving niece."

"She always suspects something when someone is kind to her, as you have experienced in full force. But in the case of Willow, I believe that she has allowed herself to hope."

"Then I'm going to allow myself to hope that she did indeed leave the necklace somewhere for you to find this morning." Lauren knew even as she said it that this was not the case.

"I've already cleaned her room, so that is hardly likely." Frances looked toward the house, shaking her head. "Do me a favor and don't mention this to her. I'm not asking you to lie, if she should ask, but unless she brings it up, don't you bring it up either. Let her just believe the necklace is still lost."

"Really? Don't you think it's better for her to know the truth?"

"I think her heart has had one too many blows. I hate to see her dealt another one at this point. Let me have a week or two to try to get the truth, and the necklace, out of Willow. Eventually we will have to tell her, if Willow doesn't come clean. But let's give it a little time."

"Whatever you think is best." Even if this went against everything inside of Lauren. She would try to hold out for a little longer before she either blurted out the truth or wrapped her hands around Willow's scrawny neck.

Frances grasped Lauren's arm again. "Thank you. Whether she realizes it yet or not, you truly are the first ray of sunshine that poor woman has seen in a long time."

"I'm pretty sure she does not realize that." Lauren grinned, but she didn't feel like smiling. She felt like crying. She walked back toward her home, pondering Frances's words. Was she indeed a ray of sunshine? A light in the darkness? She certainly hoped that she was, but it didn't feel that way.

twenty-two

On Monday, Lauren drove to the school, fitted Priscilla, and then spent the rest of the day hand beading the dress. Her fingers were aching when a text message came through from Kendall.

Can you meet me at the little turnout outside the gate? I've got something to show you.

Surely that could only mean good news.

I'll be right there.

Lauren needed to stretch her legs after a long day of stitching, so she pulled on her running shoes and sprinted down the lane. She waved at Sam as she made her way past the guardhouse.

Kendall was sitting in her car, parked in the little gravel turnout area. It was obvious that she was texting. Lauren waited until she looked up. "Hi. What have you got?"

Kendall waited just a moment before she said, "You first. Anything new in the neighborhood?"

Lauren opened her mouth and started to speak but then stopped herself. Something definitely felt wrong about sharing what was currently happening. Miss Montgomery had been deceived by the one relative with whom she had contact, and Lauren did not want to add to her list of betrayers. "She doesn't want anything to do with me. You said yourself, she is very secretive."

"I need you to put forth a little effort here. Believe me when I say I am putting forth more than a little effort on your behalf right now. I know you have been over there enough to meet Willow. Are you really going to try to tell me that you have no contact with anyone at that house?"

"I have spoken to her a maid a few times. As I have already told you, I returned something from the potting shed and had a conversation with Willow."

"What's her maid's name?"

"I'm sure her maid has nothing to do with the

murder you're investigating, so I don't see that it matters."

Kendall turned her head away for the space of a deep breath, then turned back toward Lauren. "You're right. Just forget Charlotte Montgomery, and I'll forget Marisa Remington. I'll forget anything about the photo I was going to show you about Marisa's mystery helper."

Lauren's heart raced. Could it be this close? "Who is it?"

Kendall shrugged. "Doesn't matter, because I'm tired of talking about this. If you're not willing to so much as tell me the name of the woman's maid, then I'm heading back to LA now. See you." She started up her car.

"Wait . . ."

"I'm tired of waiting." Kendall put the car in gear.

"Her maid's name is Frances."

Kendall looked up, her expression hard. "What's her last name?"

"I have no idea."

"Have a nice evening." Kendall pushed the button to start rolling up her window.

"Stop. You might be interested in the item that I returned to Miss Montgomery from the potting shed." Lauren pulled out her phone and held up the picture of the necklace.

Kendall immediately put the car in park and shut it off. She reached for the phone through the window.

Lauren pulled it back. "You're withholding info. . . . Well, I can, too."

Kendall narrowed her eyes. "You're more cagey than I'd given you credit for."

Lauren shrugged, trying to look nonchalant, while inside she already felt sick at the betrayal. "Maybe so."

Kendall nodded, then grinned. "I like it. All right, then. Let's get down to some serious business." She reached over for an envelope in the passenger's seat. "I got an additional piece of information about Marisa's trip to the bathroom." She pulled out a photo and handed it to Lauren. It showed Marisa and a second woman coming down a hallway, and this time it showed the other woman's face. She looked vaguely familiar. She was maybe thirty, very thin, with sharp features, and wearing an over-the-top hot pink gown.

"The woman with her is Cindy Salmon, an up-and-coming designer. She's the one who went into the bathroom, and according to rumor, Marisa told her if she would help rig some sort of malfunction, in the future she could count on her wearing Cindy Salmon designs on the red carpet. Of course, there is no way that Cindy Salmon will ever admit this to anyone, because that kind of truth is not going to help her reputation. You know that for a fact, I daresay."

"So that's how it happened. Marisa certainly

wouldn't know enough about design for it to work out like it did."

"That's right." Kendall sat silently and looked toward Lauren's phone.

Lauren pretended not to notice. Maybe she should do a little more research into the murder, but for right now, she felt nothing but guilty for having shown the picture at all. Even if it was apparently going to save her in the end. Even if Charlotte Montgomery was a truly disagreeable person. "Do you really believe that Charlotte Montgomery had something to do with that man's murder?"

Kendall studied Lauren's face, glanced back toward the gate, and then looked back at Lauren. "Absolutely, I do. Just remember, anything you show me may help finally bring closure to a family that's needed it for the past sixty years."

Lauren nodded but didn't say anything else. Something about all this didn't feel right. "You prove to me you're actually going to do something about this, and we'll talk more about the picture I've got."

Kendall let out a sigh. "I'm almost ready to go public with Malfunction Gate, as I have affectionately termed it. You need to be prepared to share the picture before I share my story." She glanced again toward the phone.

"Okay."

"Speaking of pictures, I have another one that's

rather interesting." Kendall flipped through the photos on her phone for just a moment, then held it out. It was a picture of an African woman holding up a purse. "I believe your friend Chloe is involved with the manufacture of these purses, is that true?"

"Yes. She started a nonprofit for widows in Uganda. Those purses are their main means of support."

"I've been doing a little research. It seems to me your friend might be working with some sort of sweatshop. It sort of looks that way here, doesn't it?"

"That is not a sweatshop. That is a cottage industry that they have started for those women so they can have gainful employment."

"Yes, but the purses are sold here in America."

"Those women are paid a fair wage, and every bit of the profits goes back into helping them. They are being lifted out of poverty by these jobs."

"I'm betting I could run an article that would convince people otherwise."

"But it wouldn't be true."

"No, and eventually it would come to light that it had all been a misunderstanding, sort of like Malfunction Gate. Although, in the meantime, that could prove disastrous to your friend, couldn't it?"

"Why would you want to intentionally do something to hurt a *nonprofit* that is helping women living below the poverty line in Africa?"

"Why would you want to protect a woman living above the wealth line in America? It's all just perception, everything is. All I'm asking for is basic details. I'm not asking for you to eavesdrop on conversations or riffle through her personal papers."

Lauren turned to leave. "I think we've talked enough for now."

Kendall started her car. "Talk to you soon, then. Got to run." She drove away.

Lauren walked slowly back toward the cottage, taking deep breaths of fresh air, hoping to clear her mind. She sat on the steps to her front porch and looked toward the mansion next door, silhouetted against the starlit sky. Did a woman live there who needed her help? Or was it a murderer who needed to be exposed?

Neither seemed all that likely to Lauren. She thought of Miss Montgomery as a grumpy old lady who had too much money and not enough kindness.

Then she thought back over her own life. What would have happened if Chloe and Rhonda had looked at her based on outside appearance only? A poor girl with a mother who was drunk or high most of the time and a father who lived with one woman and then another for years, Lauren had been the girl a lot of parents didn't want their children to spend time with.

Rhonda had looked through all that immediately. She had taken Lauren under her wing and shown her what true mother-love was like. Lauren was thankful that Rhonda had looked past assumptions. It had changed her life.

She still didn't know what to believe about Miss Montgomery, so she decided to pray. "God, forgive me if I've judged her unfairly. In fact, forgive me for judging at all. I know I've got my own issues. Please help me to show your love to Miss Montgomery. Show me the right thing to do about giving anything to Kendall. Just show me what to do, one minute at a time. That's all I ask."

She went inside and closed the door, having no idea what to do next but believing that when the time came, God would show her the next step.

twenty-three

By the time Lauren got out of bed the next morning, she was full of remorse for even half showing the necklace picture to Kendall. Another voice inside her head tried to convince her that it was fine, that the necklace was something she had found, after all, not something in the privacy of Miss Montgomery's home. It was not like she had gone snooping around looking for it. Maybe it was something she was supposed to find, so she could show it to Kendall and the truth about that murder could come out.

As much as she tried to convince herself of this, even a little bit, she failed. Showing even a flash of that picture felt wrong. Then again, she reasoned that Kendall might run an unflattering story about Chloe's work in Africa, and she needed to do what she could to protect her friend.

That was the reason. Right?

It surely had nothing to do with saving her own career. It was to keep her friend from being falsely accused of having a sweatshop in a country where she was doing everything she could to help widows provide their own means of support.

But, if Kendall Joiner was the kind of person who would blackmail someone who was doing charity work in a third-world country, could she really be depended upon to tell the truth in any dealings?

The answer was more than clear. No, she could not.

How Lauren wished she could get back that moment when she'd flashed the photo. But she'd done it in a fit of desperation, and there was no going back. Was it really any different than ripping up the flowers by the root? She was no better than Miss Montgomery, and now she knew it. She reached for her phone, pulled up the pictures of the necklace, and hit the Delete button. At least she wouldn't be tempted to take it any further.

There was nothing left to do but make up for it in any way she could. She walked over to the blue fabric. She carried it to her work bench, determined to sketch the most beautiful gown she'd ever made. She vowed that she would never again be taken in by Kendall. At that moment, she received a text.

I've gotten the green light from my editor to run the Malfunction Gate article. Stay by your phone, because I'll be calling you for some quotes in a while.

> I'll be at the cottage all day, so call whenever you need something.

Perfect. Make sure you take good care of that photo. My editor is dying to see it.

> Too late. I deleted it a little while ago.

You are joking. Right?

> No. I really did.

The article about the malfunction was going to run tomorrow. My editor is going to pull it if I tell her this.

Lauren looked at the screen on her phone. What had she done? Had she really thrown away her final chance to be proven innocent? For a woman who was possibly guilty? The sudden cessation of texts seemed to drag on forever, but what more was there to say?

Wait, I know how we can salvage this. Do you remember what the engraving said? We might be able to still work with just you describing the necklace.

Lauren released her breath. There was still a chance for her name to be cleared. But what was the cost?

I do remember it, but I would be crossing a line of privacy I promised not to cross when I was allowed to move in here. Rent-free. I cannot repay the Edwards family that way. You will have to decide whether or not it is worth telling the truth about Marisa with things as they are.

No, I'd say it's up to you whether or not you're willing to help me tell the truth. The decision of whether this article runs is 100% up to you.

Her rescue was so very close. Rhonda's verse came once again to her mind. *Be careful not to make a treaty with those who live in the land where you are going, or they will be a snare among you.* Only then was the answer clear to her. The people who lived in the land were those who at first would appear to be helpful allies, but in the end would be a snare. Just like Kendall. Cooperating with her was the treaty that shouldn't be made. Lauren took a deep breath, worked up her nerve, and sent her response.

> At this point, I'd say that article is not going to run, then. The cost is too high. Good luck to you.

And to you. You're going to need it.

"Miss Montgomery, Mr. Winston is on the phone for you." Frances stood at the doorway of Charlotte's bedroom, looking grim. "He said it was urgent."

"Yes, thank you, Frances." Charlotte sat up in bed, smoothed back her hair, and reached for the phone at her bedside table. "Neil, to what do I owe the pleasure of this early-morning call?" Her voice had that just-awakened scratchy sound that she hated. It made her sound old.

"Miss Montgomery, I received a call last night from Sotheby's auction house. It seems that they have been approached about quietly selling a piece of jewelry. I suspect it is the very piece that you notified me as being stolen, and I told them so."

"And?"

"They are awaiting my further instructions."

At last the trap had worked. Now they could take care of that little thief once and for all. "How was it they came to contact you?"

"It is such an unusual piece, the people at Sotheby's made some inquiries, which eventually led them to your estate, and hence, me. They were concerned it could have been obtained in a less-than-legitimate way."

"And, of course, it *was* obtained in a less-than-legitimate way. When did Lauren Summers bring it to them?"

"It wasn't Lauren. It was a young Asian woman. They believe that she is simply working as the runner for someone else."

"I am sure they are correct about that. That necklace was stolen."

"What do you want me to do about it?"

Charlotte drew back the draperies in her room and looked out toward the ocean. She thought about the girl who walked the path every morning to go down to the beach. The one who had pretended to be so kind, planting flowers out of neighborly goodwill. Well, her true colors had been revealed. "I want the thief arrested and prosecuted to the fullest extent of the law." She savored the thought of watching the police car pull up and take that lying, thieving girl away.

"Are you sure about that? There will be quite a bit of publicity. This will likely blow up all over the news."

Charlotte thought for just a minute. She did not want to reinsert herself into the limelight, that was true. But the thought of putting that girl where she belonged outweighed that. "As a matter of fact, I am quite sure. Please notify me as soon as you have more information."

Tuesday night, Lauren had the sewing machine running at full tilt, so when she first heard a distant banging, she dismissed it. It was during a pause when a louder knock sounded, and there could be no mistaking it. She went to the door, wondering who it could possibly be. Frances was standing there, a pleasant look on her face.

"Good evening, Frances. What can I do for you?"

"Miss Montgomery has asked you to come round for tea tomorrow. Would that suit you?"

"Tea? With Miss Montgomery?" Lauren couldn't imagine an invitation that would surprise her more than this one. But if the offer was made, who was she to refuse? "Well, sure. Tea would be great."

Frances nodded once. "She'll be glad to hear it." Frances didn't move. She looked at the ground, her face growing a bit red. "There is one more piece to her invitation. I hope you don't find it insulting."

"Go on."

"She asked that I tell you to . . . make certain that you are dressed appropriately."

Lauren laughed. "Well, that does take a bit of the flattery out of the invitation. Now that you've brought up the subject, though, I know what to wear in a modern-day tea room in Los Angeles, but I'm a little less clear on what one should wear to tea with Miss Montgomery."

Frances grinned. "A nice dress will do fine."

"All right. Something between *Downton Abbey* and *Titanic*?"

Frances looked confused. "I'm sorry?"

"I was speaking of the television show set in early-1900s England and the *Titanic* movie—there was a scene where they were having tea."

"Oh, sorry. I don't get out to many movies, and Miss Montgomery only turns on the television for the evening news, so I'm afraid I'm a bit behind on all those kinds of things."

"I have to tell you, for the most part, you're not missing much."

"So I've been told." She nodded then and turned to go.

"Thank you for the invitation. I find it strangely touching."

Frances stopped and turned. "I'm pleased to hear you say that, because it's the first one I've issued in some time."

"Really?"

"Really. In fact, I believe it may be the first one ever." She turned and walked away.

Lauren closed the door, quite stunned. She resisted the urge to pump her fist, although she couldn't quite understand why gaining an invitation from a grumpy hermit meant so much to her.

twenty-four

The dress Lauren had worn to Chloe's tea was the most obvious choice, she decided. She'd always liked the dress, even if it was sixty years out of style. It was fun to have a chance to wear it again. She took one last look in the mirror, took a deep breath, then headed across the road, wondering what the next hour might bring.

When Lauren arrived at Miss Montgomery's house, Frances led her past a large living room. Lauren glanced toward it as she walked by and noticed the heavy velvet drapes that flanked the floor-to-ceiling windows along the curve of the back wall. The hardwood floor was polished to a gleam, making a lovely setting for the Persian rug and the Queen Anne furniture arranged all around it. They kept moving until they made their way around to the back of the house. There Frances led Lauren into a small sun-room, surrounded by windows on three sides. There were plants around the perimeter, and in the middle sat an oval glass-topped white wicker table, which currently held a multi-tiered serving dish. It looked so similar to the setup at the Great Dane that Lauren smiled at the happy memory.

There were serving dishes of clotted cream and several other kinds of condiments that Lauren did not recognize or have any idea what to do with. Miss Montgomery was sitting on the far side of the table. "Thank you for coming." She gestured toward the seat across from her.

"Thank you for the invitation." Lauren sat down, unsure of what to do next.

Frances arrived with the teapot just then and set it on the table in front of them. Miss Montgomery poured some tea into a floral cup, then placed it on a matching saucer along with a small silver spoon, and handed the cup and saucer to Lauren. She then repeated the process, putting the second cup in front of herself. "How are you enjoying the neighborhood?"

"It's beautiful."

"Yes, it is." Miss Montgomery poured cream into her tea, then used her spoon to delicately fold it in. "I would think that someone your age might be a little lonely out here." She looked at Lauren evenly, clearly waiting for an answer.

Lauren supposed there wasn't any reason to be anything less than truthful here. "Actually, being away from most people is a good thing for me right now."

Miss Montgomery continued to look at her and nodded once. "Ah yes, the dress issue in Hollywood. I did hear about that. I also have seen with my own eyes that you do indeed have a talent when it comes to dresses."

"Unfortunately for me, negative publicity seems to outweigh talent, effort, or hard work."

"That's something I understand all too well." She took a sip of her tea, then reached up and took a scone off the middle tier of the server and set it on her plate. She took a small bite, then looked toward Lauren as if she expected something that had not yet happened.

Lauren was a bit at a loss as to how to proceed with this conversation. Miss Montgomery clearly did not want people prying into her personal life, so she couldn't very well ask the usual "tell me about yourself" kinds of questions. So, what were they to discuss? She finally managed, "Your home is beautiful." It was true—and obvious enough that anyone would make the same observation. Nothing prying in that.

"Thank you."

The silence grew long and loud. Finally, Miss Montgomery said, "Have you noticed anyone in the area who is not supposed to be here?"

"I really haven't been in this area long enough to know who is and who isn't supposed to be here. But I don't think I've seen anyone out of place. There's Frances and your niece, George and Edna, and Christi and Elliott and their dogs. The only other people I've noticed were the contractors at the cottage, and oh, some of my friends drove up a couple of weekends ago to help me with some kitchen repairs."

She took a deep breath, waiting for the interrogation, but Miss Montgomery just kept waiting. Lauren was racking her brain for what it was she was supposed to be saying. The silence grew longer and more awkward. Lauren added, "Um, why do you ask? Is there someone skulking around?"

"I couldn't say for sure, but my gardener told me that several times recently he has seen a blue sports car parked not far outside the gates. There usually isn't anyone in it, which makes me think the owner might be walking around here some-where."

Lauren shrugged. "Not that I know of. Is there a way to get past the guard on foot? There's not another way in, is there?"

Miss Montgomery shook her head. "Not really. The beachfront at the end of the road is quite far below, and there are no stairs or access points there. Even if there were, it would be very difficult to make it around the rock wall to our own beach. You haven't seen anyone down at the beach, have you?"

"No, I've never seen anyone else on the private beach. Not at all."

Miss Montgomery took another bite of scone, took another sip of tea, then turned her attention back on Lauren. "Your friends who came—does one of them drive a blue sports car?"

"No, it was a red truck. I don't believe I've seen a blue sports car . . ." No sooner had the words left her mouth than Lauren realized the identity of the car's owner. It had to be Kendall Joiner. She sat for a moment and considered what she should do. Telling the truth was one thing, but what if Miss Montgomery really was a murderer from all those years ago? Did Lauren really want to tip her off that someone might be on to her? Still, Kendall had proven quite sleazy. "You know, I'm pretty sure I do know who that car belongs to."

"Oh really?" She sounded as if this did not surprise her. "Please tell."

"It took me a minute to put the pieces together, but there is a reporter who has been contacting me ever since I moved in here. She has some information about the whole wardrobe incident."

Miss Montgomery nodded. "Why would she need to drive out here about that?"

Lauren studied the trail of pink flowers around the rim of her saucer. The gold edging was so delicate. So beautiful. Why couldn't life be more like a teacup? "She also keeps asking me for information."

"Oh really? What kind, exactly?"

"Well, uh . . ." Lauren looked up to find Miss Montgomery watching her closely. "She wanted information about you."

Miss Montgomery's right eyebrow quirked in the old-time movie-star manner. "And have you given her any?"

Lauren's face burned. "A little." She wanted so badly to look away, but she was determined to face whatever was coming head on. "She was particularly interested in your clothes and jewelry. I hadn't told her much, but after you ripped out my flowers that last time, I was angry and . . ." She looked down at her plate. "I'm ashamed to say it, but I took a picture of your . . . uh, of something you were wearing and showed it to her. I'm so sorry. I was just angry and hurt. I didn't let her look at it for long, and I realized right after I'd done it that it was the wrong thing to do."

"What was the picture of—the one you showed her?"

To answer this truthfully would be to let her know that Willow had taken her necklace. Lauren didn't want to be the one to do that, so she simply said, "I . . . uh . . . it was . . . a close-up of a necklace I saw you wearing."

"I see." She took a sip of her tea. "You *saw me wearing this,* you say. Would it by any chance be the necklace that I'd told you I lost?"

Lauren stared at her plate. "Yes."

"I thought so. Which might explain why I got a call from an *LA Times* reporter, asking for comments about an article they are about to run. It seems to involve a long-ago murder and my missing necklace. How do you think they might have linked those two things?"

Since Lauren had never shown Kendall the photo for longer than a moment, or told her what the inscription said, this made no sense. "I don't understand how this could have happened."

"I think you more or less told me how it happened. It probably happened in a very similar way to how my necklace seems to have disappeared." She placed her napkin gently back on her lap. "Trust me, that necklace will be found and the guilty parties held to account."

"Miss Montgomery, I do not have your necklace."

"Then you have nothing to worry about, do you? No matter, you have broken the neighborhood privacy policy and, rest assured, you will pay for it." She picked up a sandwich and set it on her plate. "My manager will be in touch in the next few days. Until then, I don't think we have anything more we need to say."

"Yes, ma'am." Lauren pushed back from the table and stood. "I really am sorry. All I ever wanted was to be a friend to you or, at the very least, a caring neighbor."

"It would seem that you did not succeed on either account, then, wouldn't it?"

"I guess you're right. I am truly sorry." Lauren walked from the house, feeling once again like the failure she kept turning out to be.

twenty-five

Charlotte sat in her tower as the evening shadows fell across her. Still, she felt no need to turn on the lights. Sometimes darkness suited her.

That Lauren girl troubled her exceedingly. She seemed so nice, so believable, so unselfish. But those kinds of people were never real. Surely, if nothing else, Charlotte had learned that. She had hoped that by now the police would have been able to link Lauren definitively with the person who had brought in the necklace for sale. Since that was taking too long, Charlotte had invited her over for tea, wanting to see what this girl might say on her own behalf. Nothing surprising, she supposed, except that it was odd that she admitted to showing that reporter the necklace. That was something she'd need to inform her lawyer about. Of course she couldn't trust the girl—she'd known that all along, hadn't she?

She thought back to the day her father died. She was in her room, crying her eyes out, while her mother was drinking heavily in the other room.

Her friend Alice had come over, stayed with her for the whole night—held her, cried with her, commiserated with her. Alice had been one of the friends who had never judged her for her parents' lack of marital status, which was odd, because she was the only one of her friends who was a churchgoer—the ones who usually were so quick to judge.

Alice spent nearly every moment with Charlotte during that week. She helped answer the phone when Charlotte's mother was too drunk or Charlotte too overcome. She had done everything a friend could do. Alice had been her one friend, too, who had never tried to work her way into one of her father's films. She was the only one who wasn't after something.

At least it had appeared so for a while.

The whispers of the church crowd grew louder and louder after Charlotte's father died. It was as if something of his clout and power had protected them from the judgmental comments and condemnation. Once he was gone, once the will had been read and it was apparent that no more power was held by Charlotte or her mother, well, the gloves were off.

Alice, in her defense, did continue to come around for a while. She kept inviting Charlotte to the same youth group, and the leader there was nice to her. The other kids, though—well, the whispers grew louder and louder. Until they weren't even whispers anymore. The leader had to hear them, he had to see what was going on, and yet he did nothing. He chose to ignore it, turn a blind eye, and pretend that nothing was amiss. Looking back, Charlotte wondered if he simply hoped to avoid a bigger controversy and thought if he waited, it would fizzle out. At the time, she could only conclude that the reason for his silence was that he agreed with them. She left that group and never returned.

Alice had tried to visit a time or two after that, but Charlotte shut her out. She was done with people who only wanted to put her down. That turned out to be just about everyone.

On Thursday evening, after attending rehearsals at the school, Lauren allowed herself the luxury of soaking in a long, hot bath. When the water had cooled to little more than tepid, she finally climbed out, put on her comfy flannel pajamas, and went to sit in front of the TV, looking for a little mind-numbing distraction before heading off to bed. Tomorrow she would drive down to Los Angeles and begin the festivities for her best friend's wedding on Saturday. At least she had a nice diversion to look forward to.

After yesterday's tea, it was pretty obvious that she was about to be kicked out of here. And as much as she wanted to blame the circumstances, blame Kendall, and blame Miss Montgomery, she knew she deserved it. One of the rules clearly spelled out from the beginning was that the homeowners valued privacy and that privacy was to be respected at all times. There could be no arguing the fact that Lauren had broken that rule when she showed Kendall the picture. Although she still couldn't believe that Kendall had acted on that small amount of information, she had. And it wouldn't have happened if Lauren hadn't shown it to her to begin with.

She thought of one of Rhonda's favorite Robert Anthony quotes and spoke it aloud. " 'When you blame others, you give up your power to change.' " Then she knelt beside the couch. "God, please help me to gracefully suffer the consequences that I deserve, in spite of the fact that they are so overwhelming. Give me the strength I need to change. Thank You, Father."

The classic movie channel was showing *To Catch a Thief.* Cary Grant and Grace Kelly in all their old Hollywood glamour. The costumes in this movie were absolutely amazing. The first sight of Grace Kelly, in a long chiffon evening gown, caused Lauren to think about Miss Montgomery's blue silk. She supposed there was no reason to continue working on that now. Lauren likely wouldn't live here long enough to finish it.

Just then her phone rang. "Hello?"

"Lauren, it's Ralph Edwards. How are things going there?"

This was it, then. The call from the landlord to tell her to start packing her things. "Things are going all right."

"Great, just great. Hey, listen, my wife and I are going to be up your way in the morning. Mind if we stop by? Say ten o'clock?"

"I'm driving down to LA for a wedding tomorrow, but I can still be here at ten if you need me to." As if she had a choice.

"That would be great if you could make that work. We won't be long."

"All right. I'll see you in the morning."

Lauren crumpled in despair for only a few seconds. She thought back to her resolution, to her prayer. She would change herself in the way that she needed to change and leave the results up to God. She hoped those results would somehow include a place for her to live. Otherwise, she didn't know what she was going to do.

twenty-six

It was half past ten before the white Lexus pulled into the driveway. Lauren had spent some time that morning doing a little extra cleaning. Her palms felt sweaty as she grew suddenly fearful that they wouldn't like what she'd done with the place. At the time it had seemed like anything would be an improvement, but now . . . well, she wondered. What if they hated it? She could not bear the thought of it.

She opened the front door and went to stand on the porch, waving a greeting to them as they emerged from the car. Ralph Edwards's wife was a very attractive fifty-something-year-old. There could be no doubt that there had been some work done on her face, but it was to a lovely effect. Her white-blond hair was artfully curved around her face, and she wore large designer sunglasses. Lauren remembered his earlier comment about his family being the type that preferred a hotel and spa. Her appearance seemed to testify to the truth in that.

Mr. Edwards approached, wearing a finely woven short-sleeved shirt and navy trousers. "May I present my wife, DeeDee? DeeDee, meet Lauren."

"It's nice to meet you." Lauren shook the extended hand, then looked back and forth between the two of them. "I've been doing some work on the inside of the place. I hope that you are happy with it."

Ralph Edwards had taken to turning in a 360-degree circle on the front porch. "Yes, Derek told me you had a nice touch when he called to tell me they were going to finish the work early. I can tell by looking at the lawn that he did not misspeak. It looks lovely."

"I'm glad you like it." She opened the front door

and waited for the two of them to precede her. "I refinished the kitchen cabinets. I tried to retain the original stain and texture as much as possible."

Ralph Edwards walked over to the one cabinet front that Cody had replaced. "Wasn't this piece broken? What did you do here?"

"Some friends of mine who are gifted in that sort of thing found a piece of wood that would match. We had a little work party and replaced that piece altogether."

"I haven't seen any bills for this coming through my contractor."

"Well, no. This was just something I did to make the place a little more aesthetically pleasing. Since you're allowing me to live here rent-free, I felt I owed you that much."

Ralph Edwards's face went pink. He pulled at his collar and looked toward his wife. "That is very . . . kind of you." He continued his little walk around the cottage, making appreciative comments about the fresh paint and the new roman shades Lauren had sewn from a heavy tan-and-blue-striped fabric.

Lauren noticed DeeDee nudging him and signaling toward Lauren with her eyes. Finally, Mr. Edwards said, "We have had contact from an interested buyer for the place. They are willing not only to jump through the extraordinary hoops to get qualified by the homeowners' association, but they are willing to pay cash and close quickly. The only problem is, they need to move in by the middle of next month. That is right at three weeks from now, so we'd need you out before that."

Lauren felt what was left of her hope breathe out through her lungs. It wasn't like Ralph Edwards owed her anything, and she wondered at his giving this explanation, when clearly Miss Montgomery had called to have her kicked out. She supposed he was trying to ease the embarrassment. In truth, it did help a little to know that he was thinking of her feelings, and it helped that she would have a few weeks to find another place to live. Lauren bit her bottom lip in an effort to keep her composure. "Of course. I understand." Her words came out thick.

"I am dreadfully sorry to do this, especially seeing how much you've done with the place. Please send me your receipts for the supplies. The least I can do is reimburse you for that."

Lauren shook her head. "There's no need. I did it to repay you for your kindness."

"And now that I'm behaving in a less-than-kind way, it's only fair that you get some credit for that. Please. I insist." He looked toward his wife then, clearly uncomfortable. "We do have to be going. We have a couple more stops to make."

"Okay. Thanks again for letting me use your beautiful cottage. I can't begin to tell you how much I've enjoyed it." She nodded toward DeeDee. "Nice to have met you."

"Likewise. Good luck on your hunt for a new place. I'm sure something fabulous will turn up."

"I'm sure you're right." Although Lauren was anything but. Her savings account, small to begin with, had dwindled to almost nothing. She knew that, with her salary, affording anything in Santa Barbara was going to be almost impossible, but her job would keep her here for the next two months. She'd just have to find something short-term. And perhaps add a second job?

She watched the Lexus pull out of the driveway and waved. She waited until they were out of sight before she allowed herself to sit down on the front porch and burst into tears.

"Frances, what's going on across the street?" Charlotte called the words down the stairway as she slowly made her way down. "Frances?"

"Yes, ma'am?" Frances appeared from somewhere at the back of the house.

"I want you to find out what is going on next door. Ralph Edwards and his wife just paid a visit over there. They were all smiles and friendly, until they pulled out and left. Then that Lauren girl collapsed into a crying fit on the front porch."

"Really?" Frances walked toward the front of the house and looked out the large window. She shook her head. "I have no idea."

Charlotte wondered if they'd found some other reason to kick that girl out. While she would be glad to have her gone, she'd wanted to have the pleasure of being the one to deal the blow, so she purposely had not yet made the final call. Whatever this was, it wasn't from her. She knew that Neil Winston had not yet contacted the Edwardses about anything. "Find out for me, will you?"

"Yes, ma'am."

"Good." Charlotte climbed back up to the third-floor turret and picked up her phone. There were a couple of calls she needed to make.

Teenaged Charlotte watched out her bedroom window as the Bentley limousine pulled up to the curb in front of the house. It was mostly silver, polished to the highest shine, with black on just the top portion. The chauffeur exited and quickly made his way to the front door, looking rather silly, Charlotte thought, in his dark suit and cap.

Her mother's voice could be heard from down the hall, issuing some sort of instruction Charlotte could not make out from here. She heard footsteps moving toward her just seconds before she saw the chauffeur struggling with the weight of her mother's trunk as he carried it toward the car.

There was a quick knock at her bedroom door before her mother entered. "The driver is here." Even from across the room, the strong smell of stale liquor was overwhelming.

This was wrong. All of this was wrong. There

had been a mistake. Her father hadn't died, it was some other man and they'd just thought it was him. He was so strong. So confident. So necessary. How could they go on without him? Of course they couldn't, and he knew that. He wouldn't have left them, this Charlotte believed with all of her heart. And since she and her mother had not been allowed anywhere near the funeral, how was she to know for sure? She didn't. She refused to believe it. Grief wrapped its long fingers around her neck and squeezed until she could barely breathe. "I don't want to go. I want to stay here for when Daddy comes back."

"He's gone, baby. The sooner you get that through your head, the better off you'll be." Mother had taken a deep drag of her cigarette, then taken a couple of steps into the room. "That's why we're going to start a new life. You like our house in Santa Barbara. It will be nice to stay there. Won't it?" She walked directly up to Charlotte and took her face between her hands, her voice growing firm. "You listen to me. I paid a lot of money to hire that car. We are not going to be seen leaving this place with our heads down like we're some sort of criminals. No, we are not."

She dropped her left hand, took another puff of the cigarette, then used just her right hand to squeeze both Charlotte's cheeks. She drew her face to within mere inches. "Do you hear me?" Her teeth were gritted as she spat out the words.

Charlotte tried to nod, but her mother's grip was tight. Tears flowed freely down her cheeks. Her mother let go, looked down at the moisture on her hand, then raised her hand back up and slapped Charlotte full across the face. Hard.

From her mother's perspective, the gesture worked, because Charlotte did stop crying from the shock of it. She looked at her mother's vacant eyes, unable to believe what had just happened. "Now, that's better," Mother said. "Here's what we're going to do. When we walk out of this house, I want your head up, your shoulders back. We are leaving here with our pride and dignity, you understand me?"

"Yes, ma'am."

"Good. Now, let's get going. We're paying the driver by the hour."

And then Charlotte and her mother had walked out of their Hollywood bungalow for the very last time. The two of them took the long walk down the cobblestone path side by side, shoulders back, heads up, eyes straight ahead. Charlotte did chance a quick look around and saw that several of the neighbors were out in their yards. They were all simply standing there, watching. Enjoying the show.

The chauffeur opened the back door. Charlotte and then her mother climbed in.

As the car pulled away from the curb, Charlotte had the strongest urge to turn around for one final look. But she would not allow herself the luxury. She knew at that moment that two things were true. She had no one she could depend on but herself. And there was no good in looking back. Ever.

twenty-seven

Lauren dragged herself back inside, thankful that no one had come by to see her outburst on the porch. At least her pride had been spared that much. She sank down on the couch and tried to form a prayer. Nothing came out. Soon she found herself facedown on the floor. "God help me. Show me what to do." There were no other words she could say.

She took only a second to get herself calmed before pulling herself up and out to her car to drive to Los Angeles. She was not going to let this ruin one second of Chloe's special weekend. Time to be strong and push through.

By the time she pulled into Rhonda's driveway a couple of hours later, she had worked up every bit of her strength to put on a good front. She would keep silent and act happy. No one needed to know anything.

Rhonda came out the door and hurried down to meet her. "There you are, my sweet girl. I'm so glad you're here."

Lauren hugged her back, so thankful for the love Rhonda had always shown her. "I'm glad I'm here, too."

Rhonda drew back and held her at arm's length, her eyes squinting. "What's wrong?"

"Wrong? Nothing. My best friend is getting married tomorrow, and I am so excited I can't stand it."

Rhonda shook her head. "Nope. Not buying it."

"What makes you think something is wrong?"

"I know you too well. You're in one of your 'acting brave' modes. In fact, I'd say this is about as strong as I've ever seen that. What are you trying to cover up?"

"Rhonda, I am not going to unload my burdens on Chloe or you this weekend."

"Well, maybe not Chloe, but you tell me and you tell me right now. Maybe I can help carry a bit of your load, and it will give you more strength to make it through this weekend with your chin up, since that's obviously what you're trying to do."

"I really don't—"

"Eh-eh." Rhonda held up her hand. "A mother does not tell her daughter to keep her problems bottled up so that she can enjoy the weekend. So you tell me what's wrong right now. Don't hold back a thing." She nodded toward the house. "No one else is here right now. They've run out for some last-minute errands. We've easily got a half hour. Now go."

"I'm getting kicked out of the cottage." Lauren sobbed out the words.

"You are? Why?"

"The owners say they have found someone who wants to buy the place, and they need me out in less than a month."

"That's not right. How could they treat you like that? I thought the deal was that you could stay there until next summer. Surely there is some way to fight this."

"We didn't sign anything when I moved in, and they were letting me use the place for free, so it's not like I can claim unfair treatment. He even offered to pay me back for the materials I've put into the upkeep and seemed to feel truly bad about it."

"As he should. It seems the least he could do." She paused, as she always did when she was collecting her thoughts. "It seems so strange, doesn't it? That place has been sitting empty for all these years, and now all of a sudden he's going to sell in a hurry. It's ridiculous, that's what it is."

"Here's the thing, though—that's not the real reason, and I know it."

"What do you mean?"

"Miss Montgomery. I went to tea at her house on Wednesday, and I told her everything about Kendall Joiner. Everything. Including something that you, and even Chloe, don't know."

"Which is?"

"I'm too ashamed to answer that question. Needless to say, it does give her a valid reason to get rid of me. I deserve it. And I've totally failed at being the light I was trying to be to her. I'm leaving in shame, and she will never know that I really, really did want to help her. She's always going to believe that I was just like everyone else in her life who wanted to use her. I won't get the chance to prove anything different."

Rhonda nodded thoughtfully and stared at the roof of her house for just a moment. "Well, listen, here's what you need to do. I want you to finish making that new dress for her that you told me about, and I want you to make it your best job ever. This is actually perfect timing, as far as it could possibly be at a time like this. When you give that gown to her, you will have absolutely nothing to gain from it. Fact is, you've already lost anything she could do for you. This will be a true gift. Even she will have to see that."

Just the thought of putting in so many hours of work for a woman who would likely not even accept it, much less appreciate it, made Lauren weary. Would it even matter? Miss Montgomery would likely just toss the thing in the trash.

But something about what Rhonda said was right, and Lauren knew it. This was the point where the gifts of the heart were separated from the gifts of convenience. Where what she professed she believed collided head on with what she felt like doing.

"You're exactly right, Rhonda. I'm going to get back to work on that dress as soon as I get home Sunday evening." She sighed. "And then I'll go in search of another place to rent."

Saturday dawned as a beautiful Southern California September day. The sun was out, the temperature was warm but not hot, and there was not a hint of humidity. It was the perfect day for a perfect wedding.

Lauren helped her best friend into the wedding dress she had designed and sewn for her, and tears filled her eyes at just how right Chloe looked in it. The silk chiffon dress had a ruched waist and a tiered, flared bottom, giving it something of a 1920s look. The bodice was shirred across the top for a strapless look, with a single layer of transparent chiffon making up the sleeveless top. So simple. So elegant. So Chloe.

She twirled around and around. "Never in the history of the entire world has there ever been a dress this perfect." She twirled again, then came over to hug Lauren.

"I'm so glad you like it."

"It's absolutely amazing." There were tears of joy in her eyes.

Those tears remained as she made her way down the aisle on her father's arm, then looked into

Jasper's eyes and recited the vows that she'd written herself. It was a beautiful moment, a beautiful day, and for just a little while, Lauren forgot every single problem in her life and lost herself in the beauty of it.

After the ceremony, each of the thirty or so attendees picked up his or her folding chair and moved it back so the tables could be carried into place for the dinner. After dinner, again the attendees helped clear the tables and chairs so the small backyard was transformed into a grassy dance floor. The sun set, and the lights strung all around twinkled. It was magical.

Cody came to stand beside Lauren. "You look amazing."

"Thanks." She felt the flush on her cheeks, then nodded toward him. "You clean up rather well yourself."

"Don't let it get out. I wouldn't want to ruin my reputation as the redneck transplant."

"Your secret is safe with me."

"How about a dance?"

She nodded. "Sounds good."

Chloe, being true to herself, was playing all vintage music. Lots of Glenn Miller and Frank Sinatra and the like. Cody pulled her onto the dance floor with a loose hold around her waist. "I like the old music," he said as "Moonlight Becomes You" came out through the speakers. "It's easier to dance to, and the words actually mean something."

Lauren let him lead her across the grass. "I couldn't agree more."

"You know what?"

"What?"

"Moonlight really does become you." He spun her around, and for just a moment, she felt almost happy. This day had been magical.

It wasn't until several hours later, when the birdseed had been thrown and Chloe and Jasper were on their way to a week in Palm Springs, that the magic of the evening wore off. Looking around at the work to be done tomorrow, Lauren knew there was a lot of mess to clean up. In almost every area of her life.

twenty-eight

"It needs a bit of cleaning up, but I'll knock a hundred dollars off the first month's rent to make up for it." Paula Caine was a tired-looking woman in her late thirties. Her pale brown hair was pulled back into a droopy ponytail, which somehow managed to convey the idea that even her hair was exhausted and spent. She led Lauren up a narrow set of wooden stairs that barely managed to fit between the tall shrubs at the fence line and the vinyl siding on the garage. The shrubs were over-grown, and several branches stuck out well into the already-narrow stairway. Paula yanked at one particularly long branch and looked over her shoulder. "I'll knock off another fifty if you want to get a set of shears and clear this out a little."

The thought of moving into yet another fixer-upper was more than a little disheartening. The high school was just getting into the thick of the play, and her time was at a premium now. That was the reason Lauren had hurried to do the work on the cottage—so she would have a decent workspace and time to concentrate on the play. So much for that plan.

Well, as Rhonda would say, the best view came after a hard climb. This rental unit was just another step on the path.

Paula pushed open the door and led the way into the above-garage unit. Lauren followed her inside.

Although it was not as dusty and cobwebby as the vacant-for-years cottage had been upon her first arrival, this place had the kind of filth and grime that comes from recent uncaring tenants. There were oil splatter marks on the back wall of the kitchenette, the corners of the floor had a thick layer of something that had never been mopped away, and it appeared a ball had been bounced off the ceiling repeatedly, as there were telltale dirty little circles all around the space that served as both living room and bedroom.

"The Murphy bed pulls down like this." Paula

went over to a cabinet on the far wall, reached up, and yanked down the bed.

The place smelled of mold and must, with just a hint of stale urine. And yet, beggars could not be choosers. Fact was, the rent was affordable, it was in a fairly safe neighborhood, and Paula Caine wasn't asking for a long-term lease agreement. Month-to-month was fine by her, since she was in the process of a divorce and wasn't sure whether or not she'd be able to keep the house when all was said and done.

"I have my kids Monday through Wednesday and every other weekend. When they are here, I need you to make sure the noise level is low to nonexistent after eight o'clock. It's hard enough being a single mother without having someone living in the backyard making noise and keeping them awake. Lord knows I had enough of that when my ex lived here."

"Not a problem."

Paula rubbed her palm against her forehead and nodded. "Glad to hear it."

Lauren left half an hour later having signed up for the place. She had to be out of the cottage in two weeks, and Paula had already given her the key to the above-garage unit and told her she could come work on it anytime. At least she could get this place cleaned up before she had to live in it. A wave of exhaustion broke over her as she drove back toward the cottage.

Once she arrived, the first thing she did was return to the dress form and the pieces of muslin she'd draped across it last night. She marked and pinned together the fabric to see if it worked the way she wanted it to, then went to cut out the pieces of the blue silk. Many of her friends considered this part tedious and boring to the extreme. Not Lauren, though. To her, it was relaxing. Studying the lines of the garment, looking for the perfect placement of every single piece, well, to her that was like working a puzzle. An intricate puzzle with the potential for incredibly beautiful results.

She spent extra time on each stitch, making sure it was perfect, because this was going to be the finest gown she'd ever produced, and she would settle for nothing less. There would be light beading around the neckline to give just a hint of sparkle, but not too much. This fabric was more than able to stand alone. With each stitch, her determination began to grow. She would do the right thing. Yes, she'd blown it up to this point, but from here on out, she knew her path.

Two weeks passed in a swirl of dizzying activity as Lauren balanced her work on the play—the rehearsals of which were now going late into the evening—cleaning up her soon-to-be new apartment, and working feverishly on Miss Montgomery's dress. By the time moving day rolled around, Lauren felt as though she'd been chasing herself around in circles. Today she would be leaving the little cottage she had come to love and the location she loved even more. She had completed Miss Montgomery's dress last night, and the new rental was at least clean enough to be livable.

Lauren loaded the last of her possessions into her Ford Escape. Several times she'd noticed the curtain on the third-floor turret window across the street pulled back. By the time she took her final two loads out, Miss Montgomery was standing out on her porch, not even pretending to do anything but what she was doing. Glaring.

Lauren waited until she'd loaded every single one of her own possessions before she drew a deep breath, picked up the gown, and headed out the door.

As she approached, Miss Montgomery watched her evenly. "What's that you've got there?"

"I found this gorgeous fabric several weeks ago, and it reminded me of you. I just couldn't leave it behind, so I took the liberty of making a gown based on the measurements of the other dresses."

"I did not ask for that, nor did I pay you for it."

"I know. I did it out of . . . well, I did it because I wanted to do something nice for you. Given all that's happened, maybe we should call it an I'm-so-sorry gift. I do hope that you will wear it and enjoy it."

"I do not take charity."

"This is not charity. It's a gift. There's a difference."

Charlotte Montgomery made no move to take the dress. Lauren finally laid it across the nearest porch chair. "If you choose not to accept it, then please do know it is given with the best of intentions. I purposely didn't bring it over until I was leaving, because I didn't want you to think that I had an ulterior motive. Since I'm leaving now, and we'll likely never meet again, it's obvious that there is nothing I hope to gain from this."

Miss Montgomery's hand stroked up near her throat, as if feeling for a necklace that wasn't there. She said nothing, simply looked back and forth between Lauren and the dress.

Lauren nodded toward her, eyes suddenly starting to burn. "I'm sorry about how things ended up. That was my fault. I really wanted nothing more than to be your friend." She turned and made her way down the sidewalk toward her car, her heart heavy that she had failed. Maybe this just wasn't her time in life to be helpful to anyone. Something she should keep in mind in the future.

Her first evening in the new place, there was a knock on the door. Lauren supposed that it must be Paula coming to check and make sure she was settling in. She pulled open the door, ready to offer her assurances that everything was fine.

Instead she found Kendall Joiner standing there, her arms folded across an LA Marathon T-shirt. "You've come up in the world. I like your new place."

Lauren didn't bother to respond, as it was obviously meant sarcastically. She pulled the door a little closer to her shoulder to block any expanded view of the interior or any crazy idea that Kendall might actually be granted entrance. "Why are you here?"

"You know why I'm here." She kept her voice low and looked over her shoulder behind her, as if expecting to be overheard.

"I told you, I don't have anything to say to you about Charlotte Montgomery."

"You told me that before she made certain you were kicked out of your place. Before you ended up in this dump." She put her hand on the rail and pulled back and forth, watching it rock precariously with the motion. "Doesn't it bother you at all? That old woman is living in that big ol' house, living a life of luxury, not doing one single thing for anyone except spinning her webs so that people like you, people who are doing their best, get kicked out of their dwellings when they are already going through a hard time that was not of their own doing."

"What do you know about why I'm here? Come

to think of it, how did you even know where to find me?"

"I told you before, I'm a reporter, it's what I do." She made a point of touching the splintered wood on the doorframe. "I will say, to be as detail oriented as you seem to be in your work, it's amazing how clueless you are in your life. Otherwise you would have noticed my car following you from the old neighborhood. My sources had told me you were moving out. I simply waited until you drove by and followed you here."

"That's creepy."

"I'll tell you what's creepy. Doesn't it bother you that a woman who was very likely involved in a murder some sixty years ago is still able to wreak all this havoc on other people, including yourself? Don't you think the family of the victim would like some closure? Don't you think we owe it to them?"

"I don't believe that the gowns and jewelry Miss Montgomery wears have anything to do with a murder from sixty years ago. You're not asking for evidence, you're asking for gossip."

"You just don't understand the significance of these items like I do. If you did, you wouldn't say that."

"I don't believe that a person who is truly searching for the truth, about a murder no less, would need to or even be willing to resort to threats about ruining a nonprofit that is doing amazing work in Africa. No, the only reason I could see for someone to do that would be to sell more tell-all books and to make herself more money. Well, I wish you all the luck in the world, but you're not getting any information from me. Not one more bit."

"Have it your way. It's not like you're protecting her, you know. I have another source. An inside source. I was simply giving you one last chance to get on board, so I would have an excuse to give my editor about why I was so determined to spend valuable time working on Malfunction Gate."

"Why is it that I don't believe you?" Lauren paused, trying to get a grip on her temper, but it didn't work. "I'm sure your 'source' "—Lauren made air quotes around the word—"will just be full of new information."

"Oh, I'm quite sure of it. Say, for instance, that the reason you're living here now has something to do with a fiction about a buyer suddenly materializing for that little cottage. Or say that Miss Montgomery has a brand-new dress. It's a blue silk thing made for her by some pathetic little loser hoping to get on her good side. Well, according to my source, it didn't work. In fact, I'm pretty sure the dress has been sent to the dump by now." She turned and made her way down the stairs. She didn't stay to watch Lauren's face to see if her words had found their mark. There was no need. It was a direct hit, and there could be no doubt about that.

Lauren somehow managed to move slowly and calmly back inside and closed the door behind her before she lost it.

twenty-nine

Traffic on the 405 was barely moving. Lauren's Escape crawled down the fast lane while she reflected, not for the first time, that there were definite advantages to living outside of Los Angeles, even if it was in a tiny studio apartment that was falling apart. Thankfully, she had built lots of extra time into today's drive, knowing that the 405 was almost always backed up. Things didn't begin thinning out until after the airport, and then only slightly.

As she approached Long Beach, the water came into view, surrounded by the giant cranes ready to off-load the containers from cargo ships arriving from all parts of the world. The sight of them sent a wave of memories washing over her, both good and bad, of childhood trips to this area. She remembered thinking the giant cranes looked like mechanical brachiosaurs and wondering if they came to life at night when no one was looking.

She followed the signs to the Queen Mary, the

majestic ship sitting in the harbor, thankful that she was about to spend a nice evening with the people she loved most in the world. Chloe had planned this dinner months ago. Two weeks after the wedding, they would have a magical dinner on the Queen Mary. Chloe and Jasper would be spending the night on board. Their "second honeymoon," they were jokingly calling it. Rhonda and Jim would also be here. Since Jasper's family and his best man all lived out of state, it would just be the five of them.

This was the first of the "wedding season diversions," as Chloe was calling them, that Jim had participated in. He was not a tea room or arboretum tour kind of guy, preferring to stick close to home. They had convinced him that the Queen Mary was worth his while because, being a history buff, he couldn't resist seeing the ship that Winston Churchill had traveled aboard. When he found out the restaurant was named Sir Winston's, he was in.

Lauren made her way inside the ship and through the lobby of the hotel portion and then followed the signs down the stairs to the restaurant. It was a large, elegant room, with a wall full of windows overlooking the harbor. It was breathtaking. No wonder Chloe had chosen this for the last hoorah of her wedding season.

The maître d' looked up as Lauren approached. "May I help you?"

"Yes, I'm here with the . . . well, either the Inglehart party or the Yoos party, I'm not sure which name the reservation is under."

He looked down at his ledger. "Yes, right this way, please."

Lauren could see the table filled with her friends at the far wall and was more than a little surprised to see Cody in the midst of them.

Chloe saw her, jumped out of her seat, and ran halfway across the restaurant to greet her. "It's so good to see you. It seems like it's been years." She drew her into a hug.

"You didn't tell me there was going to be a surprise guest," Lauren whispered, even though they were a good distance from the table.

"That's because I wanted it to be a surprise," Chloe whispered back.

"It worked."

"Of course it did. And it's time that you start coming out of your little funk and start experiencing life again."

As the two of them approached the table, Rhonda walked over to give Lauren a hug. Jim, Cody, and Jasper all stood up. Cody came around and pulled out the chair for her.

"So, tell us about your new place." Rhonda leaned across the table toward her. "I'm sure the location can't be as amazing as the last, but very few people ever get to live in that kind of area. Give us some details."

"It's nice." Lauren had no plans to tell them the truth about the dump of a place she lived in. "A small unit atop a detached garage. Quaint neighborhood closer to downtown, which of course has some advantages over the old place."

"That grumpy old lady. I can't believe she got you kicked out." Chloe folded her arms and leaned on her elbows. "Somebody needs to put her in her place, that's what I think."

"You know what, though? I brought some of this later stuff on myself. I kept hearing that verse about not making a treaty with the enemy running through my mind. I always assumed that it was warning me against making a pact with Miss Montgomery. What I've realized is that I completely misunderstood. The treaty I was supposed to avoid was one with Kendall. She was the one who dwelt in the land that I wasn't supposed to make a treaty with."

"I know you know that verse because I quote it all the time. But do you remember the story? From the Bible?" Rhonda asked.

"Vaguely. I know it was the Israelites who were not supposed to make a treaty when they entered the Promised Land."

"That's right. But they did. And why did they? Because they were tricked. Much like you were tricked. The people dressed up in worn rags and pretended to have come from a long distance off, so the Israelites assumed that it was fine to make a treaty with them because God had only told them not to make a treaty with the people *in the land*. These people appeared to be from somewhere far away. They realized too late that they had been duped."

"But it was their fault for not going to God and asking before making the treaty. Just like I assumed that what seemed obvious was indeed correct."

"Perhaps there is some truth to that. The Israelites were sworn to protect the people of Gibeon, which caused them some hassles they weren't meant to have, but God continued to bless them. In fact, He gave them a miraculous victory when they went to war to defend them, remember? The hailstones that killed more of the enemy than their swords did?"

Lauren nodded. "I guess you're right."

"Of course I am." Rhonda smiled her cheeky grin and reached out to hug Lauren again. "You made a mistake. You are paying for it. But it doesn't mean that God will not continue to bless your endeavors. You have not messed up so badly that things can't be all right again. Just you wait and see."

Charlotte had hardly been able to contain herself. They were leaving in less than two days for Europe. Europe! Could life get any better than that?

She was dancing around her room beside her mostly packed trunks, dreaming about what the three-week journey would be like. Just then, her mother came bursting through the door. Her face was flushed with excitement. "Guess what, baby, guess what? You're not going to believe who will be on the crossing with us."

"Who?" Charlotte plopped on her bed, still as could be, waiting for the answer. It was rare for her mother to be this worked up. Surely something amazing was about to be revealed.

"Mr. Walt Disney himself! He's taking the Queen Mary over for the European premier of *Alice in Wonderland*. Can you believe it?"

They both squealed and jumped up and down. This was Charlotte's big chance. She was fourteen—the perfect age to break into a Disney film. Her father's influence couldn't really help her in this respect, so the dream had seemed mostly unattainable. But now—now they were going to spend the better part of a week locked aboard the same ship as The Man himself. What could be better? Charlotte thought she might burst with happiness.

That same feeling stayed with her until the morning they were to begin their journey. Charlotte was dressed and ready over an hour before their scheduled departure from the house. She heard the phone ring down the hall and knew it was her father calling to say that he was on his way to get them. She ran over to look in the mirror one final time, and that was when she heard the first crash down the hall. Followed by another, then another. She ran out of her room and down the hall, terrified of what she might find.

Her mother was standing at the kitchen door. There was a huge gash in the wall across from her and piles of broken porcelain all around the floor. "Mama, what happened?"

"We're not going to Europe after all, baby. Go unpack your things." She turned then and made straight for the liquor cabinet.

It was over a week later when Charlotte saw the first picture in the paper. Her father, waving from the deck of the Queen Mary, his wife and son standing by his side. Charlotte never did find out the reason for the last-minute change.

Her new living quarters were so tight Lauren could barely walk around when the bed was down. She had to cram all her costume accessories over to one side, and then there was the task of pulling out the sewing machine and starting all over again each morning. After a week, she had grown accustomed to the process. This particular day it was gloomy and overcast, a good day to spend inside working, which was a good thing because she had quite a bit to finish.

She picked up the wedding gown, which had been assembled and fitted. She was now deep in the process of the hand beading. She bent and straightened her fingers a few times, trying to get them limbered up for the job ahead, and then she turned on her little television. She liked having noise while she worked.

Today the classic movie channel was showing *Pillow Talk*, with Doris Day and Rock Hudson. Perfect. Beautiful costumes mixed with a little comedy was just what she needed on a day like today. She pulled out her OttLite with magnification so she could see the tiniest detail of her work.

A knock sounded at the door. The only other time this had happened had been over a week ago, and Kendall Joiner had been here. Lauren considered sitting where she was and continuing with her work so that Kendall would get the hint and just keep moving. She finally decided it was best to end this once and for all, so she carefully set the dress aside. She hurried across the small room, letting her anger work her up until she was ready to take a hard stand, leaving Kendall absolutely no doubt that she meant it this time.

She jerked open the door, ready to launch into her refusal. She stopped cold when she saw who was standing there. Frances, her face drawn and unhappy.

"Frances? What brings you here? Do you want to come in?" Lauren gestured inside.

Frances followed her in, looked around, and

shook her head. "Well, I . . . this is where you live now?"

"I needed a short-term lease, something I could afford, and a safe neighborhood. This place fits the bill."

Frances frowned. "I'm sorry you didn't get to stay in the cottage. It was nice having a friendly face in the neighborhood."

"Yeah, well, you may be the only one who felt that way."

"You'd be surprised." Frances stared at her for a long moment. "Which brings me to why I'm here. I've come to invite you to have dinner with Miss Montgomery tomorrow night."

"Dinner? Really? The last time I was over there it was for tea, and it didn't end so well."

"Yes, I know, and I'm sorry about that."

"Frances, I do appreciate the invitation—please tell Miss Montgomery that I really do—it's just that I'm crazy busy with the theater work right now, and I just don't—"

"Please come. Don't let the past keep you from giving her one more chance to be the person that she can be."

"I really . . ." Lauren did not want to go, but she knew what Rhonda would say. She would say that the people who most need love are sometimes the most reluctant to receive it. She would say not to give up when you believe you've been called to something. She would say to go forth and shine your light. Lauren knew that she should give it one more try, even if it was only to confirm what she knew to be the truth: Miss Montgomery did not want anything to do with her. "Sure. I'd be honored."

Frances nodded. "Good. Tomorrow night at eight."

"I assume I am supposed to dress appropriately?" She smiled at Frances, remembering the invitation to tea.

"Miss Montgomery does dress for dinner, as you know. She doesn't expect you to wear a full-length vintage gown, but I would suggest your Sunday best. That said, when Willow eats dinner there, she wears jeans and a T-shirt. I think she does it just to prove that she's not going to let someone else tell her what she can and can't do."

"Well, I'll try to find something suitable."

Frances nodded once more and backed out the door. "I'm glad I've gotten the chance to know you." Lauren watched as she held tight to the splintery bannister and made her way down the steps.

thirty

"It's all set, then?" Charlotte attempted to work a few loose strands of her blond hair into her French twist. Her fingers didn't cooperate like they used to. Neither did her hair, which had taken on a wiry texture in addition to the gray color she spent so much time and energy keeping covered up. She shook her head and sighed. Couldn't nature leave at least something in order while time took away everything else?

Frances hurried over to help her. She worked the strands back in and secured them with a pin. "Yes, ma'am. It's all set. Just as you asked."

"And you prepared the gown I asked for? And the scarf?"

"Yes, ma'am. They're just here."

"Right, then. Well, let's get ready, shall we? It's going to be something of a bumpy ride this evening, I fear."

Frances smiled. "I'd say you can count on it." She lifted up the gown and shook it out. "I believe that the final destination will make the turbulence in the middle worth it."

"I hope you're right. I guess we'll know soon enough, won't we?" For the first time in longer than she could remember, Charlotte felt nervous about something she was about to do. Beyond that, a bit deeper, was something that she almost couldn't identify. It felt like . . . hope?

Out of respect for Miss Montgomery, Lauren opted to dress for dinner in a floor-length gown. Since she owned only one such dress, it made the choice simple. It was actually her grandmother's prom dress, one that she had used for her own prom in spite of the fact that it looked nothing like what any of the other girls had worn. The era wasn't that far off from what Miss Montgomery wore on a nightly basis, so this would likely fit in better at her house than it had at the high school gym all those years ago.

The skirt was pink silk topped with black tulle. The top had pink silk around the edges, with tiny crystals every inch or so, but with a black velvet bodice that had two large crystals descending from the sweetheart neckline. Most of the jeweled portions of the dress had been added by her grandmother. She'd always liked bling—at least according to Aunt Nell, who had given the dress to Lauren when she'd visited the summer of her sixteenth year.

Somehow it made her feel safe and protected, wearing this dress. It was as if Aunt Nell were with her. At least she told herself that until she pulled through the neighborhood gate. At that point she began to feel as though a seamstress were applying a beading awl directly to her stomach. There was no reason that Miss Montgomery would have anything nice to say to her tonight. Why, though, would she want her to come to dinner? It seemed everything that could be said had already been said.

Maybe she was planning further action for breach of the neighborhood policies, but Lauren didn't think that would really be a legal issue, and why have dinner for something like that? Tea would be easier. Or no food at all.

Whatever the rant, Lauren vowed to herself that she would take it without making excuses. She and she alone had made the mistake. If Miss Montgomery felt better by telling her off one last time, then so be it.

As she pulled into the driveway, she noticed the extra car parked beside the house. A red Mercedes. Oh no. When Frances had mentioned yesterday that Willow didn't follow the dress code, she'd forgotten to mention that she would be here at this dinner. This bit of knowledge would have changed Lauren's decision to accept the invitation, which was likely the reason Frances had failed to mention it. Taking a tongue-lashing she deserved was hard enough; taking it in front of someone else who deserved it worse . . . well, that was something different altogether. No matter, it was too late now.

Lauren promised herself she would not leave here until she had confronted Willow about that necklace. She would do it privately, but she would let her know that she knew Willow had stolen it.

She stepped from the car and smoothed down her skirt. Now, knowing Willow would be here in her high-priced designer jeans, Lauren felt a little silly at her choice of apparel for the evening. She walked to the front door and rang the bell, holding her breath and wishing with all that was within her that she could turn and run in the opposite direction.

Frances offered a huge smile. She gestured toward Lauren's dress. "You look wonderful. Miss Montgomery will be so pleased." She opened the door a little wider. "Right this way, please. They will be down in just a moment."

Lauren followed her through the hall and into the library, a beautiful room with sky-high ceilings and bookshelves that were packed with books from top to bottom. In the center of the back wall, the focal point, there were rows of matching leather-bound volumes lined up neat as a pin. Toward the edges, and often disguised behind a partial door or beside a couple of artful bookends, there were more recent hardbacks and paperbacks, too. Lauren walked over to see what kind of modern reading Miss Montgomery might undertake.

She was surprised to find a little bit of every-thing, from romance, to suspense, to legal thriller. There were even a few science fiction books, which Lauren very much doubted Miss Montgomery had ever read. Seeming to read her mind, Frances followed her over. "She's a great reader. Loves all kinds of books. I think that is her way of at least staying partially in touch with the world she has mostly left behind. She can read a book and feel that she has experienced a little of it."

Lauren nodded, understanding the sentiment but thinking how sad it was that Miss Montgomery had spent so many years isolating herself from the world. While she certainly understood wanting to hide away from everyone and everything, especially after Malfunction Gate, she saw before her the danger of letting yourself escape from your problems and not deal with them. Yet another reminder that she was glad she'd made the decision to come here tonight.

"Please, make yourself comfortable. I will go tell them that you have arrived."

"No need for that, on my account, anyway. I heard the doorbell." Miss Montgomery swept into the room, looking as composed and stately as Lauren had ever seen her.

Lauren, however, knew she herself looked considerably less composed. Her mouth had flown wide open and remained that way the second she saw what Miss Montgomery was wearing.

It was the blue brocade gown. Finally she

managed to stammer out, "That color is beautiful on you."

Miss Montgomery looked down, smoothed out the skirt with her hands, and looked back up. "I've always been partial to dark blue." She didn't smile, but she didn't frown, either. She simply looked as though things were happening as they were expected to happen.

"I hope you like it." It sounded as though she were asking for a compliment, but really, Lauren spoke the truth. She really hoped that Miss Montgomery liked the dress.

Charlotte Montgomery ignored the comment and walked over to the pitcher of ice water that was sitting on the sideboard, poured some into a crystal goblet, and took a sip. She glanced back down at her dress. "The cut of the gown itself is quite extraordinary. Where did you find such a pattern?"

"I made it."

"Made the pattern?"

"Not a pattern, exactly. I sketched out what I wanted the dress to look like and then draped the idea in muslin. I used that to cut the pieces. Since I'd worked on your other dresses, I knew the general measurements."

"I see." She squinted her eyes and studied Lauren, as if trying to gauge her truthfulness. "Well, you did an adequate job."

"Thank you." Lauren gestured toward her.

"Your scarf matches it nicely." Even as she said the words, she thought about how much better the necklace would have looked. How perfect the coloring and style would have worked together. She wondered if Willow would have anything like the same thought. Probably not.

Miss Montgomery, however, lifted a hand to touch the blue-and-green silk wrapped around her neck, but she said nothing. She took another sip of water.

"Well, looky here. Don't you look like a little princess, playing in your dress-up clothes?" Willow sauntered into the room wearing a white V-neck T-shirt and jeans. She offered a hard grin toward Lauren, like a boxer smiling down at his latest TKO. "Where did you find that getup?"

Lauren simply looked at her, debating whether or not to take the bait. Finally, she decided to tell the truth. "It was my grandmother's prom dress."

"I can believe that." Willow circled her, snorting laughter. "Yep, it's an old prom dress all right."

"That's enough of that," Miss Montgomery said. "It's time to go in for dinner."

The table was set in an elegant but simple style. Thick white tablecloth, silver candlesticks, and a single bouquet of flowers in the center of the round table. In spite of the fact that there were only three of them, there were four place settings. There were place cards in silver holders at three of the seats; the fourth held none. Lauren saw her name and took a seat. She was next to Miss Montgomery and directly across from Willow.

"So, ladies, thank you for joining me this evening. I had some things I wanted to discuss with the two of you, and it just seemed it would be expedient to do it all at once, rather than dragging it out over several evenings. I don't have the stamina I used to have."

Lauren glanced across at Willow, wondering what conversation Miss Montgomery could possibly want to have that would involve them both. Willow picked up her goblet and offered a fake simper toward Lauren before taking a sip.

"I know you're wondering what this is all about, so I'll get right to the point." She paused and took a sip of water as Frances entered the room.

Frances set a bowl of steaming clam chowder before each of them, then retreated back through the door. Miss Montgomery waited until she had exited before continuing. "It seems to me that the two of you have each made less-than-subtle attempts to befriend me over the past little while. Willow, you for the last couple of years. Obviously, Lauren, yours was a bit more recent. But in both cases, it caused me to ask what you hoped to gain by doing this. I'd really like to hear your own version of this answer. Willow, I'll start with you."

"For *me*"—she glared toward Lauren—"you

already know the answer. I wanted to make some sort of effort to mend the family divide. I thought it was important that you know that you have not been forgotten and abandoned by all your relations. There are some . . . well, me in particular . . . who have always believed that you were treated unfairly, and in an almost reprehensible manner. You are part of the family. There's no reason why you shouldn't know the children and grandchildren of your half siblings. By today's standards, no one would even blink that your mother was not married to my grand-father. It's not your fault that you were born into such a narrow-minded, judgmental time. As I've always said, I want to do what I can to mend the rift."

Miss Montgomery tilted her head toward her niece. "So, it's purely a relational thing. You really were hoping that in time we could all be one big happy family?"

"Exactly." Willow smiled at her and nodded.

"And not just for you, but you have been hoping that in time I can be reconciled with some of the other members of the family, as well?" She took a sip from her soup spoon as she looked toward Willow for the response.

Willow's smile grew even wider as she bobbed her head. "So much. That has been my dream."

"And yet"—Miss Montgomery raised the spoon to her lips again and waited until she had swallowed before continuing—"you've never managed to bring a single other family member with you on your visits." She took a sip of water. "I've met your friend Janet, that fellow you're living with . . . Jonas, is it? But never one of your brothers or sisters, and most certainly not your father."

Willow shrugged. "They are not as easily convinced as I had hoped. Don't worry, Auntie, I haven't given up on it. A little bit longer and I'm sure they'll start coming around."

"Because of your great efforts." She took another sip of soup and stared hard at Willow for the space of a few more seconds. "It has absolutely nothing to do with the fact that your father cut off every bit of your funding a couple of years back and left you with nothing but the remainder of your mostly-used-up trust fund. Right?"

"Auntie, I don't know what you are talking about."

"Of course not. I was clearly misinformed." Miss Montgomery turned her attention to Lauren. "And you. You move in across the street and almost immediately begin planting flowers outside my fence."

"As I've explained, they were going to go to waste. I thought I might as well use them to try to brighten up the neighborhood. I meant absolutely nothing by them, other than that."

"Yes, so you've said." Miss Montgomery stirred

her soup. "This gown"—she gestured toward the dress—"is made from fabric you bought with your own money, isn't that true?"

"Yes."

"So this wasn't just about a few extra plants that you didn't want to waste, and this was not a cheap fabric."

"Well, no, it's not. But I did get a nice deal on it."

"What did you hope to accomplish by spending your money in such a manner? That's not to mention the time required to fabricate it. There has to be something you wanted from this."

Lauren felt her cheeks heat. "Nothing. I've always been obsessed with beautiful fabrics and beautiful gowns. It seems that both are getting harder and harder to find, and few people appreciate them when they are found. When I saw that fabric, I just fell in love with it. I'd seen some of your dresses by then, and it just seemed to me that this fabric would work well for you."

"And you were hoping to gain what by it? Entrance into my home? More information for you to share with your reporter friend?" She had leaned back in her chair and was giving Lauren the full weight of her accusing stare.

"I purposely did not give you that dress until the day I was moving out. There was absolutely nothing left that I could gain at that point." Lauren looked her full in the face. She was telling the truth, and there was no reason to back down now.

"What about you, Willow?" Miss Montgomery turned her attention back to her niece. "Do you think she still had something to gain at that point?"

It was obvious from the way the question was stated that she expected the answer to be yes.

"Clearly she did." Willow glared across at Lauren. She took a breath, opened her mouth, but then seemed to think better of whatever it was she was about to say. She closed her mouth and turned toward her aunt expectantly. "I'm sure of it. Aren't you, Auntie?"

"Yes, I do believe you are correct about that." Miss Montgomery reached up, loosened her scarf, then removed it completely from her neck. "How about this? Might this be what she was trying to gain?"

thirty-one

Charlotte watched the young women's expressions as she pulled the scarf loose. Willow could not contain her glee as she looked accusingly across the table at Lauren, who was looking back and forth between Charlotte and Willow, seemingly waiting for someone to explode. Well, chances were, she wouldn't have to wait long. Charlotte turned toward the door. "Frances?"

Frances appeared immediately. "Yes, ma'am?"

"Would you ask Mr. Winston to join us now, please?"

"Yes, ma'am." Frances left the room and immediately returned with Neil Winston in tow. She set a bowl of soup in front of him before retreating back to the kitchen.

Neil Winston was quite large. Standing somewhere near six-five or six-six, with broad shoulders and a rounded but not quite heavy physique, he was an intimidating man. He wore a dark gray suit with a red silk tie, and dark-rimmed glasses. Yes, he was well cast in the role he played. "Good evening, ladies." He smiled around the table before taking his seat.

"Lauren, may I introduce Neil Winston, the neighborhood manager? You've met his parents, George and Edna, I believe?"

Lauren took his extended hand and shook it. "Hello." Her eyes were wide, and she kept glancing between Willow and Neil and Charlotte, clearly concerned about what might come next. Charlotte smiled at the thought. No need to disappoint the girl.

"Nice to meet you." Neil nodded an acknowledgment, looking professional but not unfriendly.

Charlotte gestured toward her niece, then. "And you already know my niece Willow."

"Yes, good to see you again." He nodded toward her, his face giving away nothing of his thoughts. This was one of the reasons Charlotte liked him so much. The man knew how to hold out for the element of surprise. And tonight's was going to be a doozy.

Frances set a Caesar salad before each of them. No one spoke, each person seemingly waiting for the others to lead the way. Lauren knew one thing for certain—she wasn't going to be the one to break the silence. Finally, Miss Montgomery cocked her head in Lauren's general direction. "How do you like my necklace, Lauren?"

"I love it, obviously, but I thought . . ." Lauren looked toward Willow, swallowed hard, then turned back to Miss Montgomery. "I thought you lost it."

"No, it was never lost." She took a bite of salad.

"But you said—"

"It wasn't lost, it was taken. Isn't that right, Willow?" She smiled over at her niece and took another bite.

Willow held a forkful of romaine just off her plate and smirked toward Lauren. "That's right. Thankfully, Mr. Edwards happened across your hiding place."

"What?" Lauren's mouth went dry.

"That's right. After you moved out, I walked over to speak with Mr. Edwards as he was doing a walk-through. He found the necklace in the top back shelf of the closet. Did you forget you had left it there? Did you lose your nerve about selling

259

it on the black market and decide to leave it behind? Or were you waiting for a higher bid?"

"I did not . . ." Lauren looked to her right. "Miss Montgomery, I did not put your necklace in that closet, or anywhere else for that matter." She stopped for just a moment, considering Frances's earlier words about not wanting to break Miss Montgomery's heart by telling her the truth about Willow. Still, there came a point when a person could no longer keep silent, and when one was being accused of a criminal act, that was definitely such a time. "I did not steal that necklace. Nor did I take it over to my cottage and hide it. If I had, why would I have left it behind to be found so easily? It's more than a little strange that you"—she looked at Willow— "just happened to be there when he found it."

"Yes, I was there. Of course I was there. Unfortunately, I had walked over to let him know that I had to withdraw my offer and was no longer interested in buying the place."

"Your offer? You mean . . ." Lauren looked toward Mr. Winston. "Someone really had made an offer? And it was Willow? I thought Mr. Edwards just made up that story to be a little more gentle when he kicked me out." The extent of this girl's schemes was just beginning to sink in. Clearly she had no qualms about throwing Lauren into the lion's mouth if it would save her own skin.

If Lauren held back any truth here, it might cost her even more than she'd believed possible. It was time to tell the full truth. "Miss Montgomery, I found your necklace in the potting shed the day after you told me it was missing. No one was home here, so I did take it back to the cottage for just the afternoon. That night, I brought it over and rang the doorbell. Willow answered, and I gave the necklace to her."

"Oh really? And why did you not mention this until now?" Miss Montgomery watched Lauren evenly.

Lauren glanced back toward the door that led to the kitchen. She didn't want to get Frances in trouble, but she was not going to allow herself to be accused of a crime to spare someone's feelings. She opted to start by being vague. "I believed that it might be devastating to you when you learned about your niece's deception. It didn't sit well with me, but I decided to remain silent for a little while and hoped that Willow would eventually bring it to you."

"This is absurd. Why would I not return my aunt's necklace? I know how much she treasures it, which is why I immediately returned it to her after I found it—in *your* cottage."

"Yes, Willow, you do know how much I treasure it, don't you, dear?" Miss Montgomery quirked an eyebrow at her niece, then turned her attention to Neil Winston. "Mr. Winston, why don't you tell these ladies about the call you received a few weeks ago. From Sotheby's in LA, I believe?"

"Yes, I'd be more than happy to tell them what I know." Condensation was dripping off his water goblet as he picked it up to take a sip. He savored the coolness of the water for one extra heartbeat before he continued. "It seems that someone had brought in an heirloom necklace to sell. She wanted it appraised. The jeweler recognized several things about the necklace right away. First off, he knew the design was a Joseph Throgmorton original. He also knew that some of the particulars of this design had been at the center of a Holly-wood scandal some six decades ago—it was a story that always fascinated him. Third, he recognized right away that this was a copy of the original, a very good copy, that was stamped by the fabricator. He made some calls and came to find out that this had been made at the request of the insurance agent who represented the owner of the original."

Lauren was confused. "Why would they do that?"

Willow, whose face had gone a bit pale, rolled her eyes. "What, did you grow up under a rock? A lot of high-end jewelry pieces can only be insured if they are worn exclusively at highly secure events. So, when a woman gets a necklace worth several hundred thousand dollars, she has a copy made. These are high-quality fakes, mind you, still valued in the tens of thousands some-times."

"Exactly. And in this particular case, that is the necklace in question." Neil Winston nodded his agreement with Willow's assessment.

Lauren was only growing more confused. "So, Miss Montgomery, it was a copy that you lost? Not the real necklace? Did you not realize that it was the copy when you first lost it?"

"No necklace was ever *lost* here, I can assure you of that." She took a sip of water, set down the goblet, and let the silence grow for a few seconds more before continuing. "I purposely misplaced that one, the copy, knowing you would be the one to find it. I planned on having you kicked out of your cottage as soon as you made the phone call to sell it—either as a necklace or as a story." She looked across the table then. "Please continue, Mr. Winston."

"Eventually, as manager of Miss Montgomery's estate, I was contacted by someone at the auction house." He paused, glancing at Willow. "We explained that this necklace had indeed been stolen, and we further instructed him to inform the potential seller that this was a copy but that he was willing to buy it for ten thousand dollars because of the history involved with the necklace."

Willow shifted uneasily in her seat, but her expression did not change.

Mr. Winston continued. "When the person who brought in the necklace realized it was worth a fraction of what she'd imagined, she came back to retrieve the necklace and left the store. It can only be assumed she went in search of a more lucrative outlet."

"And then she took it back to her cottage and hid it until I found it." Willow nodded, a malevolent grin settling on her lips. "What, were you going to see if you could find a higher bidder? Or some-one who didn't know jewelry as well and would believe it was the real thing?"

"I did not take that necklace anywhere, and I did not hide it anywhere in my cottage. Miss Montgomery, I am telling you the truth."

Miss Montgomery looked across the table. "Mr. Winston, what do you have to say about this?"

"I say, a picture is worth a thousand words." He reached into a manila envelope and withdrew a photograph. He turned it so they could see it. "Anyone recognize this?"

thirty-two

Charlotte Montgomery had been an impetuous seventeen-year-old. She could still remember her younger self, so full of energy and ideas and dreams. Those dreams began to die one by one and then two by ten, until there were none left.

She'd been sitting at the kitchen table of the bungalow house she shared with her mother and sometimes her father. The new edition of *Confidential* magazine was in her lap. Her father was reading some trade paper or other. Sixty years later, she could still remember how it felt to see that picture, to read the words. She could still hear the whooshing sound of ruffling paper as she threw the magazine across the room, where it splatted against the far wall, then slid to an untidy heap at the bottom.

Her father had looked up from his newspaper then, tilted his head, and just looked at her. Finally, without saying a word, he stood up and walked over to see what all the fuss was about. He picked it up and flipped through the pages. There was no question as to the exact moment he recognized what it was she had been reading. "No wonder you're upset, reading this trash. Why do you keep buying this? I told you, this is a bunch of garbage."

He had originally made this particular observation about this particular publication after he and Charlotte's mom had been photographed together, with a story following about their decades-long affair. He had called and threatened to sue, but there was nothing they had said that wasn't the complete truth. In fact, times being different then, it seemed that the magazine had withheld a fair amount of information. They threatened to print these additional tidbits if he took them to court, and that had been the end of it. He'd hated the magazine ever since.

In this upsetting issue, there were multiple pictures of Randall Edgar Blake at the "21" in New York with JoAnne Mayfield. They were surrounded by admirers as they sipped champagne, celebrating the fact that she had just been named Playmate of the Month. The problem came in the next line. They had also announced that she was all set to star in his latest film, *The Power of Love*.

"He promised that lead role to me, you know he did. He told me the role was mine right before he got on that plane to New York." The role had meant all that much more because Randall Edgar Blake did not answer to her father in any way. This was a role she'd won on her own merit. Or so she'd thought at the time.

"Believe me when I say you're better off. The guy is a loser." Her father, she noticed, rather than folding up the magazine and dumping it in the trash, actually read every single word of the article. He shook his head, then handed it back to her. "This is not the kind of man you want to do business with, trust me. Nothing good would have come of it."

She'd started to cry then, in spite of the fact that to do so in front of her father was humiliating. "But I did everything right, and I got offered the role fair and square. It was going to be my chance to show the world that I could do this on my own."

Her father walked over and put his arm around her shoulder. "Now, now, don't you waste another tear. You deserve far better than that, and that louse of a man will eventually get what's coming to him."

Charlotte turned her head slightly to look at him. "Finally I thought I was good enough. Now I find out that I'm not."

"He's a climber, baby, and those are the kinds of people you've got to watch out for. One minute they're holding on to you like you're best friends, the next minute they're walking on your head and reaching just a little higher on the rungs."

Charlotte wiped her eyes. "They're all climbers, aren't they? Everyone we know? Everyone in this town?" And that was when she first began to realize what everyone else had known all along. She didn't fully believe it, not even then. It was too terrible to allow herself to believe. All of her roles, all of her dates, and all of her friends. Nothing but climbers, using her as just another stepping-stone.

"Not to worry, my pet. You are talented. The right role will come along, and when it does, you'll be glad to have walked away from this clown when you did." He walked over to his briefcase, opened it, and pulled out a wrapped rectangular box. "I've got something for you. It was supposed to be for your birthday, but given

267

the circumstances, I'm thinking there's no harm in opening it a few days early."

She took the package, looking up at his smiling face when she did. "What is it?"

"Open it and find out." He tapped the top of the box. "Every time you wear it, I want you to remember that you are somebody special, and that you are completely and fully worthy of anybody or anything in this entire world."

She'd unwrapped the package and been stunned by the beauty inside. It was the most gorgeous necklace she'd ever seen. Huge sapphires surrounded by diamonds encircling each individual stone.

"I've always liked you in blue. It brings out your eyes."

"It's the most beautiful thing I've ever seen."

"You're the most beautiful thing I've ever seen." He'd hugged her then and stood. "I've got to run. One thing, though, the insurance fellow made me promise to keep this locked up. You're not allowed to wear it anywhere or anytime when there is not adequate security."

"When can I wear it, then?"

"We're in the process of having a copy made for you to wear whenever you feel like it. The jeweler is fabricating it now, but I'll be out of town when it's ready. Can you remind your mother to go pick it up next week?"

"Yes, sir."

"That's my girl." He walked from the house, smiling as he closed the door. She'd had no idea it would be the last time she'd ever see him. Two days later, he was dead, and she and her mother found out exactly how many of their friends were true. The answer was . . . none.

thirty-three

"This is absurd." Willow turned her face away.

Mr. Winston handed the photo to Lauren. It showed Willow and a young stick-thin Asian woman exchanging a paper bag between the two of them. It made no sense, so she looked back up at him, waiting for an explanation.

"Yes, it is." Miss Montgomery's voice was calm, firm. "Completely absurd." She paused for just a moment, then said, "Now, what was it you were saying—the reason you were here was to heal the family rift? Did you believe somehow that selling this necklace would be beneficial to that? And then, when you realized it wasn't the real thing, you decided it could be lucrative in a couple of other ways."

"I don't know what you are talking about. Mr. Edwards found that necklace in his cottage. Ask him if you don't believe me."

"First of all, you retrieved the necklace, apparently believing that returning it to me would

269

be more beneficial to you than selling off the copy. Then you attempted to make Lauren look as though she'd had something to do with it. The problem is, that's not even the worst part of your betrayal."

Neil Winston pulled out a copy of the *LA Times* article from that morning. It showed a picture of the necklace with the engraving from Randall Edgar Blake. *New Evidence Arises in the Decades-Old Randall Edgar Blake Murder*, the headline read.

"You really should learn the facts of what you possess before you go selling information to the newspapers," Miss Montgomery said.

"There is engraving on that necklace. I don't know how you can be much more factual than that." Willow frowned toward her aunt, the hint of a dare on her face.

"Keep in mind, this was the copy necklace. We had a fake engraving added to it, for reasons that I will not go into. Needless to say, the original has a much different engraving. It was from my father. Would you like to see it?" Miss Montgomery reached behind her for the clasp.

Willow's face had gone deathly pale. "I . . . well, I . . ."

Miss Montgomery set the necklace upside down beside her niece. Willow refused to look at it.

Finally, Miss Montgomery picked the necklace back up and handed it to Lauren. "Since my niece seems to be suddenly unable, or unwilling, to even look at my jewelry, perhaps, Miss Summers, you would do us all the courtesy of reading the inscription aloud to us?"

Lauren reached down to pick up the necklace, surprised that the original seemed even heavier than the copy. She held the clasp up to the light and read, in the tiniest script, " 'To my daughter, the one who has my heart. You are worthy, beautiful, and honorable.' "

"Truth was, I was none of those things and never have been, but my father saw me that way. Being born to a single mother back in those days . . . well, let's just say that there was no shortage of reminders that I was not worthy or honorable. As for beautiful, you don't have to be in Hollywood long to begin to understand your shortcomings in that particular area. I wear this necklace now to remind myself that there was once someone who did think these things of me. Even if he was the only one." She extended her hand toward Lauren. "If you don't mind."

Lauren handed her the necklace. "Do you need help with the clasp?"

"I've worn this piece every single day of my life for the past sixty years. I think I can manage it." She fastened the clasp in the front, then turned the necklace around on her neck, before directing her attention back to Willow. "People like you are the very reason I chose to live out here in the middle of nowhere, spend time with no one, and care about no one. All my life growing up, there were people who pretended to like me, to be my friend, to love me. All they actually loved were my money and my father's power. When that power was taken away, guess what? They ran as fast as they could toward the next person who they thought could help them."

Lauren's heart ached for Miss Montgomery and for the years she'd spent here, essentially alone and miserable. How awful it must be to not be able to trust anyone. In spite of her unusual childhood, Lauren at least had Chloe and Rhonda and Aunt Nell. She felt a tear slide down her cheek. She reached up with the napkin and pretended to wipe her mouth while dabbing at her cheek. When she glanced toward Miss Montgomery, she found her watching her closely, having seen the whole thing.

"Now, you are a more confusing piece of the story, I'll admit that. You don't seem to have anything to gain here, yet you keep coming back. I still don't understand what motivates you."

"Miss Montgomery, it breaks my heart that your life has been such that you disbelieve the sincerity of even the smallest act of kindness. Most people would accept it for what it is, I think, but then again, most people have not come from your unusual background. I simply wanted to be a small reflection of God's love toward you, because people in my past have been that to me. I'm sorry if my attempts at kindness actually had the opposite effect on you. Believe me, that was never my intention."

"Truth is, I think I do believe you, strange as that is for me to say."

"Oh, come on, Aunt Charlotte, anybody can see that she is just after your money."

"That's what you see because that's how you feel. Perhaps people who think differently feel differently and see things differently, too. I'm only sorry that it has taken me almost sixty wasted years to finally understand this." She looked toward Lauren. "I'd like to start by asking your forgiveness." She turned to the side wall to study an oil painting of a young girl in a party dress, as if she suddenly found it fascinating. She rubbed her hand across the neckline of her dress, then looked back at Lauren. "Forgiveness for doubting your intentions, when they apparently were noble."

"Of course I forgive you." Lauren looked from Miss Montgomery to Willow, who was still glaring at her, to Mr. Winston, who was fidgeting in his seat as if there was more to be said. "I hope I'll get the chance to make another dress for you sometime."

"There's nothing I would love more. Thank you." Miss Montgomery rose from her chair. "Please, stay seated, enjoy your dinner and desserts. I find myself needing to lie down." She swept out of the room, her blue gown glowing in the light as she left.

Mr. Winston waited until the door had closed behind Miss Montgomery before he turned his attention toward Willow. "I've been asked to notify you that, as of right now, you are no longer welcome in this house. Miss Montgomery asks that you kindly not return, as you will not be allowed inside this house ever again."

"But I . . . she can't . . ."

"Of course she can. In fact, I'll see you to your car."

Lauren pushed back her chair and prepared to leave, also. It seemed this evening had drawn to its conclusion, however weird that conclusion had been.

Neil Winston motioned toward her seat. "Miss Summers, could you please stay for just a little longer? I do have a few more things to discuss with you."

Lauren sank back into her chair, completely perplexed about what else was left to discuss, especially now that Miss Montgomery had left the room. She nodded toward Mr. Winston. "Okay."

Willow cast a backward glare toward Lauren as she walked out of the room, then turned up her nose and disappeared out the door.

thirty-four

"Did things go as you expected?" Frances brought in Charlotte's nightgown and robe and placed them across the bed.

"More or less." She touched the necklace at her throat as she nodded. Even now, as she saw it in the mirror, she experienced wonder at the beauty of it. The face above it had never been beautiful, and it most certainly wasn't now, but these jewels, they were her constant. She had worn them every single day since her father's death—regardless of the insurance rules. How were they to know which necklace she was wearing? No one other than a master jeweler would know the difference. Except Charlotte. She knew. She wore only the necklace her father had bought for her. Never the fake. Ever.

"I'm sorry about your niece. I know you were very fond of her." Frances's voice was extra soft as she said this, although Charlotte knew Frances well enough to know that she had doubted the girl's intentions for a long time. As with most things, she'd kept her opinions to herself.

"Yes, I was." Charlotte picked up the brush from the dresser and began to pull it through her hair in long, slow strokes. "But I'm glad this happened. I'm thankful that I found out the truth about yet one more person who wanted to use me for their own gain." She reached for another section of hair. "That's one lesson I thought I had learned by now. You're the only person I've ever been able to count on, you know. You and your mother."

"There is more than just me you can count on. I would have thought you learned that tonight, if you hadn't figured it out before."

"Neil Winston is faithful, that much is true, but he is well paid to be so."

"Mr. Winston is not who I was speaking of, although I believe his loyalty goes beyond his job. I believe he has your best interests at heart."

"Maybe so. Of course, I've known his parents since the beginning. We were all exiles out here together. That does tend to build a certain deep bond."

"Yes. And I suppose if that's the way you want to look at it, Lauren, too, was an exile. Maybe that's the reason she felt such an immediate affinity for you."

"I want to believe that, I really do, but I just find it so hard to do so. She loves beautiful clothes, I have a closet full of them. Do you think she is hoping to somehow profit from that?"

"I think you've been obsessed over the profit angle for too long now. Some people are just good people. Some people truly want to be help-ful to other people. Perhaps in Hollywood there was less of that than in the real world, but I think you've been pushing people aside for too long now. It's time to make an effort to start believing in people again."

"What would make Lauren decide she wanted to do nice things for me? There had to be some sort of reason for a person to do things like that."

"I believe it probably has something to do with her own difficult upbringing and, more than that, with her personal faith."

"How do you know she had a difficult upbringing or that she has a personal faith?"

"I've spoken with her some. She is quite an interesting girl. I believe you would find that you have more than a little in common with her."

"Somehow I doubt that. Name one thing we have in common."

"Well, unlike you, her parents, I believe, were married."

"See."

"But her mother was a wannabe actress who died of an overdose when Lauren was young."

"I suppose that is similar to my story."

"I also think another reason she goes out of her way to be nice to you is that she remembers when someone went out of their way for her. Her best friend's family more or less took her in during high school. She remembers how much that meant to her."

Charlotte set down the brush. "Well, I guess that

would make us quite the trio, then, wouldn't it? You, me, and her?"

Frances came to stand beside her. "We all have more than a little dysfunction in our past, that's for sure. Thankfully for Lauren, she had another family willing to take her under their wings. Thankfully for my mother, she had a strong advocate and ally who took her in, in spite of having absolutely no reason to show kindness to her. And thankfully for me, that same ally helped me move past the grief and financial burden of being a widow whose husband left her with memories of love and a staggering medical debt."

Charlotte made a dismissive gesture. The two of them rarely spoke about the events that had brought them together, but Frances always expressed gratitude. The truth was, Charlotte had taken in Frances's mother less in kindness and more in anger at the injustice of the situation. "I still get furious when I think of your mother and how she was treated."

"She used to tell me the story all the time. How humiliated she was when that man threw all her belongings into a heap on the ground. Your actions meant more to her than she was probably ever able to express to you."

"She expressed it in many ways, and there's no need to ever doubt that. And there's no need to speak of it further."

"Whatever you think best, but it's always

seemed odd to me that you refuse to accept any credit for, or really even acknowledge, that you did something truly extraordinary that day." Frances turned the doorknob. "I'd best get back downstairs. Cook's going to need some help with the rest of dinner."

Frances left the room without saying more. Charlotte was glad to have her and her reminder of things from the past gone. For now.

Mr. Winston's face was red when he returned to the dining room after walking Willow out. Lauren was thankful that she had been spared hearing the exchange of words that she suspected happened out in the driveway. Mr. Winston sat back in his chair, picked up his napkin with a flourish, and put it back into his lap. "Now, where were we?" He cut into a piece of the tenderloin that the cook had brought not long after he'd walked out with Willow. Lauren knew it had begun to grow cold by now, but Mr. Winston took a bite and moaned. "Truly tender meat is one of life's little joys."

Lauren smiled. "I've never really thought of it that way, but I won't disagree with you." She hadn't actually tasted the meat yet. She was much too nervous about what more he had to say to her.

He reached down into his briefcase and removed a large envelope. "Now, there is a bit of business I'd like to discuss with you."

Since Miss Montgomery had obviously left him behind to do her dirty work, Lauren knew that she was about to get told off but just wasn't certain of the exact reason. Her stomach knotted up, and she waited for the inevitable.

"Miss Montgomery made some inquiries into what is going on in the house across the street. She found out that Willow was the so-called buyer for the cottage, and I say so-*called* because we believe that she never did intend to buy it, she simply wanted to get you out of there."

"I don't understand why. I never did anything to her."

"You were a threat to her plan to become the sole heir of this estate."

Lauren burst out laughing. "I hardly think that planting some leftover flowers outside someone's fence makes me a contender for an inheritance."

Mr. Winston looked at her evenly but did not smile. "Then you don't know much about how these things sometimes work, it would seem."

"That's true. I don't have a single clue."

"As soon as Miss Montgomery found out that Willow was trying to buy the cottage, she had me hire some investigators to find out what you might be up to, what Willow might be up to, and to make sure that none of it got past her."

"And what did she find?"

"Surprisingly, to her at least, she found out that you are basically what you appear to be."

How should Lauren respond to that? She finally kind of laughed and said, "Yeah, I guess that's all I've got to offer for clarification here. I am basically the person that I am."

"That being the case, it did cause her to rethink her will."

Lauren pushed back from the table. The last thing she needed was the drama that would come from whatever it was Miss Montgomery had cooked up. "Mr. Winston, that really is not something I either aim for or am seeking. I just want to live my life without having someone set me up for things that I did not do. I want to be able to use my skills with clothes and make a living and get on with life. Getting added to Miss Montgomery's will seems like the surest way to lawsuits and more of the garbage I am currently trying to avoid."

"And that's exactly what Miss Montgomery believes, as well, but she does want to recognize your kindness. She had a nice long talk with Ralph Edwards and has agreed to purchase his cottage for the price that Willow had pretended to agree upon. She felt some responsibility since Willow was only in the area because of her. She had me draw up an agreement that states that you may live in it rent-free for as long as you choose to do so, with the condition that it be your main residence. Once you have moved on with your life, then it will simply be her cottage and revert to her estate."

"There is no need—"

"Miss Montgomery believes that there is a need. She wants to do something toward making amends for problems she or her family may have caused you. As you may have seen, she does not like to feel as though she owes anyone anything."

"So I've noticed." Lauren cut a piece of tenderloin but didn't attempt to eat it.

"And she also says to tell you that she likes the idea of having a neighbor who thinks of planting leftover flowers along the street." He smiled broadly as he said this.

Lauren just shook her head. "Really? She wants a neighbor who plants flowers? Since she's ripped out every single thing I've ever planted, I would not have seen that one coming."

He smiled. "Nor I. Although I've come to understand that she did rip up the last bit out of anger because she thought you had taken the necklace."

"She what?"

"She'd seen that it was gone from the shed, so she knew that you'd found it. Yet she saw you the next morning going about your business as if nothing had happened. When you spoke with Frances, you didn't mention it. At that point, she believed that you were planning to sell it."

"I gave it back to Willow the very day I found it."

"She knows that now, but at the time, it wasn't so clear." He looked down at the list beside his

282

plate. "So . . . flowers are allowed now, I suppose. Also, she has been speaking with the curator of the Fashion Institute Museum in Los Angeles. They have been after her for years to donate some of her gowns—in particular her Angelina Browning designs. She has spoken with the curator at length about the fine job you've done on some of her dress repairs. They have agreed that, for Miss Montgomery's gowns anyway, you alone will have the job of repairs and restoration, and in fact you will be in charge of that entire portion of the exhibit. This will, of course, come with a small salary. It is part-time work and guaranteed through the length of the exhibit, which will go at least through December of next year. It won't give you a glamorous life, but you'll be able to live and work here, commuting back and forth to LA when necessary, and you'll be able to at least meet your bills while you are figuring out your next step."

"Small salary or not, that is a dream job for me."

"So I understand from speaking to Leslie Navarro, one of your professors from the Fashion Institute."

"You spoke to Professor Navarro about me? When? And why?"

"Miss Montgomery is very thorough in her research."

"So I have come to realize." Lauren stared down at her plate. "I . . . don't know what to say."

"Tell us that you can move back into the cottage as soon as possible. The neighborhood hasn't been the same without you." He grinned at her. "Even my parents say so."

Lauren thought about the cramped room at the top of the rickety stairs that she had to go home to. "I think that can be arranged. Like tomorrow."

"I was hoping you'd say so." He looked up then and smiled at Frances, who had apparently been standing there for some time, although Lauren had not seen or heard her enter the room. "I think we're ready for our dessert now."

"Right away, sir." The grin on her face was the largest Lauren had ever seen from her.

thirty-five

Lauren carried the last of her belongings to her Ford Escape. She'd already made a couple of round trips to the cottage. This would be the final one.

"Sorry I can't refund the rent for the next week and a half, but that was the deal we made. You would pay for a month at a time, and you'd pay up front."

"Absolutely we did, and I have no problem with that. I just appreciate you renting the place to me on a month-to-month basis."

"You were a good tenant for the short time

you were here. I'll be sad to see you go. You cleaned up the place well, and you were quiet and nice around the kids." Paula Caine sighed and leaned against the front of Lauren's car.

"I do appreciate all you did for me. Tell the kids I said good-bye."

Paula nodded. "I'll do it. Good luck."

Lauren drove back toward the cottage, humming as she went. As she went through the entrance gate, she waved happily at Sam, who returned the gesture with a sharp salute followed by a huge smile.

Frances knocked on the cottage's front door within minutes of Lauren's arrival. "I'm so glad to have you back here. You are the breath of fresh air this neighborhood needed for a long time."

"I can't tell you how happy I am to be back." Lauren pointed toward the kitchen table. "Would you like something to drink?"

"Oh, no. There's no way I'm going to impose on someone who is in the process of moving. For the third time in less than two months, at that."

"Believe me, Frances, you are not an imposition. I've actually been curious about you, anyway."

"Curious about me? In what way?"

"You and Miss Montgomery. How long have you worked for her?"

"That's a very long story, but the short answer is that I've really been working for her my entire life."

"Really? I'd love to hear the longer version."

Frances just smiled. "And you will. Someday."

It was several weeks later before she would tell it all, but Frances did eventually return to tell Lauren the story.

"My mother, you see, was a housekeeper for a Hollywood director back in the day. He was known as quite a womanizer, and it was a reputation that was well earned. Somehow he managed to convince my mother that she was different. That he was really in love with her, and that as soon as his career was just a bit more firmly established, he would stop any pretense of courting any up-and-coming starlets and would marry her and announce for all the world to hear that she had been his one-and-only true love for all of his life."

"This director . . . was it Randall Edgar Blake?"

Frances looked surprised. "I'd forgotten you knew anything about that." She took a sip of water and continued. "It seems that Randall Edgar Blake had been promising Miss Montgomery that she would star in his upcoming movie. Then there were tabloid photos of him with another actress and an announcement that she would be the one playing the part. Miss Montgomery came over to confront him. She pulled up in the driveway, just in time to find my mother crying over a pile of her belongings, which had been tossed out the side door." Frances ran her finger around the rim of her glass. "She was pregnant, you see. He wanted her to get rid of . . . me."

Lauren reached across the table and grasped the woman's hand. "Oh, how awful."

Frances nodded. "Abortion wasn't legal then, of course, but that's not to say someone with that kind of power and money couldn't easily arrange it. My mother wouldn't even consider it. He beat her, kicked her out, and refused to give her even the previous month's pay she was owed. Miss Montgomery heard my mother crying and came to see what was the matter. Randall Edgar Blake realized what was happening and quickly came outside. He called my mother every name in the book, said he had never touched her and that she was trying to extort money from him now because she was a slut."

"Oh, your poor mother. I can't imagine how awful that must have been for her."

"Truly awful, for so many reasons. Thing was, if his words were meant to turn Miss Montgomery away from her, they had the opposite effect. You see, her entire life she'd been talked to in a similar way by more than a few people. She immediately felt a great surge of compassion for my mother, loaded her up, and took her away from there. Miss Montgomery brought her home with her and told her mother the whole story.

"Miss Montgomery's mother didn't have quite the same compassion level, and her response was more or less, 'There wasn't anyone here to help *me* when people turned against me. She's going to have to figure it out on her own.' Miss Montgomery, however, would not be deterred, and she finally convinced her mother that since my mother was a housekeeper, they could use her in the house near Santa Barbara." Frances paused and gestured across the street. "This very house. It would get her away once and for all from Randall Edgar Blake, and even give her the chance to start over somewhere fresh."

"So your mother was the housekeeper there before you?"

"Yes, for many years. Miss Montgomery even bought her a little house in a family-friendly neighborhood in the city so that she could raise me around other kids. I still have that very house. She also helped my mother construct a story about how my father died on the boat when they immigrated. No one ever knew that I was an illegitimate child. Miss Montgomery was adamant about that."

"I don't understand, though—the engraving on the copy necklace. Why did it have the initials REB?"

"A couple of different reasons, actually. Apparently Miss Montgomery's father had originally concocted the idea because he was so outraged over the betrayal of his daughter. He was going to let it be spread around the gossip columns that Randall Edgar Blake had given this outrageously expensive necklace to Charlotte Montgomery, thus hopefully inflaming JoAnne Mayfield, causing her to demand her own expensive bauble—because that is the way she operated.

"He would not have been able to afford anything close to that necklace, and JoAnne Mayfield would likely have left him and his movie project in a fit of rage. She was famous for those types of tantrums, and Mr. Montgomery planned to sit back and enjoy a bit of revenge. Unfortunately, he died before the ruse was carried out, and so did Mr. Blake. But it was about that same time that Miss Montgomery realized that most of her friends and all of her admirers had just been pretending to like her so they could get in the good graces of her father. She kept the fake engraving to remind herself—and my mother— just how false men could be. They both declared that they would never chance their hearts again.

"My mother eventually did find love, and Miss Montgomery was happy for her. She, on the other hand, has mostly hidden herself away in that big house for the past sixty years. She has one friend from her past, Alice, who still calls every now and then, but Miss Montgomery has always refused to see her."

"That is so sad." Lauren's heart ached to think

of how lonely these past decades must have been. "How did you come to work here in place of your mother?"

"My husband passed away about fifteen years ago. I fell into a deep depression and was so far in debt from years of his cancer treatments that I lost everything. I came back to stay with my mother, who by that time was finding her work here more and more difficult due to her age. Miss Montgomery hired me, strictly out of kindness to my mother, to help assist her. Somehow she found out about everything, and before I knew it, the medical debts had been mysteriously paid off. When my mother died a few years later, I continued on in her stead, and I've been here ever since."

"Do you have other members of your family?"

Frances shook her head. "I truly consider Miss Montgomery my family, in an unusual sort of way. I take care of her, and I know that she would take care of me, too. My husband and I were never able to have children, though, so to answer your question, I really don't have any other blood relatives that I know about."

"I'm glad Miss Montgomery has you in her life."

Frances stood and carried her glass to the sink, washed it, then set it in the drainer. She walked to the doorway and turned just before she went through it. "I'm glad she has both of us."

thirty-six

Opening night found the entire backstage area full of chaos and clamor. The theater was sold out, and everyone behind the curtains knew that somewhere in those sold-out seats were the Disney representatives. The very ones who would make the decision about which schools would be chosen for next season's premiere. The student seamstresses were all busy with needle and thread, making last-minute adjustments, while Lauren checked and double-checked every garment. All appeared to be in order.

In the very first scene, when Guinevere was singing about the simple joys of maidenhood, Priscilla tripped but somehow managed to grab the arm of one of her maidens. Lauren held her breath, praying that nothing had ripped in the exchange. The scene went on, everything still intact, and soon Priscilla was back in the changing room, Lauren helping her get the wedding gown over her head.

After she was dressed and they'd started working on the buttons, Priscilla said, "Tell me again why we couldn't just put a zipper in? It would have made this whole process a lot easier."

"Because they didn't have zippers in this time period, and it wouldn't be authentic." Lauren continued to work the satin buttons through their respective loops.

"Yes, but who really cares?"

"Mr. Rivers cares, for one, and the Disney people, and believe me, there are plenty of people in the audience who care about those kinds of details. And even if none of that were true, I would still care. I like for things to be done correctly."

Priscilla turned toward her then and cocked her head, and Lauren braced herself for one of the usual biting comments. "That sounds so crazy to me, that anyone could be so uptight about anything. But"—she flipped her long hair over her shoulder—"I will be the first to admit that you have made an amazing dress here, and the play will look better because of it."

Lauren kept buttoning, waiting for the punch line. It never came. Finally, she looked up and replied, "Thank you."

Priscilla swept out the door and toward the stage without further comment. Still, what she had said had been enough.

"Thank You, Father, for sending that encouragement." Lauren made her way to the wings so she could watch part of the wedding scene. Priscilla was not only beautiful, the girl had talent by the bucketful.

After the curtain closed for intermission and the house lights came up, Lauren chanced her first peek toward the packed house. She scanned the first few rows, looking for anyone who appeared to be more official than the others. Perhaps the man in the gray suit? No, he seemed to be with a large extended family. They must be here to watch someone in particular. She kept scanning until she stopped dead on the second row, center section, directly on the aisle. She couldn't believe it. There sat Miss Montgomery and Frances, the sapphire and diamond necklace barely visible inside Miss Montgomery's collared shirt.

Later, when the show was over, Lauren rushed out to find them before they left. "Why didn't you tell me you were coming? I could have gotten you some tickets."

Miss Montgomery swiped the air dismissively. "I think we can afford twelve dollars for a high school play. Besides, the whole point was to surprise you."

"Well, you accomplished that, all right."

"It's about time those tables were turned, then." Miss Montgomery smiled, then gestured toward the stage. "That wedding dress was amazing."

"I'm rather pleased with the way it turned out, I have to say."

"Have you ever considered designing wedding gowns for a living?"

The question, innocently asked, still hit like a blow. "Not really. I haven't considered much in the way of true designing for a while now. It seems like a dream that's a bit too far out of reach."

"Don't be like me, dear. I gave up on my dreams instead of fighting for them. I'd give anything if I could go back and do some of those things over again. Don't hit my age with a heavy heart full of regrets."

On Saturday morning, Lauren went to the school to oversee the costumes for the matinee performance. Theodore Rivers had sent out a group text that he wanted everyone at the theater half an hour before call time because they had a "few rough spots they needed to touch up."

Lauren toyed with the idea of skipping the extra half hour. She would not be rehearsing, after all. But her built-in work ethic wouldn't let her do it. She needed to be there in case there were adjustments needed.

She was in the costume room, steaming out the wrinkles from one of the cavalier's jackets, when a student named Megan Preston came into the room. "Mr. Rivers has asked that you come to the meeting, too."

"Really?" Lauren couldn't imagine why, but who was she to argue?

She stood at the back wall of the theater while the cast and crew all gathered round Mr. Rivers in a giant circle of chairs. He was looking at a sheet of legal paper, which appeared to be filled with suggestions. This meeting was going to take a while.

He looked up and said, "First of all, nice job last night, everyone. We have a few things we're going to review this morning, but as a whole, the evening went smashingly, I thought."

"What did the Disney people say?" one of the girls called out from the back.

Mr. Rivers looked at her, his face growing extra serious. "What did I tell all of you about the Disney results?" He looked around the room but then began to answer his own question. "They have several schools they are planning to look at. They will not pick their final schools until all schools have been considered."

"Do you think they liked the show?" Priscilla asked.

"Mom said the people from the newspaper really liked it. She said they said it was our best show ever," a boy chimed in.

Mr. Rivers looked around the group, his expression growing angry. "What did I just tell you? What have I told you all along? We have to be on our toes and do our very best performance every single day, because what if they come back for another look today?"

The kids shifted in their seats.

"We're going to review the 'Simple Joys of Maidenhood' number, but before that, I do have a couple of announcements to make. First, we still have some open seats for tomorrow's matinee. Make sure you have posted signage in all your assigned spots. And second, I will tolerate no further inquiries or speculation about the Disney decision. Mr. Champion told me last night that they have already looked at several excellent productions, and that they still have five more schools to go see . . . and . . ." His tone was even angrier now. "And . . . one of the available slots will definitely be ours." He paused for a second, his face still so serious that the students seemed to be doubting what they had just heard. Then he slowly broke into a smile, and he threw his paper into the air. The room erupted.

Once he quieted the group, he scanned the room. "And you all thought I was too old to act anymore."

The kids all cheered and shouted their acknowledgment of just how thoroughly he'd gotten them. He continued, "The committee was in agreement about the fact that our production far surpassed any they'd seen so far. They made special mention of your performance, Priscilla." Priscilla's grin was huge. "And of the sharpness of our dance sequences." He nodded toward Faye, the student choreographer. "And in particular they mentioned the professional quality of the costumes." He nodded toward Lauren. "Well done, everyone."

The whole cast and crew began to jump up and

down and hug one another. Mr. Rivers came over to Lauren. "Really well done. I believe the day is coming, in the not-too-distant future, when we will all say, 'Lauren Summers? I knew her when.'"

He walked to the front of the stage. "Okay, 'Maidenhood' scene, let's take it from the top."

On the Monday of the second week after the play had ended, Lauren was in the process of pulling weeds when she heard a car pull up. She turned and was surprised to see a white Lexus in her driveway. The cottage had officially sold to Miss Montgomery, but maybe Mr. Edwards needed something from the attic? Lauren stood and waved as he emerged from his car.

"Hi, Lauren. I hate to just drop by like this, but Miss Montgomery told us that you were home."

Told *us?* Lauren looked to see DeeDee climbing out of the passenger's seat and another younger woman exiting the back. She was a drop-dead gorgeous blonde in her late twenties or perhaps early thirties. Her high-end silk sweater and wool slacks practically screamed *money.*

"I wanted you to meet my daughter, Rebecca," Mr. Edwards said.

Rebecca walked toward Lauren, the fact that she was wearing four-inch heels not slowing her down regardless of the uneven pavement. She extended her hand. "So nice to meet you. I've heard a lot about you."

"Nice to meet you, too." *Heard a lot about me?* Lauren looked down at her sweatshirt and jeans, both a little dirty from the afternoon's gardening adventure. "Sorry, I've been working in the yard. I wasn't really expecting to see anyone."

"Yes, we apologize about dropping in on you unannounced like this, but we weren't sure about our own schedule and didn't want to set up something we weren't sure we would make." Rebecca smiled. "I hate it when people don't keep appoint-ments, don't you?"

"Yes, I guess I do." She looked back and forth between the three of them, waiting to find out what this was all about. Finally, she said, "Is there something I can do for you?"

"Maybe," Rebecca said. "You see, here's the thing. I'm getting married next summer, and once Miss Montgomery found out about it, she began to *strongly suggest* that I speak to you about the wedding gown. I'd like to have a custom gown, you see, and in fact, I have a couple of designer appointments already on the books, but I wanted to think outside the status quo. Then, when I heard what an honor you've been given at the museum, and when I saw the pictures of the wedding dress you did for *Camelot* and heard about Disney's response to it, well . . . it seems to me that if you can make a dress that lovely with such fine detail on such a limited budget, then I believe we should maybe speak

298

about what you could do with fewer constraints."

Lauren felt her heart begin to beat a little faster. "Really? Well sure, come on in."

She looked down at the dirt on her hands. "Just let me wash up for a second. I'll get my sketchbook out, and we can talk some ideas."

An hour later, Lauren and Rebecca had settled on two sketches. One for the wedding dress itself, the other for the three bridesmaids. They made an appointment to look at fabric as soon as New Year's was over. Rebecca also left a sizable check as a deposit. "This has been just fabulous," she said. "I can't wait to see the final product."

"I'm happy to be working with you. See you in the new year."

And the white Lexus pulled off down the street. It looked as if Lauren's dreams might actually be coming true. At least for just this once. *Thank You, Father.*

thirty-seven

The white lights twinkled on Lauren's tabletop Christmas tree and Christmas music came from the tiny speakers attached to her iPod as she hunched over her work table, carefully repairing a loose section of lace that had pulled away from the silk charmeuse. She was making a lovely dress for Frances to wear tomorrow evening to the opening event at the fashion museum.

The complete display wouldn't be ready for another month, but they had pulled together all of the more important pieces—especially the gowns that might be considered "holiday attire"—and they were going to open a smaller display now, hoping to catch some of the Christmas shopping crowd. The dress for Frances was a surprise, and Lauren needed to get it finished by this afternoon in order to take it over and make certain it fit. Her concentration was so deep that the knock on the door caused her to jump.

Frances was standing on the front porch, a newspaper rolled in her left hand. "Good morning, Lauren. Are you beginning to get excited?"

"I'm well past *beginning to* at this point. In fact, I'm pretty much off-the-charts excited by now." She gestured toward the living room. "Please come in."

"I don't have time to stay. I have a lot to do, and I'm sure you're busy, as well, but I wanted to make certain that you have seen today's paper."

Lauren shook her head. "I've never been much of a newspaper reader, and in spite of the fact that Miss Montgomery has procured someone to deliver her paper all the way out here, I somehow doubt that I could be included in that deal without a lot of expense."

Frances smiled. "There's probably some truth to that, and that's what we concluded, which is why Miss Montgomery insisted that I come over here right away and show this to you."

"Really?" Lauren assumed there must be some sort of dress or costume Miss Montgomery had found amusing in the Thursday Arts section of the paper. "What've we got?"

Frances handed her the folded paper, her face no longer containing her smile. "Look at the front page."

The headline read *Marisa Remington Admits to Staging "Wardrobe Malfunction."* Lauren stared at the headline, then back up at Frances. "This can't be true. What does the article say? Did you read it?"

"Yes, I did. And I'll leave it here with you so that you can enjoy it at your leisure. The gist of it seems to be that she double-crossed the designer who helped stage it all. The designer became so angry that she went to the press. Marisa, it seems, is so full of herself that when a tabloid reporter, disguised as a seamstress working for the designer, started questioning her about it, she laid it all out there. Every bit. Including laughing about how gullible you were. They have the entire thing recorded, and although the legality of such a recording may be challenged in court, the fact is that it has been heard. Loud and clear. The whole world knows that you are blameless—and that includes Miss Montgomery and me."

Lauren leaned back against the doorjamb. "I can't believe it."

"Well, believe it. It's for real." Frances glanced back toward the Victorian. "Did you know anything about this?"

"Yes." Lauren looked again at the headline. "Kendall Joiner, that reporter, told me about it early on. She said she would help me get the true story out there if I would help her get information about Miss Montgomery."

"Really?" Frances put her hand to her mouth and nodded. "You had quite an incentive to give up information, didn't you?"

Lauren shrugged. "The truth came out anyway."

"And it couldn't have come at a better time. With the grand opening tomorrow night, it will not only remove any negative publicity that someone might have dragged up about it, but now it can only bring more good publicity to the display at the museum."

"You're right." Lauren shook her head, still unable to believe this. "I just hope that this whole Marisa thing doesn't overshadow the exhibit. The dresses truly are astounding."

"We are so looking forward to the opening event."

"As am I. And speaking of . . . would you mind looking at something? I took the liberty of making this, thinking it might be something you'd like to wear to the big night." She couldn't help but grin as she watched Frances's face and the realization that this dress was meant for her.

"I thought the gray color would look nice with your eyes."

"It's the most beautiful dress I've ever seen, let alone that I've ever owned."

"I'm so glad you like it. I'll need you to try it on, but I'm not quite ready yet. Okay if I bring it over in a couple of hours for a fitting?"

"I just don't know that this day could get any better," Frances said.

"You know what? Neither do I."

It was midafternoon when Lauren's phone rang. "This is Rebecca Edwards," said the voice on the other end. "I couldn't believe what I saw in the paper—everyone is talking about it."

"I hope you don't feel that this will be a distraction for your wedding-dress plans."

"Are you kidding me? It seems I've got first dibs on the hottest new designer in town, which is one of the reasons I called. My friend Mitzi just got engaged, would you mind if I gave her your number?"

"No. I wouldn't mind at all."

thirty-eight

"The front panel, it's a bit poofy. We can't have that at the grand opening reception tonight." Miss Montgomery used her cane to point toward the offending piece of yellow silk.

Lauren smoothed the fabric on the mannequin, then reached down and tugged on the hem. She looked up. "Better, don't you think?"

"Yes, that is better." Miss Montgomery nodded with satisfaction and actually smiled a little, something she'd begun to do over the past month, but still only rarely. She looked resplendent in her Angelina Browning dress. "I think tonight's opening should be quite satisfactory."

"How could it not be? These gowns are amazing." Lauren reached out and touched a satin sleeve. "True works of art."

"Yes, they are." Miss Montgomery turned her attention toward Frances. "That dress suits you very well."

Frances blushed. "Why, thank you." She had beamed all afternoon, and she kept looking down and touching the dress, as if to confirm that it was real. "It's my first designer dress." She nodded her head toward Lauren.

"It's not exactly a *designer* dress, but I'm glad you like it."

"Hmmph. Of course it is a designer dress. You may not be world famous yet, but you are a designer, you are very good, and you did make that dress. Don't downplay the truth, it's not at all becoming."

Lauren wasn't certain if she felt more chastened or complimented by Miss Montgomery's rant. She decided she would go with complimented and nodded her head. "Yes, ma'am, I'll keep that in mind."

"See that you do."

Half an hour later, the doors were open and a crowd of Los Angeles fashionistas were sipping champagne, eating hors d'oeuvres, and oohing and ahhing over the gowns. Lauren and Chloe were in the background, merely spectators at this event, but Miss Montgomery was front and center, holding court. In spite of her hermit-like existence, the woman could still command an audience. Photographers were there from the major local papers, as well as *Vogue* and *Harper's Bazaar*. They all wanted a picture of the famous necklace and its reclusive owner.

The police had spent time investigating the murder, as well as Miss Montgomery's necklace and its part in it, and had cleared her completely, leaving Kendall embarrassed in more ways than one. Not only had she missed the scoop on Marisa because she'd chosen to hold back to pressure Lauren, but every single fact she'd named in her recent Randall Edgar Blake article had proven to be gossip and conjecture. Rumor was she'd been fired.

Lauren was perched on a bench beside Chloe, nibbling on a canapé and enjoying watching people's reactions to the magnificent dresses in front of them. Several of her friends from design school were there, as well as Professor Navarro and most of the other teachers. While it was still painful to see them in some ways, now that her name had been cleared she no longer carried the abject humiliation around with her, and she could face them with her head held high. This evening was turning out to be a success in every sense of the word.

At least, that was true until she saw Elyse Debowesky across the crowded room. "You know what?" Lauren said. "I think I'm going to step outside for some air." She stood and darted toward the door, working her way around the edge of the room.

Chloe hurried to keep up with her. "You're not leaving here without me. I saw who just walked in, so I know what you're doing. You're running. Why don't you want to sit there and let her see you? She's got to be embarrassed, now that she knows the truth."

"I'm pretty sure that woman doesn't know the meaning of the word *embarrassed*. She will look at me like I'm the little minion she sees me as—if she even bothers to remember who I am. I can't do it, Chloe. I just can't." The strength of her reaction surprised her a little. This wound went deep—perhaps deeper than she'd realized.

Lauren reached the door and turned to cast one final look over her shoulder in the general direction of Elyse Debowesky. She found the woman staring directly at her, as were the two other women she was currently engaging in conversation. One of them Lauren recognized as a reporter. Lauren hurried out the door and down the steps of the museum complex. She found a bench along the sidewalk and sank onto it. Chloe came to sit beside her.

Lauren held out her arm straight in front of her and could see that her hand was shaking. Chloe watched it, too. "Wow. That woman is totally messing with your head."

"I guess so." Lauren returned her hand to her lap and took deep breaths.

Chloe grabbed her hand and bowed her head. "Father, You know Lauren. You know what a wonderful person she is. You know all the unfair things that have happened to her over the past few months. I ask You to heal the hurt she feels inside. We ask for Your will in whatever direction her life may take as a result of this, but I ask You right now to begin to heal this pain that has obviously been left in the aftermath. Your word tells us that You are near to the brokenhearted and save those who are crushed in spirit. Father, her heart is broken. She is crushed in spirit. Please bind up her wounds and heal her. Amen."

"Thanks, Chloe. I recognized some of Rhonda's verses in those prayers." Lauren smiled.

"Yes. I love praying back scripture. It's always a good reminder as to what we already know to be the truth."

"You're right. Do you know any scriptures about cowering in the corner and being a coward?"

"Um . . . no."

"That's probably because there aren't any telling us to do that, and I think maybe that's what I'm doing. It's not the right thing to do, and I'm not going to cave this time. Come on, let's go back inside."

"Are you sure?"

Lauren took a deep breath and nodded. "Yes. I have no intention of going anywhere near her, but I am not going to hide outside. This is Miss Montgomery's big night, and I'm going to be there. For her."

Lauren walked inside, her shoulders squared. Once she entered the room, she fought the urge to again turn and run, and she overcame. She made her way over to the back of the room, where she and Chloe had been sitting before. She glanced toward Miss Montgomery, who was floating among the exhibits, currently devoid of company. She walked over to her. "Are you enjoying your evening?"

Miss Montgomery nodded slightly. "Surprisingly, yes, I am. And you?"

"Very much."

"Except you felt the need to leave the building when that Debowesky woman entered the room." Miss Montgomery watched Lauren closely.

"Yes. I needed a few minutes. But I'm back now."

"Good for you. Whether or not she ever admits it, she has to be ashamed of all that happened."

"Somehow I doubt that."

"I'd say you're about to find out. Here comes one of her entourage heading this way."

Just then Sybil Abbott came to stand between them. "Lauren, you're looking well."

Sybil was Elyse's assistant. A pleasant enough person on her own, but she had no qualms about carrying out the whims of her boss, regardless of who those whims crushed in the process. "Thank you, Sybil. So are you."

Sybil didn't bother to respond. Instead, she continued on as if Lauren hadn't spoken. "So, you've become something of a celebrity lately, haven't you? The starving fashion graduate, wrongly accused, fighting to stay afloat in this hard business."

"Have I? I don't know. I made a resolution not to read the papers or watch the news immediately after the 'wrongly accused' part of that story hit the shelves. I'll have to take your word for it."

"It is unfortunate how things were misconstrued in the beginning. Elyse wanted me to let you know that your position will be reinstated effective next week." She said this as matter-of-factly as if she were stating that it had begun to rain outside.

Lauren's stomach flopped. She managed a tight response. "That's very kind of her."

Sybil smiled and nodded. "She feels really bad about the way things happened. I think we're all happy to see it resolved."

"She didn't seem to feel too bad about it when I couldn't pay my bills because my internship was terminated."

Sybil's face did color slightly at this. "Of course she did. But what was she to do? She had the reputation of her entire company to protect. At that time, she had to make decisions for the overall good of all her employees, based on what information she possessed."

Miss Montgomery extended her hand. "Charlotte Montgomery. And you are?"

Sybil looked over at her, seeming surprised by her presence. She quickly recovered, shook Miss Montgomery's hand, and offered a brilliant smile. "Sybil Abbott. Personal assistant to Elyse Debowesky. I'm so pleased to meet you. You must be excited to be the guest of honor."

"I am most certainly not the guest of honor."

"Oh, but of course you are. It was your excellent taste that made all this possible. And the fact that you preserved all your gowns with such great care."

"Anyone who has even a lick of sense in her brain should understand—" She paused meaningfully, long enough to make certain it had sunk in that Sybil was indeed the buffoon without a lick of sense. "They've been asking me to show some of these dresses for decades now. I did not, nor would I ever have done so, had I not found the person with enough talent to pull off these repairs with precision and respect. So, the guest of honor tonight is obviously Lauren. She may not be playing the starring role, but without her, none of this would be happening right now."

Sybil nodded and smiled. "Exactly what we believe. Which is why we are so thrilled to have Lauren back on our team. Things have not been the same since she's been gone." Her smile never faded, but her eyes did dart nervously between Lauren and Miss Montgomery.

Lauren took a deep breath. She needed this job. She knew that she did. The part-time work and the couple of weddings that she had procured would not be the long-term solution for keeping her bills paid. This job would ensure that she could get her foot back into the fashion world, probably even with a leg up. But . . . there was that treaty thing again. The thing that at first looked right and looked easiest wasn't always the right path, and it often led to greater difficulties in the long run. "I'll have to pray about that one and get back to you," she told Sybil.

"Pray about it?" Sybil sounded incredulous.

"Yes, pray about it. You can tell Elyse that I will call with an answer soon."

"You know this offer will not be on the table indefinitely. In fact, it could end at any time."

"Thanks for the reminder. I'll let you know soon."

Sybil turned around and walked off toward her boss. She was clearly stunned.

"Why did you do that?" Miss Montgomery asked.

"Because I really believe I need to pray about it. I'm sure it seems that I should have taken the job without a second thought."

"Absolutely not. Why didn't you just throw that offer right back in her face?" Miss Montgomery asked this in the way that only someone who had never lacked the money to pay monthly bills could ask it.

"It would have felt good, I admit that. But taking what *felt like* the right path has gotten me into a fair amount of trouble in the past. I'm trying to learn from my mistakes." She glanced toward Chloe and Rhonda, who had just walked up to join them. "As Rhonda would say, I'm going to say my prayers before I make any more treaties."

"I hope you know what you're doing." The tone of Miss Montgomery's voice said she very much doubted this.

"Good for you," said Chloe. "Way to stay strong." She nodded toward the entrance. "Speaking of strong, will you look at what just walked in the door?"

Jasper and Cody were making their way across the room. They were dressed to the nines. Only the uncomfortable look on both their faces gave a hint that this was not their usual world. Cody raised a hand and smiled as they drew closer.

"Cody's looking good, isn't he?" Chloe asked.

"Yes, I'd have to say that he is." Lauren felt her face heat.

"Do you think you're ready for a relationship yet?"

Lauren looked at Cody, felt the butterfly feeling that she hadn't felt in a long time, then nodded. "You know what? I think I might be."

"Yes." Chloe gave a fist pump.

"Time for me to clear some room, then." Miss Montgomery smiled as she turned to make her way to the next group, but then she stopped. "You won't be home until tomorrow, is that right?"

"Yes. I'm staying at Chloe's new place tonight."

"When you return, please see to the poinsettias at the gate. I noticed today that they are looking a bit dry. You should probably water them more than you are. Especially the red ones."

"Yes, ma'am. I'll get right on that when I get home tomorrow afternoon."

"I should hope so. Especially since my friend Alice is coming to visit next week. We don't want the neighborhood to be looking shabby, now, do we?"

"No, ma'am. Definitely not."

epilogue

One Year Later

"Miss Montgomery, will you please do the honors with me?" Lauren held out her hand for her neighbor.

"I'd be delighted." Miss Montgomery made her way out of the small group and over to the red ribbon. She placed her hands on the other side of the oversized shears.

"On the count of three. One, two, three." And just like that, the ribbon was cut and *Brides by Lauren* was officially open for business.

The building was small, and it was well outside of the downtown area, but it was perfectly suited for what Lauren needed. There was a well-lit front showroom, a midsized dressing area, and a work-room in the back.

Chloe beamed. "This place is perfect for you."

"I couldn't agree with you more," Lauren said. "Fortunately for me, I know a great real estate agent."

Cody ducked his head in mock modesty. "Aw, shucks." He leaned down and kissed her. "I figure since I'm going to relocate to Santa Barbara, it's a good thing I'm selling some real estate here."

"When is your final move?" Chloe asked,

although Lauren was more than sure she already knew the answer.

"Not for a couple of months. I'm still transitioning between both offices."

It had been several months ago that Cody had first started talking about relocating because he was "getting tired of burning up the pavement between LA and Santa Barbara." He had asked Lauren her opinion, and she knew that he was basically asking for her approval. His moving here would obviously put their relationship on a fast track. He'd wanted to be sure she was ready.

Her response had been immediate. "How fast can you get here?" They had sealed that answer with a kiss. Lauren was smiling at the memory when Miss Montgomery's voice brought her back to the present.

"I'm sure we'll be seeing even more of you around the neighborhood, then?" Her gaze was fixed on Cody.

"I'd say you can count on it." He grinned and drew Lauren into a hug.

Miss Montgomery nodded. "Well, if you're going to be coming and going up and down the lane, you need to learn how to slow that truck down. Every time you come around, it kicks up enough dust to coat every window in the neighborhood."

Cody had the good sense to look sufficiently chastised. "Thank you for drawing that to my attention. I will make every effort to keep my dust to a minimum from now on." He bowed his head toward her.

"See that you do." Miss Montgomery turned away, but not before Lauren saw her smile.

acknowledgments

Great Father in heaven—thank You for the things You continue to teach me.

Lee Cushman—for being the most understanding and patient husband ever.

Melanie Cushman—your heart for the world challenges me to be a better person.

Caroline Cushman—I hope to someday have the kind of courage that you live out on a daily basis.

Ora Parrish—mother, cheerleader, and friend.

Kim Gill and Becky Reynolds—thanks for brainstorming this story with me. The wardrobe never would have malfunctioned without your brilliance.

Gayle Roper and Kelli Standish—for helping me brainstorm this story.

Angie Carobini—thank you for answering endless questions about fashion design and how the process works.

Carl, Alisa, Lisa, and Katy—I am so blessed to have such an amazing family.

Lauren Beccue—writing buddy and friend.

Wendy Lawton—for your encouragement and guidance.

Kristyn, Brenna, Denice, and Judy—you are great friends, prayer warriors, and booksellers.

The good folks at First Baptist Church, Lawrenceburg, Tennessee—even though I've lived across the country for over two decades, you are still my biggest supporters and always treat me like family.

about the author

Kathryn Cushman is a graduate of Samford University with a degree in pharmacy. She is the author of eight novels, including *Leaving Yesterday* and *A Promise to Remember*, which were both finalists for the Carol Award in Women's Fiction. Katie and her family live in Santa Barbara, California. Learn more at www.kathryncushman.com.

Center Point Large Print
600 Brooks Road / PO Box 1
Thorndike, ME 04986-0001 USA

(207) 568-3717

US & Canada:
1 800 929-9108
www.centerpointlargeprint.com